A Bedlam of Bones

Also by Suzette A. Hill

A Load of Old Bones
Bones in the Belfry
Bone Idle
Bones in High Places

A Bedlam of Bones

Suzette A. Hill

Constable • London

Constable & Robinson Ltd
3 The Lanchesters
162 Fulham Palace Road
London W6 9ER
www.constablerobinson.com

First published in the UK by Constable,
an imprint of Constable & Robinson, 2011

First US edition published by SohoConstable,
an imprint of Soho Press, 2011

Soho Press, Inc.
853 Broadway
New York, NY 10003
www.sohopress.com

A copy of the British Library Cataloguing in Publication
Data is available from the British Library

UK ISBN: 978-1-84901-458-8

US ISBN: 978-1-56947-959-9
US Library of Congress number: 2010052556

Printed and bound in the UK

1 3 5 7 9 10 8 6 4 2

PEFC
PEFC/16-33-111
CATG-PEFC-052
www.pefc.org

To the memory of my cousins Alan and Auriol Palmer.
Thanks for the warmth, the wine . . . and all
that jazz.

1

The Vicar's Version

'You don't think, do you,' I ventured, 'that you are making rather too much of this hat business?'

'Certainly not,' my sister replied briskly. 'One doesn't take tea with a murderer every day, does one?'

'What about me?'

'That's hardly every day . . . and besides, you don't count.' She refilled her cup and scrutinized the two hats perched at the end of the dining room table.

Suitably chastened, I said nothing and resumed my struggles with the crossword. Such struggles are small compared with the larger conundrums of guilt and concealment, not to mention the problem of ducking the demands of bishop and Mothers' Union. Being a clergyman is an exacting matter at the best of times, but the difficulties are compounded if one is also an assassin.

I had not always been an assassin, and indeed for most of my time – as undergraduate, soldier and eventually vicar – had led a life of blameless ineptitude. But that was all changed (the blameless part at any rate) by Mrs Elizabeth Fotherington on that fateful day in the wood – when in the vain hope of retaining my sanity and a measure of peace I had dispatched her to kingdom come. Since then, as you might expect, life has turned complex and precarious and I have been subject to a variety of discomfiting entanglements. The most recent of these was what might be termed the 'French fracas', a gruelling time spent in the Massif Central amidst soaring peaks and base pursuers.* Mercifully the latter came to an abrupt end (none of my doing, I hasten to say), but the repercussions were arduous, and involved me in issues which I had confidently assumed to be resolved once back in England in the safety of my parish of Molehill. Delusion.

'On the whole,' Primrose continued, 'I think I prefer the one *without* the veil. I know you say you like it, but I don't wish to give him a false impression.'

'What sort of false impression?' I asked.

'Of being anything other than what I am – i.e. an Englishwoman of impeccable credentials and honest intention. The veil has a *foreign* air, and I wouldn't like him to think . . .' She left the remainder unsaid, and picking up the grey hat with the assertive green bow placed it firmly on her head and gazed into the mirror.

I shrugged and lit a cigarette. 'If you say so. But why on earth Rupert Turnbull should think you are remotely foreign when he knows from our encounter in France that you are as British as he – or me for that matter – I cannot imagine.'

She sighed impatiently. 'Really, Francis, you are so literal! You know perfectly well what I mean. It is imperative that he sees me as *sound* and not one to be trifled with. There's a great deal at stake in this transaction – we're not talking peanuts, you know. And I'm damned if I am going to let that bludgeoning scoundrel think he can get his hands on my paintings for less than the market price – more would be preferable. A tiny hat with a veil looks either frivolous or dubious, and if things are to go smoothly it is essential I wield the moral advantage.'

'By wearing a hat without a veil?'

'Precisely,' she snapped.

There was a pause while I pondered this. And then I asked what she would like me to wear.

'Well, a suit, of course, but the essential thing is the dog

* See *Bones in High Places*

2

collar. You didn't wear it much in France and it is important that Turnbull be reminded of your status. Just because he battered Boris Birtle-Figgins to death and got away with it, he needn't think he can run circles around the Oughterards!'

'But Primrose,' I murmured, 'we still don't really know that he did it. It's not as if he—'

'If you mean he wasn't so foolish as to confess to anyone in the way that you blurted your idiocy to slippery Nicholas Ingaza, you're perfectly right. But as we all agreed at the time, the circumstantial evidence was overwhelming. Make no mistake – the man is a ruthless, calculating killer and highly dangerous!'

'All the more reason,' I said testily, 'to stay out of his way. I cannot *think* why you arranged to meet him back in London. We should have severed all connection the moment the steamer left the quayside at Dieppe. In fact, until the arrival of your telegram last week, I thought we had done just that. It really is too bad!'

She stared at me in wonder. 'But I have already explained, Francis. Rupert and I have a commercial contract. I am to supply his new London language school with at least six of my rustic church and sheep paintings. This is not something he can be permitted to renege upon, however tasteless or violent his private life. And if things go appropriately I could well get a further order for a batch to the Oxford one as well . . . No, as I said, we must rendezvous with him at Brown's Hotel next Tuesday afternoon at four o'clock sharp – and don't forget the collar.'

I heaved a sigh and returned to the crossword. Five across: 'Dog mad as a hatter.' Seven letters. I swivelled the propelling pencil and carefully wrote in 'Barking'.

An hour later, with Primrose and hat boxes safely en route to her home in Lewes, and with the phone off the hook, I made further inroads into the crossword, accompanied by a small packet of peppermints and a large gin. It had been a strenuous day – sorting the drifts of diocesan edicts

3

heaped up during my leave, parrying the inanities of Mavis Briggs, being lambasted by a mother whose child had failed to be chosen for the Sunday School prize, and last but certainly not least, being faced with the unexpected arrival of my sister.

It was not so much Primrose's presence per se that had been unsettling (siblings, after all, grow thick skins – and in fact we enjoy a wary closeness), but her resolution that we should renew acquaintance with Rupert Turnbull.

Pleasant and personable, Turnbull had become a source of considerable disquiet during the latter part of our stay in the Auvergne, when it emerged that in all likelihood he was a blackmailer and double murderer, and (unlike myself) confident, adroit and smoothly efficient. As I have remarked before, it is bad enough having to confront one's own fall from grace, but to be dragged willy-nilly into another's murky slipstream is distinctly disagreeable . . . especially when in all probability the party in question would not hesitate to take a hammer to one's skull if he saw fit.

Really, I thought, if only Primrose were less mercenary, sleeping dogs could safely lie and a modicum of peace be achieved. As it was . . .

I poured another drop of gin and stared gloomily at my own sleeping dog, and wondered not for the first time what on earth the creature dreamed about. Rabbits? Bones? Chasing the cat? Certainly not strolling up Albemarle Street to Brown's Hotel, sprucely dressed in clerical grey and rehearsing pleasantries to exchange with a fellow homicide . . . Lucky little beggar, innocent as the day he was born!

2

The Dog's Diary

Well, like I told Maurice, I wasn't really asleep – just think-ing with my eyes closed. And listening and sniffing. It's amazing what you can pick up that way – just lying doggo and letting them think you're dead to the world, when all the time you are alive as a CAT ON HOT BRICKS!

Maurice didn't like me saying that and started to go into one of his sulks, but he soon snapped out of it when I began to tell him what I had heard F.O. and the Prim talk-ing about earlier that afternoon. 'Oh dear,' the vicar had said, 'I don't think I can face any more of that sort of thing, we had quite enough of that fellow in France. Can't you meet him on your own if you have to?' The Prim pulled a face and said her brother wasn't exactly about to get a medal for chivalry, was he? Don't know what she meant by that, but I suppose F.O. did because he went red in the face and mumbled that he would go along if she thought he could really be of help.

When I mentioned that bit to Maurice he started to laugh – in that weedy way of his, like a mouse gargling with nettle juice – and said something about there being a thin line between help and hindrance which he didn't think the vicar had ever quite grasped. Matter of fact I couldn't quite grasp what the cat was saying either, but then I often don't. Gets a bit carried away with himself sometimes.

Anyway, the more we chewed things over and reckoned that F.O. (our master the vicar) was about to put his foot in things again, the more gloomy we got . . . No, that's not quite right: the cat got gloomy and *I* got all sneezy and bristly (the old sixth sense playing up, telling me there's fireworks ahead). Most times I don't get gloomy, except when O'Shaughnessy the Irish Setter beats me in the peeing game or F.O. snatches one of my bones and puts it on the mantelpiece where I can't reach.

But Maurice is often out of sorts. It's his own fault. He's what you might call a *disapproving* cat, and so all manner of things get up his nose and on his tail and he goes ratty. Which is why he is jolly lucky to have me as his chum. I sort of help him along and make him look on the bright side of things. For instance, I told him once that every cat-litter tray has its silver lining – which struck me as quite a useful thing to say. But he didn't seem to get the message and muttered something about being tired of stupid dogs spouting fatuous platitudes (whatever they are!), and that in any case nobody could ever say the same for my basket . . . Oh well, just goes to show, Muncho before mogs! Mind you, he has his moments – lots of them in fact. Like that time in France when he attacked one of the goons who was after F.O. and sent him flying over the cliff edge, or when he scared the living daylights out of Mavis Briggs and she nearly fell into the open grave at one of those corpse-burying things our master is always having in the churchyard. (It's nice the way the vicar and me share the same interest in bones – though I've never actually seen him gnaw any. Offered him a chew of mine a couple of times, but he didn't seem too keen. Prefers his fags I suppose.)

Anyway, the point is that Maurice and me know that the business in France with whatshisname – Turnip, I think – is going to catch up with F.O. and make big trouble. But what the cat *doesn't* know and I do – because my bones tell me – is that it won't be long before Ingaza the Brighton Type shows up again. And oh my arse, then there'll be a buggers' shindig, MAKE NO MISTAKE!

3

The Cat's Memoir

It was too bad! I had been fondly hoping that Primrose's intention to resume connection with that smooth villain was a passing whim. Apparently not, and I should have known better. The more I see of the vicar's sister the more I realize that unlike her brother, she is possessed of a rare and steely obstinacy . . .

You see, Bouncer had informed me that during her recent visit to the vicarage he had heard her instructing F.O. to prepare for a trip up to London for the purpose of taking tea with the Turnip man in some Mayfair hostelry. As it happened, I had already learnt something of this notion soon after we returned from the deprivations of France but had foolishly assumed that for once the vicar might allow common sense to prevail. As I frequently have to remind the dog, I am a cat of sharp and sage perception – and it was galling to have been caught in the snare of wishful thinking. However, as the humans glibly put it, no use mewing over spilt milk. The immediate necessity was to confront the current development and cope as best one could with human frailty – i.e. the vicar's gaffes.

These gaffes were much in evidence in France – an experience from which I had barely recovered – where, accompanied by his sister and the manipulative Brighton Type, F.O. fell foul of all manner of alarming idiocies and dangerous ruffians. (I do not include the bishop and

7

his female entourage in this latter category, though their presence there hardly contributed to peaceful harmony. Neither, I suppose, should one count the Curé of Taupinière – a specimen even more suspect than the Brighton Type.)

Fortunately, two of those ruffians were eventually disposed of – with, I might say, no small help from myself. But the principal one, Turnip, remained at large and was clearly destined to be a thorn in our master's flesh – or more to the point, in the flesh of Bouncer and myself. Being a canine, the dog lacks the sensibilities of us cats and is given to spluttering that he finds our master's entanglements 'GOOD SPORT!' Even so, he is not so foolish as to forget that F.O. is a source of food, comfort and relative protection, and that it would be unfortunate were those things to be withdrawn on account of laxity and oversight. There have indeed been some near misses, and naturally the whole issue of the original Fotherington murder continues to pose a niggling threat to our welfare. However, on the whole I have learned to live with the vexations; and while I would not agree with Bouncer about the 'good sport', it has to be said that balancing on the high wire with the vicar does have its moments of sprightly amusement.

Not that there was anything sprightly or amusing about the dog's inane attempts at French conversation that afternoon. Just because we spent time in the Auvergne he now imagines he is a native speaker and goes around shouting absurd gobbledegook accompanied by much shoulder movement and paw waving. It is a tiresome and raucous display and I cannot think why the poodle, Pierre the Ponce, seems so impressed. My own grasp of the language, selective and academic as it is, does not lend itself to such exhibitionism ... But then, of course, one has to make allowances for the braggadocio of dogs.

And talking of dogs, I also gathered from Bouncer that we could expect another visitation from the toping Gunga Din – yes, if you please, that corpulent hound attached to the lady crime novelist who had descended on F.O. when he was once being forced to house Ingaza's ill-gotten swag.* It had been bad enough our master having to cope with the Brighton Type and his oily manoeuvres, but to be encumbered with Mrs Tubbly Pole as well, not to mention the dreadful bulldog drooling at her heels, was really the last straw. And now Bouncer told me they were coming again. Horror!

My instinct of course was to ignore the dog's prognostications – based as they were on that questionable 'sixth sense' of his – but the recent news of the proposed London meeting with Turnip made me suspicious, and I feared the worst.

Thus, as a corrective to drooping spirits and a means of stiffening the fur in readiness for the coming ordeal, I decided that a gentle session with the Special Eye would be helpful; and repairing to the quiet of the pantry, I proceeded to caper with my favourite toy. This, I must explain, had been presented to me by Bouncer in one of his more rational moments. Indeed, in view of the pleasure it has since given, one might almost say it was an offering of inspired thoughtfulness. I say *almost* for it doesn't do to lavish too much praise on the dog as it creates mayhem. But at the appropriate times I am careful to express my gratitude.

The item in question is the blue glass eye which Bouncer encountered under the neck of the corpse battered by Turnip. Details of the discovery appear in an earlier volume of my memoir and so need no further reference here. Suufice to say that the little trinket affords much gaiety, and for the time being permitted me to ignore the looming confusions.

* See *Bones in the Belfry*

4

The Vicar's Version

I had decided to take the train up to London, feeling that meeting Primrose at Victoria station would be fraught enough without having the worry of parking the car as well.

It was pouring with rain, and pacing on the platform I irrationally feared there might be delays on the line. In fact she arrived punctually, sporting a rather nippy coat and skirt and having stuck to her choice of the veilless hat. I was surprised at how smart it looked. Fortunately, despite the wet the cab queue was short and we were soon installed and driving out of the station forecourt.

'Now,' Primrose said, 'our best plan is to get the tea business over first – you know, soften him up with scones and cream and all that stuff, and then when he's sated and charmed by my—'

'Hat,' I broke in.

'What?'

'Your hat.' I smiled. 'After he has succumbed to its undoubted elegance.'

She frowned impatiently. 'No, not my hat – my thoughtful interest in his wretched language schools of course! Once all that's over and he's suitably malleable, I'll get down to brass tacks about the pictures while you make an excuse to visit the gents and settle the bill.' I knew I had some role, I thought wryly.

As the taxi trundled into Albemarle Street, Primrose snapped open her powder compact, scanned the mirror, pulled on her gloves and tapping me briskly on the knee, said, 'Now, best foot forward, Francis. Much depends on this. And don't overtip the driver!'

Rather to my relief, Brown's tea lounge was almost empty. Apart from a mother and a small girl in neat school uniform (half-term treat and merciful respite from Matron?) and an elderly couple holding hands in rapt tête-à-tête, the room was empty and we could take our pick of a suitable corner. Primrose summoned a waitress, and I was just about to order tea for three when she stopped me and said, 'You had better make it four, just in case.'

'In case of what?'

'In case he brings Lavinia. She's still with him, you know.'

I changed the order and, a little surprised, asked how she knew.

'When he accepted the invitation last week. He said something about how nice it was to have his cousin back in London and hoped she could find something suitable while selling the French property.'

'So you think she's intending to settle here? Hmm – quite a change from the lofty peaks of Boris and the Massif Central, I should think.'

'Yes, but I think that's exactly what she's after. As we observed at the time, not entirely the prostrate widow. And with Boris conveniently dead she's all ready to immerse herself in the flashing fleshpots of the gay metropolis.'

'Oh really, Primrose, your imagination!'

'Not at all,' she protested. 'Remember what she said to you at his funeral – about her passion for fast cars and how she longed to learn the tango? And after all, we did see the pair of them zooming off to Paris only days after boring Boris was lowered into his grave . . .'

'So you still think she was complicit in the murder?'

11

'Undoubtedly. In fact, if you ask me . . . Damn!' she muttered. 'Here they both are. I told you so. Now, I don't want her lurking around while I'm getting him to sign on the dotted line. You'd better take her for a walk or something.'

'But how . . . ?' Before I could protest further, Turnbull and Lavinia had spotted us, and with ingratiating smiles we rose to greet them.

Seeing the pair so soon after our time in France, there seemed nothing remarkable about their proximity. And apart from the fact that Lavinia was wearing azure blue eyeshadow and stockings with startlingly black seams (a change from the pale lids and drooping smocks of the Auvergne), neither looked any different. Nevertheless, despite the social normality of our meeting, I felt a frisson of fear as I watched Turnbull being the perfect guest amidst the starched napkins and bone china of our decorous sur-roundings. I stared down at the low table and saw not gâteaux and cucumber sandwiches, but Boris sprawled and bloodied on the sunlit flagstones. Had he *really* done it? Oh lor!

'Nice to see you both again,' I lied. 'And Lavinia, how well you look!'

'Oh,' she cried, 'it must be the relief from strain. So much to do and organize after poor Boris's end. And there's been all the business of putting the house on the market – the French are so awkward over these things! Anyway, now that I'm back in good old London town and away from it all I feel *so* much better!' She sank on to the sofa, arrang-ing her bouffant skirt and stretching out a neat toe, shod in what Primrose assured me later was a Rayne original. ('His latest model,' she had fumed. 'Must have cost at least thirty guineas. Tainted spoils, that's what!')

'Good, good,' I said vaguely, not quite sure whether I was supposed to show sympathy or give a cheer, and turn-ing to her cousin I asked how his plans for the language school were coming along.

'Couldn't be better,' Turnbull replied. 'The Oxford one is opening in a couple of months and the one in Kensington at the end of next week – which is why I need your sister's paintings in place.'

We went on to chat about this and that, asked after Lavinia's search for a suitable London base and tactfully skated round all but the barest mention of Boris and his putative killer Herbert Castris. At one point the name of Inspector Dumont was mentioned ('such a charming man and with such Gallic politesse!'), but the conversation quickly slid away into neutral matters – namely Primrose's latest accolade for her sheep pictures. 'Do you know,' she laughed, 'the reviewer actually said he had never seen such soulful faces in his life!'

'Huh,' I responded. 'Obviously hasn't seen my flock when the sermon's too long and they're dying for their G and Ts!' And then, as I was lifting a cup of Lapsang Souchong to my lips and speculatively eyeing the impressive array of cakes at my elbow, I sensed a movement in the doorway.

The round furrowed face of a brindle bulldog appeared, followed by its squat and hefty torso. Breathing heavily, undershot jaw firmly clamped, the creature stood four-square and staring. I stared back nervously, and then in horror – as with a rumble of recognition, the creature lumbered over to me and thrust its head on to my lap . . . I gazed down at the snuffling form of Gunga Din.

In startled silence my companions also gazed. And then clearing his throat, Turnbull said, 'Is that another of your pets, Oughterard? I thought you just had Bouncer and the cat.'

'Er, no,' I said uncomfortably, contemplating the rolling eye. 'I think it belongs to a friend . . .' And before I could add anything further, Maud Tubbly Pole came billowing into view.

'Hello!' she boomed, unsettling the trysting couple in their mutual absorption. 'First it's the Channel ferry and now it's Brown's. We're obviously destined, Francis!' She advanced with beaming purpose. Gingerly pushing aside the encumbrance, I rose to greet her and made the necessary introductions: 'This is Maud Tubbly Pole, lethal crime writer,' I said with a laugh – and instantly regretted it. (What a tactless comment in front of that pair!)

They smiled politely and shook hands, but I thought I noticed the merest start of surprise from Maud when Turnbull's name was mentioned. However, she gave him an affable nod, and turning to Primrose, said stoutly, 'I like your paintings, my dear, the sheep have such intelligent faces – unlike most!'

Lavinia gave a silvery laugh. And then gesturing toward the snuffling pet, said, 'Is this your dog? What a sweet little fellow.' She regarded Gunga Din with mild distaste.

'Not sweet,' his owner chortled, 'but *sterling*. Mummy's sterling boy, that's what he is!' And she prodded him fondly on the backside. This brought forth a pained grunt, and with a loud hiccup the sterling boy rolled over and went to sleep.

After a pause, pleasantries were resumed, and I asked Mrs Tubbly Pole if I could get her an extra cup and saucer. She waved this aside. 'Oh no, my dear, I only popped in to secure a table for tonight. I can't have caviar *and* cakes! Alfred's secretary – I'm standing him dinner for helping me to clinch matters with the Great Man. You'll see, your name will be up in lights before you can say "Holy smoke"!' She grinned toothily and delivered a prod not dissimilar to that received by Gunga Din, but fortunately mine was on the knee.

I smiled wanly and hoped that nobody had heard. No such luck. And for Lavinia's benefit I had to endure a lengthy synopsis of the whole saga – i.e. her successful novel inspired by the infamous Molehill murder*, the invaluable help given by the 'kindly parson' in her quest for local detail (yes, I recalled ruefully: hoisting her and the deadweight Gunga up the belfry ladder in search of 'atmosphere'), and finally her 'masterly' persuasion of Alfred Hitchcock not only to turn it into a film, but – horror of horrors – to give 'my friend Francis here' a walk-on part.

* See *A Load of Old Bones*

14

'Goodness,' Lavinia laughed. 'To think that we have a rising film star in our midst. Hidden talents, Francis!'

With a more caustic tone, Primrose also laughed. 'Well, better a film star than a murderer in our midst. Hitchcock's films are so sinister he'll probably cast him as one!'

I froze. How *could* she be so brazen? Did she think it a game to jibe Turnbull thus! I shot him a covert glance to see the reaction, but he was preoccupied with his napkin and a particularly lush choux bun, and seemed not to have heard. I certainly hoped not ... And then the thought struck me that perhaps the jibe had been directed at *me* – exactly the sort of flippant observation Primrose would make! Either way, one could do without such intemperate innuendos and I scowled in her direction. She ignored my look and plied Turnbull with more tea.

I turned to Mrs Tubbly Pole and was about to enquire after her niece, Lily, when I noticed that she was staring at Turnbull intently. 'I think I knew your ...' she began. Then stopped short, and bending down started to drool over Gunga Din. A moment later, still smiling affably, she yanked the dog's collar, and murmuring something about a hair appointment made ready to leave. Amid effusive farewells I escorted her to the foyer and then out on to the street to hail a taxi.

As one came near she grabbed my arm and said hastily, 'You want to be careful with that one, Francis. *Very* careful ... Anyway, I'll telephone you shortly with news of Alfred – and *other things*.' She shot me a meaningful look, and before I had a chance to say anything, the cab drew up and she had bundled herself and her companion into its depths.

The very last thing I wanted was news of 'Alfred' and the tiresome film proposals. But I did want to hear about the 'other things'. What had she meant about Turnbull – and whom had she known connected with him? His father, his brother, wife, mistress ...? It could be anyone. But whatever the meaning, Mrs T.P.'s warning certainly seemed to confirm my own earlier fear: that Rupert Turnbull was a dangerous piece of work and best avoided.

15

I returned to the hotel and caught a brief glimpse of Lavinia mounting the stairs en route for the ladies. With luck she might be there long enough to allow Primrose and Rupert to complete their business. Well, let them get on with it; and the sooner Primrose detached herself from the wretched man's orbit the better! I lit a cigarette and sat down on one of the sofas in the hallway. If Lavinia returned too soon I could always divert her by bland social chit-chat, i.e., 'How's life without saintly Boris? And did you really egg on your cousin to do him in?'

'I think that all went rather well,' Primrose chuckled as we walked down towards Piccadilly. 'Very well indeed. No problem with my terms and he'll take delivery of the pictures on Friday. Excellent.'

'Good,' I said. 'So that's that and we don't have to see them again.'

'No we don't *have* to see them again, but it might be polite all the same.'

'Why? What do you mean?' I asked suspiciously.

'You were probably too busy with your novelist friend, but while you were both gassing Lavinia invited me to go with her to a new art gallery launch in Brighton. Belongs to an old school chum. Apparently it's likely to be quite a big event and I think she wants a running mate.'

'What about Turnbull, can't he go with her?'

'She didn't mention him. I had the impression she was going on her own.'

'How is she getting there? Return ticket on the Brighton Belle?'

'Actually she's staying the night with me in Lewes.'

I groaned. 'Oh for pity's sake, Primrose! I thought it was agreed that we were going to keep our distance. That palaver in France was frightful to say the least, and the sooner we put the lid on it the better. You may remember we had all voted to keep our heads well below the parapet, and here you are waving a blooming flag!'

'Don't exaggerate, Francis. Overreacting as usual. I simply want to find out a bit more about Lavinia, i.e. discover if she really did encourage Turnbull to bump off her old man. You must admit it's quite intriguing!'

'Only to the officious.'

'Don't be so pompous. Just because you've got your own skeleton doesn't mean you can't be interested in another's.'

'I consider that remark in very poor taste,' I replied stiffly.

'Hmm. But if I did find out anything I bet you'd want to know.'

'Possibly.'

'You bet you would! Quick! There's a taxi. Take me back to Victoria and I'll buy you a shandy in the buffet.'

I set her safely on the Lewes train, and with some relief took the tube to Waterloo and thence the train on to Molehill. One way and another it had been a tiring day and I was glad to gain the comfort of my armchair, switch on the Home Service and doze to the emollient voice of Frank Phillips apprising the nation of its latest scandals.

5

The Vicar's Version

The following morning was marred by the realization that my cigarette case was missing. I don't use it very much, being generally in too much of a hurry to make the transfer from one jacket to another. However, it's handy for social occasions and I was annoyed not to see it anywhere. I tried to think when I had last had it; and then wondered perhaps if it might have been dropped in Ingaza's car on our way back from France. Typical of him not to say anything. It was a long shot but worth a try, and I went to the telephone and dialled his number.

'Well 'ee's in bed, yer see,' explained Eric. 'What you might call *languishin'*.'

'Languishing?' I snapped. 'What's Ingaza got to languish about? He was perfectly all right the last time I saw him.' (Swirling off from the Newhaven docks in a cloud of exhaust and brilliantine.)

'Ah, but 'ee's gorn down since.'

'Huh,' I said without sympathy. 'Aunt Lil on the war-path, is she? Didn't get her quota of postcards from the Auvergne, I suppose.'

'Nah, she got those all right,' said Eric, 'thought they was very nice, she did. It ain't that, Frankie,' (I winced at the name, but knew I was stuck with it), 'it's what you might call *rav-vah* serious . . . not too nice at all, old son, if you get my meaning.' I did not get his meaning and was about to say as much, when he added, 'And of course the old bish won't like it much either. Put him in a pretty pickle I shouldn't wonder . . .'

I stiffened. 'Old bish'? Surely he couldn't mean . . . I cleared my throat and said tentatively, 'You're not by any chance alluding to my superior, Bishop Clinker, are you?'

'Got it in one, mate. That's the geezer – Clinker.'

'So what has the bishop got to do with things?' I asked warily.

'We-ll, not for me to say really. I expect His Nibs will fill you in when 'ee's stopped languishing.'

'Oh yes? And when is that likely to be?'

'Couldn't say, old son. Most like when he gets a good tip from 'is Cranleigh pal.' He gave a hoarse laugh. 'Abaht time that ferret earned his commission! Toodle-oo.' He rang off, leaving me perplexed and uneasy.

Ingaza's languishing was no concern of mine, but I was ruffled by the link with Horace Clinker. Whatever Eric was referring to, it was clearly something affecting the two of them and evidently unwelcome. If Ingaza was sufficiently exercised to be 'languishing', what then was the bishop in his 'pickle' doing? Searching around for someone to complain to . . . or to blame, no doubt. Over time I had noticed that in periods of pique or discomfort, more often than not it was F. Oughterard who bore the brunt of Clinker's fulminations. Would this be such an occasion? In view of my association with Ingaza it most probably would.

I sighed irritably. Really, after all our recent tribulations in France the last thing I wanted was to be embroiled in the bishop's problems – particularly if they involved Ingaza. Coping with each separately was bad enough, but a joint onslaught was more than nerves could stand. No peace for the . . .

I whistled for the dog, shoved his head in his collar, slammed the front door and set off grimly to view the defective brickwork around the church porch.

* * *

When I returned, the lunchtime post had arrived. Rarely does it contain anything much except bills and diocesan circulars, and I was about to sweep it aside when I saw a large cream envelope postmarked Maida Vale with my address scrawled boldly in purple ink. Judging from both locality and script I guessed it could only be from Maud Tubbly Pole, and never quite knowing what to expect from that quarter, slit it open with a certain trepidation.

Devastated, it ran, *Alfred tells me he cannot find a slot for you in the screenplay of my book, and the work itself is to be postponed for at least a year! All very vexing and I know you will be so disappointed. He sends his heartfelt apologies and trusts you will find stardom with another director (and mentions something about the Ealing comedies). However, the* good *news is that I am scheduled for a signing session at your local bookshop, and two days after they want me to give a talk to the Molehill Lending Library followed by some sort of bun fight in the evening. Thus, rather than dash up and down to London, I have decided to take a room for a week at the Gravediggers' Arms a mile down the road from you. They were so kind to Gunga last time I was in your neck of the woods and I know he will appreciate the change of scenery – and who knows, perhaps renew his* special *friendship with dear little Bouncer and Maurice!*

Anyway, my dear, it will also mean that I can fill you in a trifle more about your handsome friend at the jolly tea party the other day. I have been giving the matter some thought and one or two bells have begun to ring rather dissonantly.

She went on to supply dates and times for her visit and breezed cheerfully about other topics, but I gave scant heed to these, being too elated by the Hitchcock news. I was also intrigued by the laconic reference to Turnbull. Well, I would just have to wait and see. Meanwhile, there were psalms to be sung and pews to be addressed . . . I donned my cassock and prepared for both.

* * *

Later that day I was ambling along the High Street, minding my business and trying to look as anonymous as a vicar ever can, when I was pulled up short by a sharp tug at my sleeve. I looked down and was confronted by the intent face of Mavis Briggs.

'Canon,' she breathed, 'can you spare a moment? I was about to have a coffee, and perhaps you would care to join me – there's something rather urgent I need to discuss.'

I did not care but was caught nevertheless. And having no ready excuse, dutifully followed her into Mrs Muffet's Tea Room. Mavis ordered only coffee, but stung by the hijacking I compensated with a jam doughnut.

Mavis does not hang about. That is to say, when she has some point or request to make she cuts to the chase and gives her victims little time to collect their wits.

'I am really very concerned, Canon,' she began earnestly. I bit into my doughnut, looking impassive. 'You see, I can't help thinking that that new librarian is getting above himself.'

'How far above?'

'What? . . . Oh, I see. Well in my opinion, much too far.'

'In what way?'

'You may not have noticed, but it has become fashionable for authors to be invited to the library to give readings from their books, answer questions and discuss *literary* matters with their readers.'

'Yes,' I replied, 'I've heard about that. Rather a good idea I should have thought . . .'

'Indeed,' she agreed, 'but it rather depends on what *sort* of author! After all, a library does have certain standards to maintain, one can't have just anyone. I mean,' and here she lowered her voice, '*some* might be a corruptive influence on the young! Mr Hoylake would do well to bear that in mind.'

'Perhaps,' I agreed uneasily, wondering who on earth Mr Hoylake had invited that was to exert such a malign influence on the local youth . . . Frank Harris was rumoured to be ill, and I doubted whether Henry Miller would see

Molehill as a lucrative trading post for his books. 'So who are you talking about?'

'Haven't you read today's *Clarion*? It's that woman crime writer, Mary Tubbly Pole. She's coming in a fortnight's time!'

'Maud,' I said mechanically.

'Well whatever her name, I don't think she's at all appropriate.'

'But she's very popular,' I protested. 'Probably be quite a draw.'

'She may be popular, but is she *literary*?' Mavis squeaked sententiously.

I wondered whether we were to embark on an exploration of what constituted literature and whether entertainment and intellectual stimulus were mutually exclusive. If so I should need to be fortified by another doughnut. On the other hand, such a course would surely lengthen proceedings and prolong the agony. Thus I decided to forego the doughnut and say nothing. 'Hmm . . .'

However, it became clear that Mavis's question had been largely rhetorical, for in the next instant she rushed on: 'You see, Mr Hoylake has been more than negative about my own little publications. After all, it is not every Surrey town that has a *poet* in its midst, and yet whenever I broach the idea of holding a series of readings with a chance for the public to ask me about my *philosophy of life* he clams up and says nothing. Or at least, he did until yesterday.' She paused pointedly and I felt that I was supposed to say something.

'And, er, what did he say yesterday?'

'Well,' she twittered, 'it was the third time this week that I had approached him, and I was just about to enquire if he would care to reconsider my useful offer, when he swung round and said that he had no intention of permitting his library to provide a platform for pappy piffle, and would I kindly move out of the way as I was making a barrier between Colonel Dawlish and the Hank Jansens! I may say, Canon, I was more than shocked, but I stood my ground, oh yes!'

22

'Good for you, Mavis,' I said, awed by Hoylake's nerve and his alliterative zeal. 'So what did you say?'

'I told him that although *he* might not possess literary discernment, a number of people did, including Canon Oughterard who was only too eager to write the introduction to my third volume. That gave him pause for thought!'

It also gave me pause to wipe the smug smile off my face; and I emerged into the High Street wondering how on earth I was ever going to summon the nerve to enter the library again.

6

The Dog's Diary

He was in a right old bate this evening! Muttering and spluttering and yanking my lead as if he was dragging rocks out of a well. I can tell you, I wasn't having it. No thank you! And to quote the cat, I made my position clear – i.e. crouched on the pavement outside the organist's gate and did the business. Tapsell saw from his window and came hurtling out cursing the vicar up and down dale. There was an awful row and F.O. looked a bit sheepish. Generally he gets the better of Tapsell but this time he was short of ammunition. Serves him right – a dog like me deserves a bit more POLLY TESS, as Pierre the Ponce says.

Still, mustn't grumble. He's all right generally – pretty kind, really – but just now and again he gets ratty. I suppose it's being a murderer that does it. Gets on his fins I daresay . . . Mind you, I don't think that was the cause this evening. It was something to do with the Brighton Type and the bishop person. The vicar was on the blower, and after he put the thing down I heard him say, 'That's all I need – bloody Nicholas and bloody Horace!' So for some reason they are at him – and *we* get the flak.

I told all this to Maurice, but he didn't say much. Just gave one of those God-awful miaows and then went silent and sort of huffy. Hasn't spoken since. I'm not complaining, mind. Sometimes it's quite nice not to have the cat's pennyworth shoved under my nose all the time. Still, it won't last. He'll soon find his tongue again and start telling me what's what. But in the MEANTIME I'm off to the graveyard for a bit of peeing practice. O'Shaughnessy has bet me his new ham bone that I can't outdo him. We'll see about that!

So, I've had a nice little caper, emptied the old bladder at a rate of knots *and* discovered a shortcut through the big tombs by the side gate. O'Shaughnessy doesn't know about that – or if he does, the rotter's never mentioned it to me. So if everything goes to plan and I can keep up my pace and my peeing, that ham bone should be in the bag – or, better still, in BOUNCER'S BASKET!

As guessed, Maurice has now crawled out of his huff and started to talk again. But before he got too carried away by the sound of his own voice I thought I'd give him a blow-by-blow account of my fun in the cemetery. And I had got halfway through this when he suddenly said, 'Yes, yes, Bouncer, all very fragrant I'm sure, but there are issues of greater moment than bones and urine, and we need to discuss them.'

Well, I didn't know what he meant by moment and urine, but I understood the word bones all right, so I told him coldly that as far as I was concerned bones were JOLLY IMPORTANT and that I didn't think many things mattered more.

'Haddock and murder,' he said.

'Stuff the haddock,' I said, 'but what about the murder?'

He looked sniffy, and then said in his best cat voice, 'It has come to my notice that our master is more than worried about the Turnip villain, he—'

'Well, yes of course,' I said, 'we guessed that when he rushed up to London with the Prim to meet him at that special place you were on about. So what's new?'

'What is new, Bouncer, is that one's suspicions are now fully confirmed: he is indeed destined to see more of that dangerous ruffian.'

'How do you know?' I asked.

'I've heard him talking.'

'Who to?'

'To himself, in his sleep.'

'Huh!'

'I can assure you it was very revealing. If you recall, when he returned from that London hotel he put on his slippers and collapsed into the armchair, and despite the racket coming from the wireless went straight off to sleep. You retired to your basket in the kitchen while I stayed on the hearthrug. From there I could hear exactly what he was muttering.' The cat stopped here and asked if I was listening. Well of course I was listening – no chance not to when he's giving tongue! Just because I was having a bit of a scratch and a look down below didn't mean I hadn't got my ears cocked! Anyway, he went on to report that F.O. had said something like, '"Prim's put her hoof in it now . . . Can't face being caught up with Turnip again, slippery customer! Mrs T.P. nearly swallowed her teeth when she saw him, said he was murky. He's that all right! Enough murk with Elizabeth – can't stand any more following me around . . . Oh God!" So you see, Bouncer,' the cat went on, 'if this Turnip is skulking about *and* the Brighton Type and the bishop person are on his wick, then clearly there is more than a nip in the air and I fear storm clouds gather!'

I didn't really understand that last part because it seemed quite a nice day to me – and besides, I don't know what the weather had to do with it . . . Still, like I've said before, the cat's got a tricky mind. Anyway, *I* think we shall have to watch our rumps – not to mention the vicar's . . . Funny that bit about the Tubbly. Sounds as if she must have been in that London place too – and I bet old Gunga was with her! So I expect we shall be seeing him before long . . . Probably just as fat – and tight. Soon find out I expect.

But right now I think I'll go and do a bit of Frog-speak with Pierre the Ponce. I learnt a lot of useful stuff in France, such as *merde*, *salope*, and *ne toochay par mon os*. It's a good thing to keep up with the old parlay-voo, but Maurice says he's got better things to do with his time. Probably just as well – he talks enough in ordinary lingo (though being Maurice it's not as ordinary as all that, of course). But perhaps I might practise in the crypt with those gabbling ghosts – I'll ask after their crumbling osses. That'll fox 'em!

7

The Vicar's Version

As threatened, Mrs Tubbly Pole did indeed install herself at the Gravediggers' Arms, and her advent there was preceded by hue and cry both from the bookshop and the local library. Posters were displayed, flyers distributed, personal invitations circulated, and the reading public earnestly urged to drop everything and hasten to avail itself of 'such exciting literary opportunities'. 'A Rival to Agatha', ran a headline in the *Molehill Clarion*, and even the normally snide Edith Hopgarden was heard to murmur she might grace one of the occasions with her presence. (Though I suspect this was as much to do with needling Mavis Briggs as with satisfying any particular enthusiasm of her own.)

Personally I was delighted that Maud should receive such acclaim, but was still distinctly apprehensive that her diagnostic ramblings about her book, *Murder at the Mole-heap*, might in some way implicate me. But in this respect there was little that I could do other than to keep as low a profile as possible and hope for the best.

As expected (and, in view of the promised Turnbull data, partially hoped for), I received a telephone call from the Gravediggers' to alert me to an impending visit. 'My dear,' she bellowed, 'all very cosy here of course, but nothing like having a drink with an old friend. What about tonight?

Gunga could do with a little outing and I'm sure your beasts would so love to see him!'

I looked at the 'beasts' sprawled comatose and snoring on the carpet, and rather doubting her words said I was sure they would like nothing better.

'Six o'clock it is,' she said briskly. 'All news then. Line 'em up, Francis! Toodle pip!'

Hastily I searched for my wallet and bustled out to the off-licence to replenish depleted stocks and buy extra crisps for the dog, recalling it liked a little blotting paper with its gin.

Six o'clock approached and I made the necessary preparations: stoked the fire, plumped the cushions, rallied the animals, got out the glasses (plus a saucer for Gunga Din) and as instructed, lined up the hooch. There was a sound of a taxi drawing up, and a few minutes later the doorbell rang with clarion ferocity. Maud and companion were upon us.

With a broad grin and grasping the equally broad drink I had poured her, she eased herself into the chair by the fire. Taking its cue, the dog too settled heavily on the hearth, and I was about to offer it the usual saucer when she forestalled me, saying, 'Not just yet, Francis, he must mind his manners and say hello to his hosts first. Where are the little fellows?'

I went into the kitchen, scooped up Maurice from the window sill and hustled Bouncer ahead to the sitting room. Here the due courtesies were enacted. The cat emitted two of its more gruesome screeches and Bouncer made a bee-line for the bulldog's bottom, sniffed liberally and then gave a matey bite. Gunga Din rolled on to his back, waved his stumpy legs in the air and let out a falsetto howl of what I took to be pained horror. I started to apologize and remonstrate with Bouncer, but the victim's guardian cut me short, saying, 'Oh don't worry – that's just his way of saying, "I'll get you next time and what else shall

29

we play?" Give him his gin now and he'll be as happy as Larry.'

I dispensed the statutory four drops. And from amidst the rumpled features and to the sounds of heavy breathing, a small and startlingly pink tongue emerged to toy with its evening cocktail. Mrs T.P. watched indulgently. Bouncer meanwhile had retreated to the far end of the room, and begun – rather ostentatiously, I thought – to worry his marrow-bone. I think it was his way of showing who was top dog and who the lounge lizard.

With characteristic gusto my guest started to hold forth upon her imminent book-signing session and plans for the talk in the local library. She was obviously keen that I should lend support, something I was perfectly ready to do were it not for my fear that in her zest for her theme, i.e. the murder of a rich and respectable local widow by person unknown, she would exaggerate my role in her earlier researches.* As the unsuspected subject of those researches, I had found those investigations a particular embarrassment. Thus I was reluctant to retrace old and painful ground and be quizzed yet again (least of all in public) about my ideas regarding the dispatch of 'poor Mrs Fotherington'. Regretfully I pleaded a prior engagement but promised to look in on the book-signing and pledged the purchase of six copies. (A gesture not quite as cynical as you might imagine. I had become genuinely fond of Mrs Tubbly Pole and was happy to contribute, however scantily, to her literary success.) 'That's the ticket, Francis,' she crowed, 'generous to a fault! Knew I could rely on you.' I blushed and hastily proffered some of Gunga Din's crisps and started to refill her glass. 'Bottoms up and here's to crime!' was the genial response.

'Ye-es,' I agreed, a trifle tentatively. 'And here's to yourself of course.' I raised my glass.

'And don't forget Cecil, my dear!'

'Cecil? Cecil who?'

* See *Bones in the Belfry*

She wagged an admonishing finger. 'Ah, you *have* forgotten. Cecil Piltdown of course!'

Of course. Mrs Tubbly Pole's alias and beloved literary doppelgänger: a name kept specifically for her more lurid flights of fancy, and which, I suspected, provided the greater part of her considerable bucks.

'To Cecil,' I acknowledged respectfully.

She shifted her gaze to Bouncer, still absorbed in grinding hell out of his bone, and seemed about to launch into a spiel on the quirks of canine psychology. However, intriguing though dogs may be, it was another kind of psychology that drew me. 'Maud,' I said carefully, 'the other day when we were having tea with Rupert Turnbull and his cousin, I think you recognized him, didn't you? And you mentioned it briefly in your letter.'

She gazed meditatively at her whisky. 'Hmm, pretty well. It was a long time ago, so I couldn't be entirely sure if it was the same Rupert Turnbull – he was a lot younger then – but I have a feeling I was right.'

'You rather suggested that you knew somebody connected with him. Who was it?'

'His housemaster.'

I don't know what reply I had expected but it certainly wasn't this, and I felt a twinge of disappointment. My own housemaster had been so painfully dull and dry that it was difficult to credit Turnbull's with the slightest significance. And as an enlightening revelation, the statement seemed worthless.

'Yes,' she mused, 'Freddie Felter, we knew him in India. My husband Jacko was governor of the school where he taught maths – St Austin's, the British college in Jaipur. Some of the boys were being coached for the Civil Service exams, including Turnbull. Felter used to bring them to tea occasionally and Jacko would supply a few tips . . . Yes, Freddie Felter – probably the most unpalatable person I have ever met.'

'Goodness,' I exclaimed, suddenly interested. 'Whatever was wrong with him?'

'Most things,' she said simply.

'Such as?'

'For one, he had the most awful moustache, even worse than Jacko's. It made him look like a thin walrus.'

'But Maud,' I protested, 'you can hardly hold his moustache against him!'

'Oh yes I can, it was dreadful.' She grinned a grimace, and added, 'But there were *other* things.'

'Go on.'

'Well, to begin with, he was an inveterate liar. Tried to convince Jacko he took a double first at Cambridge and had turned down a Fellowship.' She gave a wry laugh. 'One didn't spin yarns like that to Jacko, he could spot a humbug from a hundred yards. "Holmes of the Civil Service", that's what they called him! Personally I called him plain nosy, but that's another story. Anyway, Jacko soon sniffed out the truth: a diploma from a teacher training college. A paltry enough fabrication, I grant you, but there were so many others. The man was a walking falsehood – and nasty with it.'

'In what way?' I asked, replenishing her glass.

'He was a manipulative bully, but not directly. He would get others to do his dirty work, Turnbull more often than not . . . there was something wrong with that boy, very wrong. Liked nothing better than to get out the knuckleduster – figuratively speaking at least. A sort of Moseley thug in the making. The younger boys hated him, but he was always perfectly agreeable when he came to tea with us. Yes, a pretty smooth little sadist really.' She broke off to water the dog's gin. ('Can't have him boozy for his trot in the park, can we?')

Thug in the making . . . That fitted. And I recalled the fate of little Castris in France, strung up on the door jamb in his own dining room. But I also pictured Turnbull in the sedate ambience of Brown's tea lounge being the model of temperate good nature. It was amazing how diverse a person could be! And then rather uneasily I started to think of my own diversity. But surely in my case there was far more consistency. From what I recalled of those fateful moments in the wood, the deed had been done almost in passing and with no obvious transformation of character. I wondered: did that make me more or less dangerous than Turnbull? Difficult to say ...

However, there was no time to cogitate, for, dilution achieved, my companion resumed her narrative: 'You see, Francis, there was one particularly unsavoury incident which involved the atrocious beating-up of a thirteen-year-old – Bobbie Timms, rather a nice kid. He and his housemaster were old enemies, and one day the boy came across a compromising photograph of Felter and another man. This he proceeded to pass among his schoolmates amidst much giggling and ribaldry. One gathers that no harm was intended other than to have a good laugh at Felter's expense. The boys were too naïve to grasp the more serious implications of the find, and there was no question of their reporting the matter to the Head. Apparently, seeing "old Freddie with his pants down" was amusement enough. However, Felter discovered what had been going on, retrieved the photograph but said nothing.'

Here Mrs Tubbly Pole paused and made a further assault on the crisps, which she proceeded to crunch loudly.

I waited, letting the sound subside, and then asked: 'So what happened? Didn't you say there was a beating?'

'Oh yes, there was that all right – but not until a month later. Pure revenge. The boy was so bruised he had to spend three days in the school sanatorium. They say his spleen was ruptured.'

'Good Lord! So the housemaster had laid into him – how frightful!'

'Oh no, not Felter – Turnbull. At the former's behest. There was an enormous brouhaha, and master and satellite left under a joint cloud, each blaming the other. I heard that Felter went back to England – joined some accountancy firm near Oxford I rather think; but what happened to Turnbull I had no idea. Didn't care either.'

'But you do think that was him at tea the other day?'

'Oh yes, the more I think about it, the more I am certain. It would be too much of a coincidence otherwise. Seems to have done well for himself with those language schools.

Perhaps he has changed his spots. But I doubt it – they don't generally, that sort.' She nodded confidently, and by way of illustration embarked on a graphic résumé of one of her wilder novels in which the detective, a man of unimpeachable probity, had turned out to be the grandson of Jack the Ripper – and with similar propensities.

'Did it sell?' I enquired innocently.

'Sell?' she boomed. 'I should say. Kept Gunga in gin for at least two years!'

8

The Vicar's Version

As predicted, after my talk with Eric and his cryptic reference to the bishop's 'pickle', the telephone rang with an episcopal summons. The thin voice of Clinker's secretary informed me that his Lordship would be obliged if I would call at the Palace at my earliest convenience, i.e. Monday, or Tuesday at the latest. Monday was Bouncer's day to have his teeth scrubbed, and as far as I was concerned if there was to be a clash between diocesan business and the dog's dentistry the latter had priority. Thus I opted for 'the latest'.

There was a displeased pause at the other end. 'Hmm, I think his Lordship would have preferred the Monday.' I murmured something about there being an urgent christening. 'Very well,' the voice sighed, 'I'll slot you in for nine thirty sharp. You've made a note of that, have you, Canon?'

I assured him I had and asked tentatively if he knew what it might concern.

'Not the least idea,' was the pained reply. 'I am merely the messenger.' He rang off and I lit a cigarette and brooded.

Clearly, after the enforced intimacies of France and its dramas, Clinker had reverted to official mode – thankful perhaps to resume the mantle of rank and distance. Provided it meant I was not to be embroiled in fresh embarrassment, this mattered not a jot. However, coming so soon after Eric's news, I suspected that the summons signalled only two things: grief and gloom. I went to the piano and embarked upon Chopin's Funeral March.

As was his habit, Bouncer came and took his place beside me, staring up intently at the keys. For a dog of such extrovert temperament, he has a curious penchant for such dirges, and I can never decide which is his favourite, the one from Handel's *Saul* or the Chopin. Either way he is apt to punctuate the notes with a series of gurgling whines which I fondly interpret as discerning appreciation – though of course one can never be entirely certain with that dog.

Maurice, on the other hand, hates all music; and the moment he sees me making for the piano stalks from the room in dudgeon ... Although there was one memorable occasion when Savage had lent me his precious gramophone record of Joe Venuti playing 'Honeysuckle Rose', and the cat had pranced in curious boogie fashion up and down the piano top. I suppose the wailing violin sounds must have struck some atavistic feline chord. He's never done it since ... but then neither have I borrowed the Venuti since. Time for another sampling, perhaps.

Apart from an overture (parried) from Mavis Briggs about my penning the introduction to her less than inspiring *Little Gems*, the weekend passed off tolerably well. There was of course the usual prima donna tantrum from Tapsell in the organ loft and complaints from Colonel Dawlish regarding the state of the banners in the Lady Chapel, but such things are par for the course and I survived to Monday no more scathed than usual.

Monday itself was a little more taxing, for as mentioned, it was Bouncer's dental date. Naturally the usual drama erupted; but eventually master and dog emerged into the sunshine none the worse for wear and with the latter sporting alarmingly chalky fangs. No, it was Tuesday that was the real killer: my rendezvous at the episcopal palace, where I arrived poised for difficulty but not imagining it would take quite the course it did . . .

I had set off at what seemed like the crack of dawn, i.e. a quarter to nine, and through lashing rain drove slowly along the Hog's Back. In better conditions and without a defective windscreen-wiper I thoroughly enjoy this stretch of Surrey, and it is amazing the speed the old Singer can get up. But that day, with visibility almost nil and my mind clouded with the prospect of Clinker's demands (whatever they were likely to be), the journey was a chore and a bore. However, I reached the Palace in good time, and after waiting only two minutes was ushered into the bishop's study.

It was the first time we had met since our time in France and I was taken aback by the sudden change in my superior. He must have shed nearly half a stone, and his eyes had that slightly hang-dog expression I've seen on Bouncer in one of his rare under-the-weather moods. The voice, however, retained its customary edge.

'Ah, Oughterard, glad you could spare a few minutes from your *frantically* busy schedule. Doubtless very tiresome having to come over to Guildford. Much obliged I'm sure.' He did not look particularly obliged. However, I made suitably tactful responses and waited.

He cleared his throat, paused, and then said, 'And, ah, how is Maurice?'

'I'm sorry?'

'Maurice, your cat. Nice little fellow. Survived the trip back, did he?'

'Er, yes,' I replied in wonder. Cat and bishop had not notably taken to each other in France, so why on earth this sudden solicitude?

'Good, good. And Bouncer?'

Bouncer? What on earth had got into him?! 'Yes,' I mumbled vaguely, 'in fine fettle, I think. Teeth have had to have their annual cleaning, but other than that he . . .' I stopped, noticing that Clinker was drumming his fingers and staring out of the window. Of course, I thought, that's what it's about – playing for time. So when is he going to lob it to me? In the next instant.

'Have you heard from Ingaza?' he snapped. I told him I hadn't – assuming that Eric's enigmatic bawlings hardly counted. 'Hmm,' he said bleakly, 'thought you might have by now.' There was another pause. And then, staring me in the eye and as if suddenly seizing the bull by the horns, he announced, 'There's a bit of a problem going on, Francis – delicate, really.' Clinker's use of my first name, although in theory a mark of chumminess, invariably spells embarrassment and trouble, and I steeled myself accordingly.

'Oh dear,' I replied, adjusting my features to show sympathetic concern. 'Not too bad, I hope.'

'Huh! Couldn't be worse,' he said curtly. And to my surprise he reached into his desk drawer, pulled out a packet of cigarettes and proceeded to light up. I had never witnessed this before, and in fact was so surprised that I even forgot to feel piqued at not being offered one.

'Yes,' he continued, amid clumsy puffs, 'distressing really. Not what one wants at my time of life – especially with the possibility of this new appointment in the offing.' (The appointment involved being a sort of supplementary aide to the Archbishop of York; a post, I gathered, that entailed few duties but much prestige. Clinker had been angling for it for some time, and it was one of the reasons why he had been so desperate to hush up the recent French shamozzle. His chances were good, the only rival being a fellow bishop, Percival Crawley, whom Clinker detested. To lose the post would be painful, but to lose to 'Creep' Percival intolerable.)

'If I can be of any help . . .' I began reluctantly.

He sighed heavily. 'I doubt it – I just thought you might have heard from Ingaza. Are you *sure* he hasn't said anything?' I shook my head, and he looked perplexed. 'Hmm – perhaps he can't have been approached yet.'

'Approached about what?'

'Blackmail,' he muttered, almost inaudibly.

I gazed in astonishment. 'Good Lord! You mean you are being blackmailed, sir? But who on earth by?'

'The *blackmailer*, of course. And keep your voice down!'

He ground out the cigarette on his desktop, burnt his finger and winced.

'I see,' I said slowly. 'And what does Mrs Clinker say?'

'Gladys? What are you talking about, Oughterard! She doesn't say anything – she doesn't know. It's hardly the sort of thing we might discuss at the breakfast table! Oxford before the war may be a long time ago now, but even so, you surely don't imagine that I would confide—' He broke off and started to scrabble through an address book. 'Where is that confounded man's number?'

I studied him, things falling into place: Nicholas Ingaza and Oxford pre-war. Oh my hat! And after all this time . . . They were both being got at! So that was it: the younger Clinker's momentary lapse, an absurd whimsical indiscretion and quickly eclipsed by Gladys and the respectable tentacles of the Church. Surely nobody could be on his tail *now*! And what about Nicholas? Who on earth would want to dig up that particular passing episode when there must have been so many scurrilous antics since, not to mention the infamous Turkish Bath incident?* He had done time for that. So who was wanting to pursue him now? Surely it was all yesterday's news . . . On the other hand, I reflected grimly, Ingaza's bathtime high jinks might be old news – but not the bishop's gaffe. That could be dynamite!

'How much?' I said to Clinker.

'What?'

'How much money do they want for their silence?'

'Don't know,' he replied shortly. 'It's not been mentioned.'

'But presumably it will be.'

He shrugged his shoulders. 'Yes, yes, I imagine . . . But it's not the money as such, it's just the – it's just the *ghastliness* of it all! That letter was brazen, taunting. It really made me feel so—' He broke off and stared at me intently. 'Of course, I'm forgetting. You wouldn't know about it, would you?'

I hesitated. 'Well, I did rather gather from Eric, Ingaza's friend—'

---

* First mentioned in *A Load of Old Bones*

'Suppose you're going to ask me to enlarge,' he cut in bitterly, 'all the damn details. Shouldn't have called you over here really, stupid of me . . . Still, it will probably all surface sooner or later. Oh my God . . .' He got up abruptly, scattering papers, and stumbled to the window where he stood chewing a pencil and scowling at the beating rain. Tricky.

I cleared my throat and said mildly, 'Think I've got the gist of things, sir. A minor aberration years ago. Small matter between you and Nicholas – no great shakes, water under a bridge really . . .'

He whirled round. '*No great shakes!* That's hardly the idiom I would use! I suppose that's how *he* described it. Typical. You do realize the matter is an indictable offence, Oughterard! Not on the scale of Ingaza's later shocking tomfoolery, I grant you, but an offence all the same. If this is raked up, I'm done for!'

'I am sure it won't come to that,' I ventured reassuringly. 'And besides, I gather they are getting much softer on that sort of thing nowadays. There's so much more to . . .'

'Look, Oughterard,' he said bitingly. 'Having led a life of such sheltered and singular rectitude, presumably you are unable to grasp the straits that I am in. The merest hint that the Bishop of Surrey and Berkshire once had a fling, however fleetingly, with one such as Nicholas is enough to scupper both my boat and my pension – and Mrs Clinker can kiss goodbye to being Vice-President of the National League for Darning and Elocution. She's set her heart on that, and I shan't hear the end of it.'

'Goodness,' I exclaimed, 'I didn't know there was such a thing. Whatever do they—' I broke off hastily. No, this was not the time to pursue such curiosities. Instead, assuming an air of cool efficiency, I said, 'Well, I had better take a look at the letter then.'

He hesitated, slightly surprised at my tone. 'Er – yes, of course. I suppose you had better.' He rummaged in his desk, produced an envelope and passed it over in silence. It bore a central London postmark, date-stamped ten days previously. Like the envelope, the single sheet of white paper was neatly typed:

Sir,

It has come to my notice that you were once a naughty boy with a bit of fluff at Oxford. First lecturing post, wasn't it? And he an undergraduate at Merton. Well, 'boys will be boys' — except of course you weren't a boy, were you? Twenty-eight, twenty-nine — an Oxford don who, as many would think, ought to have known better. Tut, tut! Still, I expect you enjoyed it all right. Gave you a thrill, did it? Walking on the edge, all that sort of thing! Do you think of it now sometimes, when you traipse around in your Mickey Mouse mitre all rigged up like a Christmas tree? Or is it swept under the rug like the filthy bit of dirt it is? Mud sticks. Dirt sticks. And make no mistake, I'll stick too.

Yours faithfully,

Donald Duck

P.S. Your old friend has been doing pretty well for himself I hear. Have sent him a note too — he'll probably relish a trip down memory lane.

I handed the letter back to Clinker. 'Seems to have a fixation with Walt Disney,' I remarked drily.

'Hmm,' he replied dismally. 'Bastard.'

He was right. It was a vicious little note, mean and low, and I suddenly began to take the bishop's plight seriously.

'As you say, he's not actually asked for money,' I mused. 'I wonder what he has in mind.'

'What he has in mind,' fumed Clinker, 'is to play silly beggars with me, soften me up and then go in for the kill and take me for everything I have. I've read about this sort of thing. That's what they *do* – keep you on hot bricks. But of course that's not something you would be aware of.'

Oh no? I thought, recalling the French nightmare.*

* See *Bones in High Places*

41

'I take it that the police would not be a good thing?'

'Too right they wouldn't!' he yelped. 'Not at this stage at any rate, though God knows it may come to that . . .' He groaned.

'But who could it be?' I asked. 'Who would have known about you and Nicholas at Oxford? Although I suppose the writer needn't have actually been there himself – it could have been dug up recently. Doesn't he say "it has come to my notice"? Unless of course that's simply a blind, or a façon de parler.'

'A façon de Christ Almighty!' cried the bishop. 'No, I've no idea who it could be! Perhaps Ingaza has. Why hasn't the wretched fellow contacted me? He must have received that note by now. What on earth is he doing?'

'Languishing,' I replied absently.

'*What?* Well he has no business to languish. He ought to be here, giving constructive advice. He's not in my address book – have you got his number?'

'Oh yes, I've got his number all right.'

'Well ring him up then! Tell him there are vital things to discuss and he must come up to Guildford straight away . . . No, wait a minute, not here at the Palace. That wouldn't do at all, it will only set Gladys off – she couldn't abide him in France. It'll have to be your vicarage. That's it: telephone him this afternoon and tell him it is imperative I see him. Now Francis, I know I can rely on you. See to it, there's a good fellow.'

The good fellow returned to Molehill, poured a large gin, consumed three cream cakes, and then feeling suitably fortified, did as requested.

9

The Vicar's Version

Emboldened by the gin, and brushing the crumbs of a meringue from my waistcoat, I seized the telephone and dialled the Brighton number. 'Ah, hello Nicholas,' I began cheerfully. 'Are you busy in the next few days?'

'What's it to you?' was the cordial reply.

'I rather wondered if you would be free to come up here for lunch.'

'Why?'

I told him that Horace Clinker was keen to discuss one or two things with him. 'He's a bit worried, you see.'

'So he should be,' he murmured.

'I've, er, seen a letter that he received. And I think you may have been sent something similar. It's not very pleasant.'

'You can say that again. Frigging disgusting.'

'So, would you like to come up and chew things over a bit? You know, try to work something out?'

'Hmm – all right. Got any whisky?' I assured him I had. 'And what about treacle tart? One of the few things you do quite well.' I told him I thought I could rise to that as well. Thus a provisional arrangement was made for three days' hence, depending on the bishop's convenience. Judging from Clinker's mood when last seen, I suspected it would be more than convenient.

I finished the call a little surprised at Ingaza's sombre responses. Accustomed to his provocative, often maddening banter, I found the subdued tone slightly deflating. Clearly the latest development had taken effect.

On the prescribed date he arrived twenty minutes early and was greeted warmly by the dog. Bouncer's approval of Ingaza had started to emerge during our stay in France. It had not been apparent previously, but there was clearly something that stirred the creature's respect. Perhaps it was their shared cussedness.

The slight tan Ingaza had acquired on the heights of the Massif had disappeared and his face had resumed its customary pallor. In a louche sort of way and in certain lights Ingaza can appear almost handsome, but on that day he looked gaunt and dishevelled. His hair, normally so carefully smarmed, was dry and unkempt, and I noticed the absence of the flash tie-pin and heavy signet ring. Set out in a hurry perhaps? Or did the sartorial indifference betray some nagging anxiety?

We settled in the sitting room and lit cigarettes. 'Well, this is a bit rum,' I began. 'Hor's in an awful stew.'

'That would follow,' he replied drily.

'You've both had these letters. Have you brought yours with you?'

He nodded and took a piece of paper from his wallet. 'Came about a week ago, stupid bloody thing. Here, read it.' And with a scowl he passed it over.

Dear Mr Ingaza,

We are not as yet acquainted, but I think over time you will get to know me fairly well – or at least if not me directly, most certainly the business that interests me. You yourself are an astute man of business and will thus not be so foolhardy as to ignore my terms.

'What terms?' you may enquire. The terms of our transaction of course. 'That being?' you ask. Simple: my silence for your money.

I was intrigued to learn of your erstwhile prowess in Classics – a double first in Greats no less; and your subsequent 'Athenian' activities have been duly noted. In this respect it also tickled my sense of irony to discover that when immersed in the delights of Horatius Flaccus at Oxford you were also courting the company of one Horatius Clinker: a charming coincidence (you roguish little pervert, you!) and one that would not escape the vigilant eye of the Daily Smut, *should news of it happen to pass that illustrious paper's front door.*

Your youthful misdemeanours within a certain London Turkish bath attracted much publicity at the time and you paid the price. But that is dead wood now and I feel that a revival of interest is in order. What better topic than a resurrection of the Horatian affair? Now that really would make the bishop move! (Yes, I grant, an egregious pun, but I fear irresistible to a veteran chess player such as myself.)

À bientôt,
Donald Duck
P.S. Financial requirements to follow.

'Cocky little shit, isn't he?' Nicholas suddenly seethed. 'I'll give him Donald bleeding Duck if he ever comes near me!'

'Yes, but he won't, will he?' I replied quietly. 'The whole thing will be done from a safe distance. There will be messages, instructions, but he's unlikely to get physically close. He'll pull his wires by remote control.'

'We'll see about that,' he snapped. 'He's not going to put one over on Old Nick. No fucking fear.' He reached for the blended whisky. 'Haven't you got something better than this?'

'Afraid not.'

'Oh well, it'll have to do.' And so saying, he filled his glass almost to the brim.

'Steady on! Clinker may want some.'

'Should have got here earlier, shouldn't he?' was the brusque retort. He became silent and I reread the letter.

Given my own discomfort at the hands of Nicholas, I suppose that seeing him so exercised should have given me a sense of *schadenfreude*. And yet curiously I felt none. His own brand of blackmail had been distinctly oblique, amiable even, and I began to wonder if perhaps the manipulation had rested more on my own fears than his serious intent. Such was the gravity of my crime that I had been ready to believe the worst and dance to the slightest of tunes . . . Assumptions are of course dangerous, but increasingly I was beginning to feel that Nicholas's capacity to shop me was entirely abstract, and his sly innuendos simply an amusing way of recruiting my services.

Well, whatever the case, he had exhibited no malice . . . Whereas the present operator certainly did. I found both letters distasteful in the extreme. Each held a note of gloating pleasure, almost as if the financial object were of less interest than the power to unsettle or humiliate. Nicholas was right – he was cocky enough. But dangerous with it, and I was concerned for them both.

There was the sound of a car pulling up; and a minute later the front gate creaked open and the bishop appeared. He was clad in the dark raincoat with turned-up collar that he habitually wore when going undercover to play tiddly-winks with Mrs Carruthers.* Mercifully he was without the black fedora – an addition which invariably gave him the air of a rather plump Chicago hoodlum.

I ushered him in and, rescuing the whisky bottle from Nicholas, offered him a glass.

'Just a small one, Francis. A busy morning, and they've closed that shortcut to Molehill. Had to go the long way round – a tedious route.' He took a sip, cleared his throat and nodded to Nicholas. 'Glad you could come. Rather important. It's not good this business, not good at all.'

'You can say that again,' was the acid reply.

There was an awkward pause, broken by myself saying brightly, 'Well I suggest you swap letters and compare notes, and while you're doing that I'll go and get lunch on the table.' I hurried into the kitchen, leaving them alone to sort things out.

---

* See *Bone Idle*

There I hovered by the stove, stirring the ham and beans, watched intently by Maurice from the window sill. Of the dog there was now no sign. Presumably it was his day for the crypt or he had bounded off to the graveyard to bawl at the dead. I addressed a few polite words to the cat; and then judging that my guests would now be more settled and mutually attuned, dished up the greens and announced that lunch was ready.

It was not the easiest of meals – Clinker huffing and puffing, Ingaza casting dire imprecations. What was notable were the differing attitudes: brooding resentment from Nicholas, blue funk from the bishop. Given the latter's position, Clinker certainly had more to lose and one could understand his apprehension. Nevertheless, Nicholas was deeply agitated – but less through fear than with indignation that anyone should try to browbeat him. I had seen some of this at Saint Bede's, and more recently in France when he had been enraged that one of our opponents should presume to call the shots (and not only figuratively). Pride, not fear, drove Ingaza, and it soon became clear that what had really riled him was the allusion to himself in the bishop's letter as 'a bit of fluff'. This he would never forgive, and were vengeance ever to be wreaked that would surely be the spur.

At one point I suggested diffidently that perhaps it might be best to grasp the nettle and show the letters to the police after all, adding without much conviction, 'One gathers they're quite used to this sort of thing ... Some actor had problems only recently and the Law was surprisingly ...'

Clinker put down his knife and fork and gazed at me. 'Look,' he said coldly, 'it may be all right for you, Oughterard, but I can tell you that Horace Clinker has no intention of being bracketed with some mincing, pansy-arsed thespian. So kindly come up with a better idea than that!'

Nicholas turned to me. 'He's on form, isn't he?' he observed.

Personally I was a trifle taken aback by the bishop's linguistic choice, but in the circumstances felt that a tactful silence was the best response. Thus I smiled vaguely at the cat and went on eating.

Discussion continued. However, we reached the treacle tart stage with little being achieved other than their resolution not to burden the police, and Ingaza's proposal that the blackmailer be booted to buggery. Neither idea got us very far. But the tart was a success.

10

The Vicar's Version

Such had been my preoccupation with the unsettling events surrounding Clinker and Ingaza, that my sister's arrangement to accompany Lavinia to the gallery launch had slipped from my mind. Some days later, however, a call from Primrose slipped it firmly back again.

'Hello,' she said cheerfully. 'Thought I'd just let you know that Lavinia is all set to come down next Wednesday and stay the night. Looks as if it's going to be quite a good do. Are you sure you don't want to come?'

'Quite sure,' I replied firmly.

'Oh well, suit yourself, but Nicholas might look in. I gather some of his cronies will be there.'

'*They* may be, but I doubt if he will,' I said absently.

'What? Why shouldn't he be – is he taking Aunt Lil to the dog track or something?'

I hesitated. 'No – it's, er, just that I think he's got other things on his mind at present. He may be keeping a low profile.'

'Huh,' she said impatiently, 'he's always got something on his mind. Cooking up some scheme or other, I bet. And by the way, he's been very quiet about my share from the last Canadian consignment. I put a lot of effort into getting those sheep pens just right – it's no use painting twentieth-century gates on to eighteenth-century palings, somebody's sure to object. So kindly tell him that Primrose Oughterard is awaiting settlement!'

'Well if you must go in for this kind of artistic chicanery—'

'It is *not* chicanery!' came the indignant response. 'If I've told you once I've told you a dozen times, I am merely supplying the Canadians with what they like and cannot obtain in the normal way. If it pleases them to think that a few classical embellishments here and there add up to the real thing, who am I to quibble?'

'Hmm,' I murmured. 'Authenticity being in the eye of the beholder, presumably?'

'Exactly, Francis, I knew you would grasp it in the end.'

I let it rest. We had gone down that path too many times. And besides, as she would occasionally point out, who was I to raise a moral eyebrow in such matters? That's one of the problems with murder, it leaves one in such an awkward position.

I steered her back to Lavinia's visit. 'Listen, Primrose, for goodness' sake be careful. If she really did connive at the disposal of Boris it could be highly dangerous if she thinks for one moment that you suspect. She's bound to tell Turnbull. Personally I think you're crazy to go near either of them. It only takes one thoughtless word or false move and things could turn very nasty indeed. No point in giving them a hostage to fortune, much better to play safe.'

'Like you did in Foxford Wood?'

I sighed angrily. 'It is precisely because of Foxford Wood that I know what I am talking about! You must stay clear!'

'My dear, you really are getting things completely out of proportion. Now calm down or you'll give yourself a hernia. When Lavinia told me at the hotel that she would be down here for this gallery event, one's social grace stepped in (something you wouldn't know about) and naturally I offered her a bed for the night. I think you can trust me to manage things discreetly. I shall be the perfect hostess, the essence of tact about matters in France and a most enlivening companion at the private view. You'll see – she'll think me wonderful, drop her defences and let slip all manner of things about the battering of Boris, without having a clue that I've twigged. It will be quite a challenge!'

'Oh well,' I said gloomily, 'if you want to play Miss Marple . . . but just watch it, that's all.'

'Of course I will,' she replied nonchalantly. 'But I don't care for the comparison – Christie's old trout is *years* older than me!'

That afternoon I was due to give a pep talk to Saint Botolph's Lay Ladies (a somewhat unfortunate title I had always felt) whose C-in-C, Miss Dalrymple, had been grumbling about falling numbers and a dearth of fresh volunteers. 'People are so lazy,' she had grumbled, 'and when they're not being lazy they are absurdly timid. They need galvanizing, that's what! We need a recruitment campaign, a sort of holy *putsch* to get them off their beam-ends. Don't you agree, Canon? You might compose an hortatory address, that should do it!'

I had hesitated, assailed by lurid pictures of Edith Hopgarden & Co. strutting down the side aisles in helmets and jackboots. But my silence was also caused by perplexity – for, to tell the truth, I had never been *entirely* clear as to what it was that the Lay Ladies actually did: anything and everything, I suspected, and doubtless in a most worthy manner. But I had always been reluctant to enquire too closely, having quite enough on my plate dealing with the frets and furies of the Vestry Circle. The Lay Ladies were, I gathered, a sort of all-female offshoot of that body, subordinate but vital: ecclesiastical scene shifters *sine qua non*.

Thus, armed with only a hazy concept of their function, I settled down to compose some sort of rallying call – a task not helped by the fact that my mind kept returning to the plight of Clinker and Ingaza. Who on earth had got hold of that Oxford business – some erstwhile crony of Ingaza's turned sour and vindictive? One of the bishop's rivals to the pending York appointment – the hand of Creep Percival perhaps? Surely not. Who in those circles

51

would stoop so low? Then I recalled the bitter professional tensions between the wretched Castris and Boris Birtle-Figgins.* (Evidently, when the chips are down gentility is no guarantee of fair play . . .) Or was it some professional operator with no personal connection at all but who knew a good thing when he stumbled on it? But would a neutral professional have adopted quite such a malign tone? The letters had been penned with a sneering relish which seemed to go beyond the mere desire for monetary gain . . . although, as the bishop had surmised, perhaps that was all part of the softening-up device, a cynical means of destroying his victims' defences before making the attack when they were at their lowest ebb. Perhaps, perhaps . . .

I sighed and returned to the rallying call. 'Service,' I wrote, 'is one of the most worthy and honourable activities we are called upon to perform, and each task from the most complex to the most menial has a special point and value, which when offered with both zest and humility will . . .' Here I paused, chewed my pen and went back to thoughts of Clinker. Supposing it *did* hit the press, would it really cause such a stir? Was the public not growing more tolerant of such indiscretions? Besides, it had all happened before the war, nearly two decades ago . . . another age! But to both questions the short answers were respectively a resounding 'Yes' and 'No', and I studied the blotter in dismay. Then, bending once more to my task, I picked up my pen and made desultory jottings about shoulders and wheels and hands and decks.

Just now and again, to my surprise, I can produce quite an effective address, and one which even the pernickety Colonel Dawlish will approve. But such was not the case that morning: the Muse was patently sulking or otherwise engaged, and there seemed little hope that the Lay Ladies' *putsch* would gain much animus from their vicar. Far better, I decided, for it to come from Miss Dalrymple herself. Of foghorn voice and gimlet gaze, she seemed eminently suited to stir the flagging cohorts. With her pennant flying

* See *Bones in High Places*

in their faces, who but the brazen would resist the call to supervise sewing-fests, tea urns, biblical beanfeasts and the Young Wives' gym displays? Yes, I would telephone immediately!

'But I think at least you ought to be there, Canon,' she told me. 'It would lend gravitas.'

'Really?' I exclaimed, going pink with pleasure.

'Well, sort of,' she modified. 'And I do feel you should say a few words as well. Reminds them who's boss.'

'Absolutely,' I replied. 'And naturally I'll give full support – be right behind you.'

'Yes, but don't stand too close. We don't want my thunder stolen, do we?' I wondered who on earth would try a thing like that; but before I could say anything she barked a laugh, and, clearly satisfied, rang off.

Relief! I lit a Craven 'A', went to the piano, and, shooting my cuffs, embarked on Fats Waller's 'The Joint Is Jumping'. It's a tricky piece but I hammered away merrily, blackmailers and Lay Ladies banished to limbo. I think the dog had hoped for something more sober, as with a disgruntled burp he sloped off to the kitchen. Hard cheese.

With the burden of address eased from my shoulders by the redoubtable Dalrymple, I was able to pass a moderately painless afternoon. Her exhortation (plus a few politely received words from myself) seemed to do the trick, and the Lay Ladies bubbled and chirruped with renewed and lively energy. I still wasn't quite sure of all their many functions, but worked on the principle that as long as I kept on smiling and asked no leading questions, I could remain safely detached.

All went well, and when the time came for tea and biscuits it seemed that escape was nigh. Not so. The breathy voice of Mavis Briggs was suddenly heard announcing she wished to give a vote of thanks to their 'quite *dazzling*' speaker, and if we didn't mind, she had a few things of her own to add as well. Dear God, I thought, she's going to spout some poems! That we were spared. But she launched into a long and meandering reminiscence about the origin of the organization and the vital part played by its founding members – of which, naturally, she was one.

If looks could kill, Mavis would have been struck thrice dead by Edith Hopgarden. But for the most part the other ladies lapsed into a resigned torpor, with one or two of the less comatose taking out their knitting. Not having any knitting to hand, I allowed my thoughts to wander back to the blackmail.

Given the length of Mavis's discourse I was able to brood at some leisure upon the identity of 'Donald Duck'. What an absurd soubriquet – only an idiot or warped mind would dream that one up! Oddly enough it was this signature to the letters that annoyed me more than anything else. It was so insufferably insolent . . . I wondered when the next approach would be made and for how long he intended to make them sweat. And what about the method of payment – one large sum or relentless instalments? He? Yes, it was likely to be a man – improbable that a woman would have such a close knowledge of that particular topic or indeed enjoy exploiting it so fully. Still, one could never be entirely sure . . . I closed my eyes, lulled by the gnat-like droning from the platform.

And then, just as I was beginning to nod off, unaccountably the amiable face of Rupert Turnbull came into my mind, and with that face the memory of the lucrative little racket he had been running at his language school in France. Learning that a number of the foreign students were domiciled without the requisite papers, he had been blithely threatening to shop them to the authorities unless they produced suitably enhanced fees. Turnbull – as smooth a blackmailer as he was a murderer . . . I opened my eyes with a start. 'Good Lord!' I gasped. 'Surely not!'

The droning stopped. 'Oh dear! Is there something wrong, Canon?' Mavis's solicitous voice enquired.

'I, er, well, not really . . . so sorry, I—'

I was cut short by Miss Dalrymple, who, seizing the opportunity, cried, 'Fascinating, Mavis, most succinct! Now, I think it's time we all went home.' And grasping handbag, gloves and next-door neighbour, she made a beeline for the exit. Others were quick to follow. I rather suspect I may have gone up a notch in her estimation.

I wandered back to the vicarage, musing uneasily upon the possibility of Turnbull being the blackmailer of Clinker and Nicholas. There wasn't a shred of evidence of course, but as with intractable crosswords, in this type of worrying mystery one grasps at the remotest straws to provide a lead. And it seemed to me that here were three straws: Turnbull had already previously engaged in blackmailing activities to supplement his commercial enterprise; although unproved, he was believed by three of us to be a double murderer, ruthless in pursuit of his own ends; and according to Maud Tubbly Pole he had an innately sadistic temperament – which would make him entirely capable of exerting relentless and teasing pressure on his victims. But why those particular victims? Because they were *known* to him: the French connection! As Lavinia's cousin, he had been a frequent presence in the Birtle-Figgins's house above Berceau, and would have become friendly with the Clinkers during their sojourn there. Nicholas too he had encountered at least a couple of times (indeed, I specifically recalled them chatting most amicably in the aftermath of Boris's funeral). What might he have guessed, ascertained and subsequently rooted out about that past liaison? And now, returned to London with a fresh enterprise and seeking additional funds, what better pickings to swell the coffers than the noble bishop and his 'bit of fluff'!

Far-flung conjecture? Possibly. But the thought had taken root in my mind and I was stuck with it for the rest of the evening, even in sleep that night it coloured and troubled my dreams.

11

The Vicar's Version

Waking early the next morning I was even more determined to persuade Primrose not to involve herself further with Lavinia Birtle-Figgins and Turnbull. If the latter really was doing the blackmailing then all the more reason to give them a wide berth. Primrose was wayward and I doubted whether she really appreciated the danger she was courting. At the back of my mind, too, was now the nagging thought that if Rupert Turnbull could rake up *their* past, might he not turn to mine as well? If he was on to rich pickings with them, they'd be even richer with me! And with a shudder my thoughts went back to France and the sneering menace of Mullion's predatory eye . . .

I was startled out of my broodings by the antics of the dog. He had been sleeping peacefully at the foot of the bed, but with a sudden flurried shake woke up and scrambled towards me, licked my face and then flopped down again with his head on my chest. I lay surprised and still, wondering what had precipitated such a manoeuvre, but oddly soothed by the snuffling closeness. The snuffling lapsed into heavy breathing as he dozed off again.

I lay unmoving, my mind still beset with images of danger. But somehow the animal's unexpected interruption and furry proximity had produced a calming effect and put things in a better light. It was absurd to think that Turnbull could possibly get a handle on the Fotherington incident. He had never known her and barely knew me; I had not been charged, nor indeed had any hints or allegations been made in the press. The matter was entirely remote to him. No, as usual the old underlying fear was playing up and I was seeing personal threats where none existed. Of far more pressing concern was the plight of Clinker and Ingaza.

In their different ways both men infuriated me, but each had become an integral part of my life and I held them in grudging if exasperated regard. The last thing I wanted was to see either of them hounded mercilessly by a prurient public. Nicholas had suffered it once and I suspected it might destroy the bishop. Yes, theirs was the real problem – but how on earth to deal with it? I gave the dog a pat, and throwing back the bedclothes went downstairs to see about breakfast.

The post had arrived and among the letters was one from Primrose. Her preferred method of communication is the telephone (or telegram if feeling especially assertive), but now and again she will resort to epistle form, partly I think to prevent me from interrupting. Thus, pouring a cup of coffee and fortified by a fresh cigarette, I slit open the envelope and unfolded the scrawled double sheets of her favourite blue writing paper.

Francis dear, the letter began,

You have no idea what an absorbing *time I have spent with Lavinia! And I have come to the conclusion that she is either completely doolally or worryingly sane – a bit of both I suspect. Anyway, the combination has certainly been an intriguing experience and in an odd way rather enjoyable.*

To begin with, she arrived soused *in Chanel (though a welcome change from that pungent herbal stuff she wore in France) and nursing a dog! (Similarly soused.) Fortunately, said dog was minuscule, a kind of mongrel chihuahua – otherwise, like your galumphing Bouncer it would have scared the chinchillas witless. She explained it was a recent present from Rupert and was called Attlee – for whom, for some obscure reason, she had conceived a yen during the war. Fortunately the creature took after its namesake,*

57

keeping silent at all times except to emit a brisk irascible bark whenever it wanted to go out. I enquired if it smoked a pipe and she said not as far as she knew.

Anyway, unpacking and pleasantries over, I took them both on a tour of the garden (looking rather good actually – though I do think you could have tied the hollyhocks more securely, they are flopping all over the place). We then sat in the summer house and I asked her if she missed France – meaning, of course, Boris.

Well, you'll never guess what she said! After gazing pensively at the distant Downs, she replied that on the whole, no, and sad though Boris's death was, had it not been for such an untimely event she would never have had the good fortune to meet Mr Attlee. She must have seen my surprise, for she explained that her husband had been allergic to all animals and would never allow her to have one. Other than observing that it was an ill wind, I wasn't quite sure what I was supposed to say. However, the remark evidently suited her for she exclaimed, 'My feelings exactly!', adding that it was strange the way things would often 'pan out', even when least expected. I agreed that it was very strange – and considered throwing in something about silver linings and the undoubted rewards of patience, but thought better of it.

By this time a breeze was getting up and my own view was that things were 'panning out' in the direction of a large gin. So we moved indoors and Lavinia said she would join me later as she had a new frock she wanted to wear for the opening and it was essential to get it exactly right. She seemed to expect the dog to join her upstairs, but it remained rooted to the sofa, unmoved and unwilling. It's a dour-faced little creature, but once it had ascertained that I had no intention of smothering it in scent and kisses we became quite matey.

Half an hour later the owner reappeared, resplendent in pearls and shimmering blue satin – with, I may say, eyeshadow and snazzy Louis heels to match. I can tell you, Francis, a far cry from the dirndls and drooping tent dresses of Berceau-Lamont! Naturally, with that as an example I felt obliged to cut a dash myself (Mother's antique earrings and dear Uncle Herbert's sequinned bolero). So there we were – two tall women decked to the nines, gadding off for the evening in the impeccable company of the tacit Attlee!

I was just pondering in which particular game of charades I had last seen Uncle Herbert sporting that bolero (a garment he would regularly struggle into regardless of theme or suitability), when Maurice leapt through the open window and, evidently in tolerant mood, settled himself on my lap. This doesn't happen very often and I felt duty-bound to stop my reading and express gratitude and surprise. Courtesies were exchanged, an inquisitive paw extended to scrabble with the discarded envelope, and then, after a few gracious purrs and a quick tweak of my tie, he was off again to harry the woollen mouse. I returned to the letter.

When we arrived, there was already a great mob of people: quite a number I knew, of course, but a whole gaggle that I didn't (down from London I think) and presumably associates of Lavinia's old school chum, a plump mousy little creature – though judging from the diamond studs and necklace, obviously loaded. Business must be booming! Certainly she had spared no expense in furnishing the new premises, and everything looked frightfully chic and à la mode. The champagne wasn't bad either.

Which, Francis, brings me to our friend Ingaza. Oh yes, he was there all right – draped over a dry martini and muttering querulously about the owner's taste in contemporary abstracts. 'If little Miss Prissy imagines the cognoscenti of Brighton are going to be dazzled by these daubings she's in for a shock,' he opined. 'So passé! You'll see – the whole thing will go bust in a month.' And deftly intercepting a passing drinks tray, he replaced his empty cocktail glass with a full one of 'Miss Prissy's' vintage champagne.

Yes, on standard form you might say. Except that I couldn't help feeling he seemed a trifle tense: dragging on even more gaspers than usual and nearly jumping out of his skin when some art-dealing crony tapped him lightly on the shoulder. I made a joke about his looking like a marked man – to which he replied darkly that he probably was. And when I asked marked by whom, he said that that was exactly what he wanted to know. Well frankly I had better things to do than stand grappling with Ingaza's conundrums – e.g. to reach the caviar canapés before they were all snaffled. So after giving him a sharp reminder that I still awaited my Canadian fee, I rejoined the hordes.

And that's when I saw Lavinia talking animatedly with some elderly gent of about ninety (sixty-five, probably, but he looked pretty decrepit to me) whom she introduced vaguely as an old friend of the family (hers or Boris's?) and whom she hadn't met for ages but so hoped to see more of now she was back in London. Apparently the hope was reciprocated as I noticed he plied her with Sidecars for the rest of the evening. Eventually he joined a group about to get the train back to London. But just before he left she whispered to me that he owned a yacht and was 'worth quite a bob or two' – an observation which personally I couldn't help thinking just a mite vulgar. Anyway, she said he was called Frederick – though whether that was his first or second name it wasn't clear. But she also added that he had once been a schoolmaster in India – Jaipur, I think – but had moved on to more lucrative things. Would need to, presumably, if he was able to afford a yacht!

I reread those last lines with startled curiosity . . . It couldn't be, surely! No, of course not. The scholastic world must abound in English ex-schoolmasters who had taught in India twenty years ago or more, and doubtless quite a few in Jaipur . . . But would so many Fredericks have gravitated to Jaipur? Perhaps not. Even so, it seemed improbable that Lavinia's elderly friend should be the Freddie Felter so luridly described by Mrs Tubbly Pole. Of course not. It was bound to transpire that this man was called John Frederick, an Oxford graduate in History who couldn't add up for toffee and had never worn a moustache in his life, drooping or otherwise. That firmly settled I continued with the remainder of the letter.

Anyway, eventually things wound up and we hitched a lift back with one of the guests, Lavinia clearly having enjoyed herself chewing the cud with her old school chum – Ingaza's 'Miss Prissy' – and then latterly with the attentive Frederick chap. As a matter of fact she had taken quite a bit on board, so when we got home I suggested some coffee but she said it was 'safer' to stick with gin. So the three of us (if you count the beloved Attlee) put our feet up in the sitting room and indulged in the usual post-mortem, in the course of which she said she had glimpsed Ingaza across the room but hadn't the nerve to approach as he had looked so grim(!)

I was going to ask her more about Turnbull's professional plans and whether she was thinking of partnering him in the language schools project, but before I got there she suddenly trilled, 'It's such fun living dangerously, don't you think?'

Without mentioning the gory French episode, I asked if that was what she had been doing with Boris. She took a sip of gin and grimaced, though I wasn't sure whether that was on account of the lack of bitters or the thought of her late husband. The latter I think, for she exclaimed, 'Good gracious, nothing dangerous there – just crashing boredom from start to finish. What a fool I was to be so influenced! Ah well, water under the bridge, things are different now.' She then turned to the dog and crooned, 'Isn't that so, mon petit cheri?' I don't think Attlee liked being addressed as 'cheri' as he gazed fixedly ahead, making no response.

Well, Francis, all I can say is that either she's totally unaware that Turnbull did in her old man or she hasn't the slightest clue that you or I suspect anything. Otherwise how on earth could she be so gormlessly indiscreet!! As said, either perfectly intelligent or as thick as they come! Make sure you give me a bell when you can tear yourself away from clerical delights. Shall be interested to hear your views.

All love – P.

I put down the letter, and tackling tomato and fried bread began to ponder the import of Primrose's news.

I didn't get far, as there was a sudden rap on the window accompanied by the lowering face of the organist. I stood up reluctantly, draping a napkin over my breakfast things. If Tapsell imagined he was going to be offered coffee and bacon he had another think coming!

I opened the window. 'Good morning, Tapsell,' I said affably. 'You're up early, aren't you?'

'Just as well,' he snapped. 'We've got mice in the organ pipes and they're all fighting! What are you going to do about it?'

'Shoot the buggers,' I said, and closed the window.

12

The Cat's Memoir

It had been an entertaining morning really. First, anguished roars from the infant next door having been foolish enough to plunge into the water butt (I had been watching its approach with interest, guessing that something dramatic might happen); then squabbles among the pigeons over a rather disagreeable piece of cake – which naturally I appropriated, leaving them gaping and furious; and then the arrival of the postman with a letter from the vicar's sister. How did I know it was from her? Well I didn't really, but I was assured by Bouncer that that was the case. And how did the dog know? Precisely the question I asked him.

'Oh yes,' he announced airily, 'definitely from the Prim.'

'Since your only reading material is the dog-Latin in the crypt,' I pointed out, 'I don't see how you can possibly tell.'

'Huh, you don't have to *read* – smelling's enough.'

'Smelling what?'

He sighed (almost as if I were defective!) 'That Sussex air and her skin, of course. Envelope's smothered in spoor of both. Obvious.'

'Really?' I said doubtfully. 'Unusual sensitivity, Bouncer.'

'Nothing unusual about it,' he replied, 'just bred in the bone. It's what us dogs have. Cats don't.' He spoke with nonchalant authority and I thought it best not to pursue the matter.

'But rather rare for her to write a whole letter, isn't it?' I suggested. 'Normally it's the telephone or those little yellow envelopes delivered by the red-headed boy. Must be something special.'

'Could be,' answered the dog. 'Why don't you go and take a look and see what he's doing? If he's grinding those humbugs and twitching his ankle it's bound to be bad, but if he's just smoking and blowing rings it's probably okay.' Thus, still feeling moderately cooperative, I did precisely that.

I perched on the window ledge, peering in, but with the subject of my scrutiny largely obscured by a haze of smoke, it was difficult to see much. So I slipped into the room and up on to his lap. Although immersed in the letter he had the good grace to pause and say a few words of welcome which I duly acknowledged. There was no sign of the peppermints or twitching ankle so it would seem all was normal.

I ducked my head under his wrist to see if anything intelligible could be gleaned from the paper in his hand. Alas, despite my several skills I have yet to master the art of deciphering human hieroglyphics (particularly when so carelessly scrawled). So all I could discern was that the writing was copious, which *might* mean that Primrose had something important to say – though if human speech is anything to go by, volume is no guarantee of interest.

Feeling it polite to tarry a little longer, I toyed briefly with the crumpled envelope, gave a playful yank of his tie, and then suddenly glimpsing my woollen mouse lurking in a corner, disengaged myself and leapt in pursuit.

I was just giving the creature a few prods with my paw when there was a gasp from the vicar followed by the exclamation, 'Good grief, not that Felter, it couldn't be!' I glanced up and saw a startled look on his face, but then calming down again he resumed reading. Nothing more was said, and losing interest I picked up the mouse and went into the hall where I met the dog bounding in from the garden wanting its breakfast.

'Things all right?' he asked.

I said that for the time being they seemed so, but that I had heard F.O. utter a name which had caused him momentary agitation and it might be useful to commit it to memory in case of repercussions.

'What name?'

I told him it was Felter, and knowing that Bouncer can be a trifle slow in these matters, patiently repeated the syllables for him.

'Oh yes,' he said carelessly, 'Freddie Felter – nasty piece of work.'

I am not often flummoxed by the dog but this was one such time, and jettisoning the mouse, I stared in astonishment. 'How on earth do you know that?'

'Easy,' he replied, 'it's what the Tubbly was gassing on about when she was here the other day. Don't you remember? When she brought old Gunga and I bit his bum again.'

I nodded. 'Yes, I do remember – a most indecorous scene.'

'But funny!'

I conceded it was funny but said I did not recall anything being said about someone with the name of Freddie Felter.

'Don't suppose you would. You had sloped off to the graveyard by then. But *I* stayed and heard everything. They thought I was busy with my bone, which I was to begin with, but then I stopped and just sat listening VERY QUIETLY!' He wagged his tail, looking pleased with himself, while I readjusted my ears. For one uneasy moment I thought he might bark out a few of the French words he had learnt in the Auvergne, but fortunately I was spared that.

'So what did you hear?'

'Enough to know that this Felt fellow is a bad lot and looks like a walrus. The Tubbly said that her mate Jacko had been very good at sniffing things. Just like me! And *also* like me he could always tell when someone didn't smell right, even from a hundred yards. And the Felt Fellow was one of those – got a very nasty pong to him. So you see, Maurice!'

'Not entirely,' I murmured. 'All you have told me is that the Felt Fellow looks peculiar and is noisome.'

He scowled. 'Not noisy, *smelly*! Are you going deaf, Maurice? I said he didn't SMELL right!!' There was a belligerent look in his eye and I thought it unwise to argue the point.

'Yes, yes,' I said hastily, 'I've got the idea – so what else was said?'

There was silence while the dog furrowed his brows and gazed into the distance. I waited patiently.

'Turnip,' he said eventually.

'Ah,' I said encouragingly. 'And . . . ?'

'Well, you see,' he exclaimed eagerly, giving me a shove with his nose, 'a LONG time ago Felt and Turnip knew each other and went around beating people up . . . What do you think of that? When the Tubbly told F.O. I could see he was quite shocked.' He paused and then added, 'But after that I rather lost the thread of things – you know how it is, sometimes they gabble so fast a chap can't always . . .' He trailed off lamely.

'Excellent, Bouncer,' I mewed. 'We are now in possession of certain facts which may come in useful.'

He brightened. 'Do you think so?'

'Without a doubt. What you have ascertained is that Felt is distasteful and dangerous and is – or was once – somehow linked with the blackguard Turnip and F.O. seems perturbed by this. Such intelligence may be of value to us. After all, forewarned is—'

'You mean a sniffy snout keeps the spies out!' the dog shouted.

'*What?*'

'It's what my old master Bowler used to say. He was always muttering it.'

'Hmm. Probably about the only time your old master was right – he was not known for his acuity . . . Anyway, it has been a busy morning and I propose we go and play lions and tigers in the graveyard.'

'RATHER!' bellowed the dog.

13

The Vicar's Version

Later that morning, having extricated myself from Tapsell and the mice, i.e. by telephoning the rat-catcher and giving church and organ a wide berth, I retreated to a rare bolt-hole – the darkened snug of the Swan and Goose – and over an early restorative reflected on Primrose's letter.

Lavinia certainly seemed brazenly insouciant about her husband's murder all right, and increasingly it looked as if she had indeed been Turnbull's accomplice – or at the very least, cheerful accessory after the fact. I recalled our first meeting with her as the earnest and whey-faced chatelaine of their modest estate in the rugged Auvergne. There, she had been the model of other-worldly piety, amiably dull and a fit consort to the high-minded Boris. But now, shot of that role and returned to cosmopolitan life, she was fast taking on a persona altogether more chic – and possibly hard-boiled. I remembered her manner in Brown's Hotel: charming and giggly – and yet somehow, beneath the suddenly fashionable attire and wide-eyed gaiety, subtly self-possessed. Interesting how a change in situation can reshape character . . .

But in a way I was more intrigued by Primrose's allu-sion to her companion's elderly chum. The more I pondered on the name Frederick, the more I began to ques-tion my earlier doubts about Lavinia's admirer having once been Turnbull's distasteful housemaster. If Primrose's assessment was right, then his age of sixty-five or there-abouts could certainly fit; but more significant was the fact that like Maud's Freddie Felter, he had schoolmastered in Jaipur before the war. It was true, Frederick *might* be the man's surname – but if Lavinia had mentioned him casually as being an old friend of the family wouldn't she have been more likely to use the less formal title – i.e. his first name? 'Old friend of the family,' I mused. How far did the term 'family' stretch? Turnbull and Lavinia were cousins of sorts . . . Did their familial link include Freddie Felter, erstwhile housemaster at St Austin's, the British college of Jaipur, and drummed out for dubious practices? Hmm.

'Francis!' a voice bawled from the doorway. 'Spotted you, you rogue!' I righted my glass and retrieved the scattered peanuts. It was Mrs Tubbly Pole.

'You weren't at my bun fight last night,' she accused.

'Er, no, I—'

'Feet on fender, screwing up a crossword no doubt.'

'Ah, well not entirely . . .' I murmured defensively.

'No matter, dear friend. You've pledged six copies as it is, so I owe you a pinkers!' She gestured imperiously to the barman. 'A large gin and bitters for the Canon, and have something for yourself. Oh, and you can top mine up while you're about it.' She proffered her glass while I looked nervously for Gunga Din.

'Left the little man at home,' she explained, 'sleeping it off. Heavy night last night *and* successful – although I have to say there were a few oddities in the audience. Somebody called Mavis – kept asking about the "moral dimension". Hadn't a clue what she was talking about. And then if you please she started to spout some plaintive doggerel. Sounded half-cut to me! Have you got many like that in Molehill?'

'Yes,' I said, 'lots.'

'Ah well, all in a day's work. One gets used to it.'

I nodded, and then asked her how she had managed to reach the Swan and Goose. 'It's over a mile and a half from the Gravediggers'. Did you take a taxi?'

She fixed me with a beady eye. 'Some of us, Francis, are sound in wind and limb and are able to drag ourselves the odd mile or so – unlike certain members of the clergy who, scraggy as they may be, evidently bust a gut getting up the pulpit steps!'

I smiled, glancing at my thin knees (but then flinched, recalling my panting efforts trying to hoist her bulldog up the belfry staircase*). 'I'll be happy to drive you back anyway.'

She beamed and we embarked on this and that. Mainly that – i.e. the current parlous state of the publishing world, the conservatism of the reading public, the peculiar foibles of forensic experts, and then – perhaps as a nod in my direction – the equally peculiar foibles of the nineteenth-century Oxford Movement. I contributed a couple of observations on the last item and listened fascinated to the rest. Eventually I ventured a question.

'I say, Maud, you know the Freddie Felter you were talking about, did he ever drink Sidecars?'

'Oh yes,' she said carelessly, 'all the time. In those days in India it was considered a bit raffish – black cha and whisky being the usual. But of course beastly Freddie had to be different.'

As Ingaza might have said: well, what do you know!

She paused and looked at me quizzically. 'If you don't mind my saying, Francis, your question strikes me as a mite inconsequential . . . What on earth does Freddie Felter's penchant for American cocktails have to do with anything?'

I told her that my sister had seen someone like him talking to a friend of hers recently.

'Is she rich?'

'Who, Primrose?'

'No, the friend.'

'Well,' I said reflectively, 'not short of a bob or two. In fact, now you mention it, probably quite—'

'Could be him I suppose. Little toad always had his eye to the main chance, snooping here, fawning there . . . If you

* See *Bones in the Belfry*

69

want my advice, tell your sister to steer clear. Felter and Turnbull: a nasty pair then and probably much worse now!' She gave a derisory snort, and then glancing at her watch exclaimed that it was long past the 'little fellow's biscuit time'. And thus we made a rapid departure to the Gravediggers' and the charms of Gunga Din.

That evening Primrose telephoned, grumbling about Ingaza's tardiness in remitting her latest dues for the 'Canadian project'.

'He's so slippery,' she fulminated. 'And besides, it's high time he increased my whack – those sketches are being snapped up like hot cakes! Can't you do something, Francis?'

I hesitated. 'Er, I don't suppose he would listen to me. But in any case, Prim, he's a bit preoccupied at present—'

'Oh yes,' she exclaimed scornfully, 'doubtless cooking up some fiendish heist with that awful Eric!'

'You mean more fiendish than yours?' I asked innocently.

The explosion was swift and predictable, but I cut her short, saying, 'If you really want to know, he is being black-mailed – and so is Clinker.'

There was a silence, broken by a spluttering whistle. 'Who on earth by? Canterbury?'

Patiently I explained the situation of the letters; and then on the principle of in for a penny, in for a pound, unfolded my suspicions about Turnbull.

There followed another silence. And then she said musingly, 'You might have something there. I gather from Lavinia that since getting back from France, Rupert and Clinker have been socializing.'

'Socializing? In what way?'

'The usual way. Apparently they bumped into each other at some education conference in Oxford, and Rupert got quite chummy with Clinker – started to reminisce about Berceau-Lamont and poor old Boris, and quizzed him about his time as a don before the war. It seems Turnbull managed to screw some funding out of Hor's old college

70

for another language institute he is busy setting up, something to do with the foreign intake on their postgraduate courses. Anyway, according to Lavinia, since then he and Hor have been getting on quite well. She seemed to find it rather amusing.'

'Well, she would, wouldn't she,' I replied tartly, 'knowing that the noble bishop is unwittingly consorting with a murderer?'

'Hmm,' replied Primrose smoothly, 'as he does unwittingly with you . . .'

I glowered down the telephone, but let it pass and instead asked her: 'Do you think I should warn him off – you know, sort of suggest that Turnbull is a bit iffy and he would be wise to steer clear?'

'Well if he *is* the blackmailer, it's a little late for that, isn't it? He has obviously delved into Clinker's past and, alias Donald Duck, already made his approach. Besides, there's absolutely no *proof* that he is involved. He may have dispatched Boris and be fundamentally nasty, but that doesn't mean he is now putting the screws on old Horace. So far it's mere conjecture . . . Best to keep quiet if you ask me. As Ma used to say to Pa, "Close your eyes, dear, and it will all dissolve."'

'Yes,' I said wryly, 'and I remember Pa's response. It wasn't pretty!'

She giggled. 'No, it wasn't. But just occasionally Mother was right: it doesn't do to jump the gun.'

I wasn't entirely convinced, but reflected that it would be tricky giving a cogent warning without also disclosing other matters to Clinker – i.e. our conviction that Turnbull had been Boris's assassin in France: a revelation whose reception could be exhausting to say the least. Yes, I counselled myself, Primrose was right – let sleeping bishops lie . . .

They were not to lie long. The following morning I was startled awake by an early phone call. And after blearily stumbling downstairs and nearly breaking my neck on the dog's bone, I was even more startled to hear Ingaza's nasal tones. Dawn raids are not his speciality.

'I've heard from Hor,' he announced. 'He's had another letter.'

'Er, sorry – what?'

'Clinker. He's had a second letter ... from the fucking duck.'

14

The Vicar's Version

'Oh no,' I groaned, 'this is really a bit much!'

'I should think it is a bit much!' Ingaza snarled. 'It's sodding too bloody much!' A rant ensued involving terms of a similarly robust ilk.

'So it is only Clinker – you haven't received another?'

'Not yet, but I'm bound to get one – or,' he added sadistically, 'you will.'

I paled. 'Me!'

'Well yes, old boy,' he replied, reverting to his usual drawl. 'He may have started with Hor and me, but you have to admit that you rather have the edge on us in the high stakes. I wouldn't be complacent if I were you.'

Complacent? That would be the day!

'I am far from being that, Nicholas,' I replied evenly, 'but for the moment I think we should address the immediate threat which is to you and Horace. No point in crossing hypothetical bridges.' (That last utterance had a familiar ring and I recalled it had been one of Pa's favourite sayings. Did my tone sound as patronizing? I hoped not.)

'Hmm. That's as may be. Anyway, Hor's in a right sweat. Wants to meet us pronto at his London club this Saturday. He's up there for some function at Lambeth Palace and it's the only time he can manage. He sounded pretty rattled so I suppose if he wants to talk about it we had better go. I gather the club is one of those swish jobs in Pall Mall and does quite a decent lunch. Actually offered to foot the bill, so he must be desperate!' He gave a hollow laugh.

There was a busy week ahead and Saturday would be the first break in the schedule. So the prospect of flogging up to London to listen to the bishop and Ingaza lamenting their collective plight was not enticing. I had enough perils of my own to consider without augmenting them with other people's.

But the instant the thought came, it vanished in a puff of guilt. It was precisely because I was so familiar with the condition of fearful panic and the isolation it brings, that I should now give what small support I could. 'That's what pals are *for*, Francis,' I heard my sister's voice pontificating in the treehouse decades ago, 'they help you out of jams!' I wasn't sure that either Clinker or Ingaza fitted the category of 'pal' exactly (bane, more like), but you get accustomed to people and owe them a jaundiced loyalty ... Besides, as Nicholas had hinted, and which had already passed through my own mind, there was always the possibility that I too might be caught in the orbit of the Donald Duck character. And as Nicholas had also so charmingly observed, in my case the stakes were higher. One did not get the chop for buggery, but one did for murder ... No, this was not a time for wry disinterest. The jam was sticky, and one way or another we were all up to our ears in it.

'Yes, Nicholas,' I said easily, 'Saturday should be fine. If the Lord Bishop requires our presence in London, who are we to deny him that whim?'

'My sentiments exactly, old cock,' was the dry reply.

The next few days were both trying and bumpy: trials via the Vestry Committee with its interminable ramblings and agitated phone calls; bumps from the Mothers' Union, the Confederacy of Church Wardens and other assorted complainants. Three funerals brought relief from their cheerless attentions, but by Friday night I was ready for some emollient rest. Not that any was in prospect, for a day in London with the bishop and Ingaza was unlikely to soothe a troubled spirit. However, I recalled grimly, all part of one's moral duty . . .

Thus with our meeting scheduled for midday, I rose at dawn on the Saturday morning. Apparently Clinker had to return to Lambeth in the afternoon to chair one of the sessions, hence the early lunch at his club.

I was just checking the timetable for a fast train to Waterloo when the phone rang. It was Ingaza, in some dudgeon.

'Change of plan,' he exclaimed, 'you can go back to bed.'

'What do you mean?'

'What I say. Hor wants us in the evening instead. We've got to meet him at the Albert Hall.'

'The *Albert Hall*! Why there, in Heaven's name?'

'You might well ask,' he said acidly. 'It's bloody Gladys – something to do with her joining him unexpectedly in London and wanting to go to a concert there. Messed up all his plans.'

'But we can hardly discuss the letter with him if she's hovering.'

'That's what I said, but he seemed to think he could manage some diversionary tactic. Apparently he's up to his eyes with meetings in the coming week and it's the only chance he'll get to give us a sighting of this thing.'

'But I was going to listen to a good concert on the Third Programme tonight,' I protested.

'Well, dear boy, what could be better? We might get seats at the Albert Hall. Far better than the wireless! Not my thing entirely, but since we're there I don't mind staying for a couple of good tunes.'

'What tunes?' I asked suspiciously.

'No idea, but I gather Sargent's conducting, and some old trout called Myra Hess is tickling the ivories.'

'Myra Hess!' I exclaimed. 'Good Lord, put me down for that!'

And that's what he did. And I met him that evening in the bar of the Rubens Hotel for a quick snifter before confronting the purlieus of Kensington Gore and the laments of Clinker.

Actually, the snifter wasn't so quick. And after we had finished making fruitless speculation about the blackmail, and Nicholas had eyed up the barman and regaled me with gruesome tales of his awful Aunt Lil, time was running out. We had fifteen minutes to find a cab and take our seats.

The resultant race was undignified and exhausting. But we arrived with seconds to spare and decanted ourselves into the auditorium, pushing our way past tutting seats and irate glares just in time for the entry of the orchestra leader. With a flourish of coat-tails he took his place to the sound of polite applause, fiddled with his fiddle, and with a look of quizzical expectation peered towards the wings from which, after a fractional pause, Sargent appeared.

Evening dress impeccably cut, carnation pristine, black hair finely sleeked and shoes polished to perfection – dapper, stylish Flash Harry took his bow to a wave of thunderous acclaim. Graciously the confident smile raked stalls and loggias. The clapping swelled, subsided . . . Then with a nod to the first violin, the svelte figure turned to face his players and with a shooting of cuffs and brisk flourish of baton, signalled the opening bars . . . Yes, as always, intelligent musician and consummate showman was in fine fettle.

'Christ,' Ingaza muttered, 'wouldn't mind a bit of that!'

'Didn't think you liked Brahms,' I whispered.

There was a pause. And then he replied sotto voce, 'Not Brahms, dear boy – the other chap.'

In fact, given our situation, there was scant chance for either of us to savour the performance – musical or otherwise. For ten rows away I could see Clinker and, despite my hopes, Gladys at his side. Just marvellous! How on earth were we going to have a chance of seeing that letter with his wife in tow?

And then my eyes alighted on someone else: Hubert Hesketh, dean of Clinker's cathedral. He was sitting next to Gladys, flapping his programme and nodding rhythmically to the music. She won't like that, I thought with some satisfaction. However, Gladys's irritation was of little concern compared with my own annoyance that we were fated to negotiate the bishop's entourage before getting a glimpse of the letter. What an absurd idea – to demand that we meet him here and then to bring his wife and dean! I slumped irritably in my seat. But unlike Ingaza, whose eyes were clearly magnetized by the figure on the platform, I soon became diverted by those plangent magisterial strains; and closing my eyes and banishing all thoughts of the Clinker contingent, gave myself up to Brahmsian sonorities . . .

With a final swirl of the baton and discreet nod to the brass, the crashing chords were stilled, to be replaced by a tidal wave of applause. The maestro turned, beamed, bowed, exited; re-entered, beamed, bowed, exited; re-entered . . .

Nicholas leered. 'Not bad at all, at all . . . Now, where's old Hor?'

'Scarpered.' I scanned the exit and just caught sight of the backs of Gladys and Hesketh disappearing into the throng.

'Who's that with her?' asked Nicholas. 'It looks like another of your crew.'

'It is,' I said shortly. 'Hesketh, the dean.'

'Good Lord, you don't mean old Hubert Hesketh – the one who was always so keen on reading the lessons at St Bede's? Fancy him turning up again! Thought he might have made his name by now at the Folies Bergère.' He sniggered.

'At the Folies . . . What *are* you talking about, Nicholas?'

Still grinning, he dropped his voice and in confidential tones said, 'Well according to the college grapevine, his balls used to light up like Christmas trees . . . on certain occasions at any rate, I gather.'

'Light up like what?' I cried, blushing to my roots.

'Yes, all silver and sort of—'

'Would you mind, Nicholas,' I protested. 'I really don't need to know these things!'

'No,' he agreed, 'you're probably right, old man. Wouldn't do your psyche any good. Now, what's Hor up to?'

Still retaining uneasy pictures of flashing baubles, I told him that in view of the latest development, he was probably trying to escape his companions or anaesthetize himself at the bar.

We pushed our way out into the foyer and glimpsed the other two, but not the bishop. 'Probably gone for a leak,' said Nicholas. 'You hang on here and I'll see if I can find him.'

'No,' I said firmly. 'Gladys has just noticed us. *I'll* go and you can hold the fort.'

Without waiting for a response, I made my way purposefully towards the gents. As luck would have it, Clinker was just coming out as I went in.

'Ah, Francis,' he exclaimed, 'glad to see you. Thought you weren't here. Couldn't see you when we arrived. Ghastly day, ghastly!'

'Yes, sir,' I said hastily, 'but what about the letter? Have you got it?'

'Of course I've got it,' he replied testily. 'You don't imagine I left it at home in Gladys's sewing basket, do you?' With a furtive glance to left and right, he delved into his inside pocket and fished it out. This time there were only a few lines:

No, my Lord Bishop, I can assure you it won't go away – and given the tasteless nature of the offence and the amount of public prurience should it become known, the requested sum will not be chicken feed! Better start approaching your brokers – and tell your sharkish friend to flog a few more artefacts! By the way, be careful where you tread – your movements are being noted.
Quack quack for now,
Donald

'Still the farmyard fixation,' I observed, 'and still no mention of the exact money.'

'No,' replied Clinker bitterly. 'As I said, he's enjoying making me sweat, spinning it out for the sudden pounce. And what's that sneaky bit about being watched? Oh my God, this is awful. Where's Ingaza? He's got to see this.' He scanned the crowd distractedly.

'Slightly tricky at the moment, he's collared by . . . er, he's talking with your wife and the Reverend Hesketh.'

Clinker sighed. 'Yes, the moment it was known I would be up in London for the Dioceses' Forum she insisted on a shopping expedition to Derry & Toms, plus this concert some friend had given her tickets for. Friend bowed out – hence Hesketh. I hadn't a chance.' He scowled; and taking the note from me, stuffed it back in his pocket.

'But you have to admit the music's rather good,' I ventured. 'Some time since I've been to a full-blown performance, and it's always inspiring under a conductor like Sir Malcolm. And with Dame Myra doing the Beethoven after the interval it will really be—'

'Yes, yes,' muttered Clinker impatiently, 'all very nice I'm sure, but I have no intention of staying for the second half. That fellow Turnbull has invited us to his cousin's housewarming party. Apparently she's putting on quite a show. It's in one of those flats behind the Hall, just a couple of streets away. So with luck one can get there before everything's scoffed. Having starved on salad for lunch and listened to the Lambeth contingent droning on about the dearth of African missionaries I could do with something substantial.' He paused, and as I was digesting the bit about Lavinia's housewarming, added in anguished tones, 'But I *must* see Nicholas, it's essential we compare notes!'

'Yes, he certainly wants to look at the letter, but I don't think there's anything to compare. So far he hasn't received a second one.'

'Really?' asked Clinker in surprise. 'Well it's about time he did. I don't see why I should bear all the brunt!'

'Probably come in tomorrow's post,' I murmured. And on that reassuring note we returned to seek out the others.

Gladys had already donned her coat and, looking like the wrath of God, was cramming on her hat. 'There you are,' she began. 'Couldn't think where you had got to! It'll look so rude if we're late.' She glared at me, obviously assuming I was responsible for the bishop's absence – which in a way I was. 'Do hurry up!'

'All in good time,' replied Clinker shortly. 'Besides, there's something I need to discuss with Nicholas first,' and he made to draw him aside.

'Can't think what,' was the brusque retort. 'In any case, people are already returning to their seats. We don't want to delay Mr Ingaza's musical enjoyment, do we?' (This said with a smile of icy politeness.)

Her husband looked mulish, so sensing defeat, Gladys declared she would go on ahead and grasping the hapless Hesketh by the elbow, propelled him towards the exit.

Clinker breathed a sigh of relief and once more taking the letter from his pocket, thrust it under Ingaza's nose. The latter read it impassively.

'So what do you think of that?' the bishop demanded.

Ingaza shrugged. 'Not much. A borderline case, I would say – unless he's assuming a persona.'

'What do you mean?'

'Well . . . so far the tone of these letters has suggested spite and obsession, i.e. the classic style of a twisted temperament. But that might just be a misleading front – or an amusement. It's possible the writer is entirely sane and detached, his very normality his insurance.'

'Hmm,' said Clinker, 'you may be right, but either way, what a scoundrel! And as for that crack about my movements being noted . . . why, he might be here *now*!' He glanced around nervously.

'Yes, it's probably Hesketh,' grinned Nicholas.

Clinker eyed him coldly. 'I consider that in very poor taste. Typical. No help at all!' He sighed heavily. 'Hmm. Perhaps I really ought to start shifting some shares . . .'

As the bishop pondered, I thought of Ingaza's earlier words: 'sane and detached, his very normality his insurance.' And again the amiable face and pleasant voice of Rupert Turnbull swam into mind . . .

'This party you've been invited to,' Ingaza suddenly broke in, 'can anyone go?'

'What?' said Clinker vaguely.

'Well, if you don't mind my saying so,' Ingaza explained smoothly, 'you did drag us up here on the promise of a few drinks and a cosy confab at your swish club, but so far all we've had is the Albert Hall; and other than Flash Harry, no entertainment. Personally I could do with some champers and a little pâté de whatsit. Do us all good!'

Clinker looked doubtful. And then he brightened. 'Yes, I take your point . . . a spot of epicurean indulgence to blot out the horror. All right then – don't suppose they'd mind a couple of extras, it's not as if they've never met you.' He turned to me and added, 'Besides, Lavinia seems to like you, Francis, and anything's better than being stuck with the dean all evening!'

I hung back, nettled by this last observation and reluctant to forego the pleasure of hearing Dame Myra. I was even more reluctant to re-encounter Turnbull. However, the other two were already striding ahead, and thus I followed in a mood of nervous curiosity . . .

15

The Cat's Memoir

'Stupid idiot!' the dog grumbled. 'He's gone and taken my bone and dropped it in the dustbin.'

'Hardly the first time,' I murmured. 'Why don't you get it out? Knock the thing over, you usually do.'

'I have. But he's clamped the lid on so tight I can't get into it. You'll have to do something, Maurice.'

'Me!'

'Yes, you can shove one of your claws under the rim and ease it off.'

'I hardly see why I should employ my undoubted dexterity in retrieving one of your beastly bones.'

'Ah, but you might if I tell you what I've heard.'

'Oh? What have you heard?'

'Shan't say,' he chortled, plunging his head down to his nether regions.

I viewed the inelegance with narrowed eyes, debating whether to succumb to the dog's blackmail or remain in ignorance. Being an enquiring cat, I eventually bowed to curiosity and graciously told him that I was always ready to help a fellow creature combat the vicar's foibles.

He frowned. 'What's foi . . . ?'

'A minor silliness,' I explained patiently.

'Huh! No silliness,' he growled, 'plain revenge!'

'What for?'

'Went arse over tip on his way to the blower. The idiot hadn't seen my bone on the bottom stair.'

'How careless,' I tactfully agreed.

He nodded eagerly. 'So you'll do it?'

'Provided you tell me exactly what you know.'

He embarked on a fractured, albeit theatrical account of F.O.'s telephone conversations, first with the Brighton Type and then with the Prim. From what I could make out there was some disturbance involving the Clinker: unsavoury letters had been received and pressure applied. I tried to read between the lines of Bouncer's narrative but could glean little other than the bishop person was in danger over something in his past and that the Brighton Type was incandescent. (According to Bouncer, F.O. had gone quite pink at the quality of the invective ... though of course those were not the dog's words, his being something about the vicar going red as a baboon's backside.) Anyway, the upshot seemed to be that F.O. was required to join the Brighton Type in London – though regarding when or for what purpose the dog was tantalizingly vague. I tried to elicit further details but he lapsed into gormless truculence and asked when I was going to rescue his bone.

Needless to say, the lid slipped off the bin with the ease of an oiled haddock and Bouncer was suitably impressed. I have a knack with such things, learnt long ago at the paws of my redoubtable grandfather, Maltravers. Under his tuition I was able to assimilate a wealth of skills necessary to the confounding of human guile ... And from the same source came my refusal to kowtow to the obstinacy of dogs. Thus if Bouncer imagined I would be fobbed off by vague evasions regarding F.O.'s mission to London, he could think again! Such is the bedlam in this household that it doesn't do to permit lapses in intelligence: at all costs a cat must keep ahead of the chaos!

16

The Vicar's Version

The flat was in one of those Victorian red-brick mansion blocks favoured by the fashionable and well heeled; and as we went up the solid steps I couldn't help thinking that Lavinia must have done pretty well out of the sale of the French property – and indeed any other remunerations accruing from her husband's murder.

We took the lift to the third floor, and guided by a buzz of voices and a slightly open door, entered the vestibule of her new abode. The room beyond was large, beautifully furnished – and packed. We hovered on the threshold, bemused by the throng but eager to forage. Out of the corner of my eye I caught sight of Hesketh, still attached to Gladys and presumably still making dutiful small talk. In his hand he held a glass of water (conceivably gin, though it seemed unlikely). Clinker, too, had probably seen them, for with a brisk clearing of throat he began to push his way in the opposite direction, muttering something about looking for his hostess. He wasn't of course; just seeking the nearest source of food.

Ingaza became similarly engaged, but in his case the focus was a distant tray of champagne – although I wasn't sure whether the attraction was the drink or its purveyor, a handsome youth whose white flunky's jacket conferred a passing air of distinction.

And then just as I was thinking that I too might go in quest of libations, I noticed the new tenant standing in a far corner talking animatedly among a group of her guests. I had not seen Lavinia since taking tea at Brown's, and her now total transformation from frump to moderate siren was striking. I had forgotten the sartorial details in Primrose's letter, but the cobalt-blue sheath-dress, elaborately coiffed hair and glittering bangles jogged my memory. I also recalled my sister's description of the newly acquired lap-dog Attlee, and I scanned the room, curious to spy the little creature, but he had obviously elected to remain aloofly out of sight. (Nevertheless, mindful of the embarrassing encounter with Bouncer at an earlier and fateful soirée, I was careful where I put my feet.*)

'I say, Oughterard,' said a voice behind me, 'awfully good of you to come. A most pleasant surprise!' I turned round and was met with the benign features of Rupert Turnbull. Slightly embarrassed, I started to explain that I had been 'swept up' by the bishop at the concert and was on the point of leaving for Molehill.

'Oh no, don't do that,' he beamed, 'all the more the merrier. You *must* stay, Lavinia will be delighted that you are here!' And so saying, he thrust a drink into my hand and propelled me towards where she was standing.

She greeted me warmly and I complimented her on the decor of the new flat. She looked almost radiant, and divested of the late Mr Birtle-Figgins was clearly in her element.

We chatted for a while, and she enthused about her cousin's language schools, saying she was helping to back a fresh project in Oxford. 'Of course they've got masses of such places there already, but Rupert's will be *ultra* up to date with all the very latest equipment, and catering *only* for the high-flying specialists ... you know, the Foreign Office bods and MI5 – and MI6 too, I gather, or whatever number they give themselves!' She giggled. 'Oh yes, it's going to be all rather special, and *so* enterprising. Mind

* See *A Load of Old Bones*

you, there's a huge outlay required. But knowing Rupert he's bound to recoup it in next to no time, he's awfully good like that!' She prattled on merrily, while I visualized Boris's fate upon the flagstones.

After a little I was able to melt away in the direction of the dining room, which displayed a still-enticing buffet. Just as I was piling up my plate and nodding vaguely at some fox-faced woman twittering on my left, there was a tap on my shoulder and the earnest form of Hubert Hesketh presented itself. Unless he had had a refill, he was still clutching the same glass of cheerless water.

'Ah, good to have a word with you, Canon,' he whispered. (Except when bawling canticles, Hesketh invariably whispers – a habit that sends Clinker mad and the congregation to sleep.)

'I trust you are enjoying things . . . though I have to say it's not entirely my cup of tea. Too many people and, er, ' (eyeing my heaped-up plate) 'so much food and noise. I always try to avoid these things in Guildford if I can. But when Mrs Clinker heard I was up at Lambeth with the bishop for the annual Forum she most kindly invited me to accompany them to the concert. And then . . . ah, well the next thing was I seemed to be *here* . . .' He smiled ruefully and took an abstemious sip from his glass.

I could see that he was indeed out of his element – even more so than myself, who was at least bolstered by Scotch and kedgeree. (And as to Gladys's 'kind' invitation, I rather suspected the dean's presence was subtle revenge on Clinker for some infringement of her domestic regime.) Dutifully I enquired after his life's work, an ongoing tome devoted to the lesser points of Canon Law in fourth-century Anatolia, and whose proportions and desiccation grew mightier by the year. He gave the customary answer of: 'So much to do and so little time!'

I smiled, observing that it always sounded like a task of daunting complexity, and rather he than me.

'Ah, but you see when one is bent on uncovering the *truth*, nothing daunts. One plods on patiently, intrigued, inspired – and liberated!'

'Liberated?'

'Most definitely,' he whispered. 'After all, every truth is a freedom. Man is but fettered by ignorance. Wouldn't you agree?'

I nodded soberly, while at the same time seeing such truth sending me spiralling down through Pierrepoint's trapdoor. Which was better, I mused: to be revealed and dead or concealed and alive? Given the biological instinct for life over death, I opted for the latter condition. It would do for the meanwhile . . . I also wondered just how liberated our revered bishop might feel if Turnbull or A. N. Other chose to blazon abroad the truth of his Oxford friendship with Ingaza. I had a glimpse of Clinker kicking up his heels on the episcopal lawn, cope and crozier flung to the winds as he tasted the novelty of his 'unfettered' state . . . The scene dissolved with uncanny speed.

Beginning to tire of both kedgeree and Hesketh, I glanced around for Ingaza. With luck he would be ready to leave. At first there seemed no sign, and rather uncharitably I assumed he had slid into the kitchen in pursuit of the white-jacketed waiter. But then I suddenly saw him with Lavinia, talking to a smallish elderly man with bow tie and pince-nez. Lavinia must have seen my gaze for she waved me over, saying, 'We were just talking about you, Francis, and I was telling Freddie here what a *strength* you and Nicholas were during that appalling business with my poor Boris in Berceau-Lamont!' She turned to her companion, adding in rather gushing tones, 'They were simply wonderful, you know, simply wonderful!' Nicholas smiled modestly, smoothly attuned to the charade, while I felt absurd.

However, feelings of absurdity quickly gave way to shock as the name 'Freddie' struck sparks in my brain. Could this be . . . ? I looked to see what he was drinking. But other than a cigarette in an ivory holder he held nothing, let alone anything resembling a Sidecar. No, I was obviously becoming ridiculously obsessed – unhinged, you might say (it doesn't take much) . . . Except that, turning to me and extending a hand, he announced: 'Freddie, Freddie Felter. A pleasure to meet you, Canon. I think I just missed talking to your sister in Brighton – Millie's new gallery launch. Lavinia was going to introduce us, but alas, I had to make a wild dash for my train. Pathetic really, how one is in thrall to railway timetables. Indeed, one gathers that the mobilization of the Great War was *utterly* dependent on such trivia!' He laughed genially, snapping open a tortoiseshell cigarette case. I accepted the offer, catching the faint echo of Maud Tubbly Pole's voice: *Felter and Turnbull: a nasty pair then and probably much worse now!*

In fact, Felter struck me as being perfectly agreeable. (But then of course so was Turnbull. And by now I knew full well that being agreeable was no test of probity! Nevertheless, given Maud's novelist's imagination and her penchant for drama I began to think that she may have been inflating his vices. It was in any case a long time ago, and people changed.) He talked engagingly on a number of subjects, not least his early experiences as a novice yachtsman in the English Channel. 'Still, nothing like the Baltic. Now that *was* baptism by fire – or wave!' he chuckled.

'Know the Baltic, do you?' a voice asked with sudden interest. Clinker had joined us, and I could see exactly where the conversation would lead: his favourite book, Childers' *The Riddle of the Sands*. I muttered an excuse and quickly slid away, disinclined to hear yet another of the bishop's paeans. I knew them too well, and in any case could not share his enthusiasm. Whether Felter could I didn't wait to learn.

Nicholas followed my cue. And carefully sidestepping Gladys nattering with some similarly lantern-jawed female, we went for a final raid on the buffet. Nicholas had scooped up yet another champagne en route, and when in a careful undertone I asked him whether he had made any further assessment of Turnbull as blackmailer, he replied loudly that he hadn't and didn't care an eff anyway, and had I seen that bloody Millie creature?

I winced, thankful that few guests were within earshot. The lady's name rang a bell but I was pretty sure I had not so far encountered her. Telling him to keep his voice down, I asked who she was.

He took a slurp from his glass and replied witheringly, 'Oh, you know, that whey-faced troll from the Brighton gallery – the owner – stacked with diamonds and without a discerning thought in her head. Some crony of Lavinia's. Had the nerve to accost me just now and suggest I give the place a plug among my own clientele!'

I realized from his description that it must of course be the same woman Primrose had mentioned in her letter and, presumably, the one Felter had referred to a few moments before.

'So what did you say?'

'Well if she hadn't been simpering up at blue-eyed Turnbull I'd have told her to take a running jump. As it was, I said that my clients were interested in *art* and not the populist posturings of third-rate amateurs.' He smirked with satisfaction, while I closed my eyes.

'Oh yes, if Turnbull really is the blackmailer that's bound to endear you to him! Insulting one of their guests will probably double the fee!'

He shrugged indifferently, and draining his glass replied, 'As I said before, and as Clark Gable or somebody once remarked, "Frankly, my dear, I don't give a fuck."'

'Damn, actually.'

'What?'

'Never mind. Let's get out of here. Party's over.' I set him carefully in the direction of the outer hall while I sought our hosts and made the appropriate farewells.

Lavinia looked pleased with the evening's success and was most insistent that we should meet in Oxford to celebrate the opening of the new establishment. 'After all, it's not very far from you really, and I'm sure the dear bishop would love the opportunity to drop in on his alma mater and relive old times!'

'As doubtless would Mr Ingaza,' chimed Turnbull blandly. His face betrayed nothing – although I thought I caught the hint of a sardonic note in his voice, but I couldn't be sure . . .

* * *

It had been a strenuous evening (whole day in fact) and I was ready to return to the vicarage and the comparatively temperate company of cat and dog. But before that, it looked as if I might have to shepherd Ingaza back to Victoria for the Brighton train. Fortunately, however, once out on the pavement my companion seemed to recover himself sufficiently to flag down a taxi, and with an airy, 'Toodle-oo, old cock,' disappeared into its depths and into the night.

Left alone, I wondered whether he too could expect a second note, and my jocular quip to Clinker about it arriving the next day prove only too true. But if so, would it really be by Turnbull's agency? And even if it were, what the hell was to be done about it? One thing was certain, such an event would certainly shift the recipient's current insouciance all right! I strolled towards the tube station, grimly imagining the sound and scale of the victim's fury. And for a brief spell the twittering inanities of Mavis Briggs seemed almost bearable . . .

17

The Vicar's Version

To my slight surprise and much relief, the next few days yielded nothing from Brighton; and thus I assumed that unlike the unfortunate Clinker, Ingaza had been spared a second approach. So clinging to the principle of no news being good news, I immersed myself in the palliative routine of matters ecclesiastical. Here I could exert at least moderate control over events . . . although not, as it turned out, in the case of the Inter-Church Flower Festival.

This was an annual affair in which churches of the diocese came together to celebrate the benisons of summer – an elaborate business involving copious processions, floral dances, decorative floats and general junketing. The week's events were crowned by a prize-giving ceremony to award a cup for the most imaginatively decorated lychgate and church porch. For several years St Botolph's and the adjacent parish of St Hilda's had been limp rivals in these floral stakes, though both were regularly out-manoeuvred by a church in the north of the county. I cannot say that this bothered me unduly – being merely thankful that we could put on a respectable show and that nothing actually went *wrong*.

However, under the directive of Gauleiter Edith Hopgarden, this year moves were afoot to smarten up our act and win the coveted laurels. 'St Botolph's in Bloom shall not be beaten!' was Edith's war-cry (to which, I gather, the response from St Hilda's was 'Buggery and bedlam to the blooming Bots!' I do not *think* this was the Reverend Pick's personal composition, but doubtless he shared the sentiment).

Anyway, the result was an inordinately lavish and convoluted display which so overwhelmed both gate and porch that access could only be gained by crab-like insinuation. To gild the various lilies, Mavis Briggs was fixated on inserting home-made pixies amid the foliage – an idea which prompted Mrs Carruthers (arch sceptic and Clinker's erstwhile tiddlywinks partner) to volunteer some of her egregious garden gnomes. Pulling rank and in my best canonical voice, I directed both ladies to where they could put their suggestions.

So far, so good. And then the blow fell. The selection committee for the prize was traditionally headed by some county dignitary who would visit each parish to make the final judgement. This year it was to be the Honourable Daphne Porringer, a rather nice old bird with whom I had always got on well; and I was quite looking forward to meeting her off the train and showing her the delights of Molehill prior to being confronted with our floral efforts. But at the last moment she had telephoned announcing she was fearfully sorry, but her diplomat godson had wired from Monte Carlo to say he had booked her into the Hotel Hermitage before dining with Prince Rainier and enjoying a little flutter at the Casino, and would I be frightfully put out if she sent a proxy to judge the flowers? 'There are some things, Canon,' she declared, 'that one simply cannot pass by! Wouldn't you agree?'

'Absolutely!' I agreed. 'Er, who is your stand-in?'

'Gladys. Gladys Clinker, our bishop's wife.'

'Charming,' I replied through clenched teeth.

And that was it. I was faced with the grating task of entertaining Gladys *alone*, and no doubt being the butt and practice for her scathing observations. Penance, penance, penance!

* * *

Inspection day dawned with an awesome sun. And closing the blinds in the kitchen I drank buckets of coffee and morosely attacked an egg. Coming only from Guildford, Gladys would not be on a train but was apparently arriving in Clinker's formal car, chauffeured by his driver Barnes. The last time I had encountered the latter was when his employer was in the process of being levered from the vicarage in a condition of mild paralysis – or legless in Gaza as some might put it.* Though hardly in a position to comment, Barnes had nevertheless conveyed tacit disapproval of what he clearly saw as my doing (which it was). Thus the prospect of the chauffeur's cold eye and his passenger's acid tongue was not a happy one, and I told Maurice so in no uncertain terms. Ignoring me, the cat looked the other way and began to groom itself with dedicated absorption.

Gladys arrived promptly at ten o'clock and I went out to the car to greet her. Barnes, as coffin-faced as when last seen and clad in Gestapo black, was already standing at the passenger door ushering her on to the pavement. She emerged looking mildly human, but I knew that wouldn't last.

'Ah, Canon,' she began, 'what a lovely day – spoilt only by the fact that here I am in Molehill instead of on the golf course *as planned*. Daphne Porringer *begged* me to do this little favour for her and so of course I could hardly refuse. But looking at lychgates decked in wilting cornucopias of grossly extravagant blooms is not my idea of a stimulating morning. However, duty calls . . .'

I replied something to the effect that I was sure she would find the flowers well watered, that matters need take no more than fifty minutes (twenty with luck!), and would she perhaps like some coffee before commencing her inspection? She said she would, and instructed Barnes to return in good time as there were other contestants to

* See *A Load of Old Bones*

see and she had no intention of letting things drag on into the afternoon. The chauffeur gave a dutiful nod, and turning to me murmured quietly that this time he was sure he could rely on 'sir' to return madam in an upright state. Then still po-faced, he had the effrontery to give me a sombre wink. The cheek of it!

Quietly seething, I took Gladys indoors, produced the coffee and sat meekly while she pontificated on this, that and the other. I asked if she had enjoyed Lavinia Birtle-Figgins' housewarming party the previous week.

'Well,' she replied with a sniff, 'at least we were spared the parsley sandwiches she seemed so keen on serving in France. In fact, with that awful husband out of the way she seems to have smartened up considerably. Mind you,' she added cuttingly, 'it doesn't do to get too grand and pushy, looks rather vulgar I always think. Personally I do not regard that Felter person as the best of influences, though Rupert Turnbull appears pleasant enough – always very courteous when he visited their house in Berceau. I daresay they'll marry once his language schools are up and running . . .'

'Er, what's wrong with Freddie Felter? He seemed very friendly at the party and I gathered the bishop got on well with him—'

'Oh, my husband will get on well with anyone who speaks highly of Erskine Childers and his tedious boat novel. The man was shot, you know – a traitor!'

I was disinclined to discuss either the politics or the literary worth of Childers, being far more interested in her opinion of Freddie Felter. It was intriguing that two women as different as Gladys Clinker and Maud Tubbly Pole should be so averse to him. Maud of course had apparently good reason from the past, but what were Gladys's objections?

'So what didn't you like about Felter?' I persisted gently.

She shrugged dismissively and twitched her nose in a way I had witnessed many times. 'Oh, I don't know . . . just rather a common little man, I suppose – touch of the parvenu if you ask me. Besides, he had the discourtesy to howl with laughter when I was expressing a very serious opinion. Can't remember what it was now but he seemed to think it highly droll. *I* did not!' She glowered at the memory, while I warmed further to Freddie.

'Unfortunately,' she continued, 'now that Horace has learnt of his shared liking for that novel and knows its setting, they have been corresponding and exchanging views.' She sighed impatiently. 'I suppose I shall be expected to ask him to luncheon next!'

Recalling my own experience at Gladys's lunch table* I wished Felter well of it. Politely I offered her another cup of coffee, but glancing at her watch she declined and intimated it was time to inspect the flower arrangements. 'One isn't here to gossip, you know, Canon. *Some* of us have things to do!'

Duly rebuked, I hastened her into the sunshine and up to the church, where, sidling through the heavily garlanded lychgate, we made our way to the west porch. Though lacking both gnome and pixie (one had feared Mavis might have made furtive adjustments during the night) this now looked remarkably like Queen Titania's fairy bower, and I have to admit that personally I found it rather charming.

Gladys did not. She had walked on ahead, pencil and notebook in hand, and was peering intently into the porch interior. Suddenly I heard a cry of horror, followed by a loud: 'Disgraceful!' Startled, I hurried to where she was standing and followed her gaze into its depths . . .

Titania's bower, did I say? Too right it was – replete with a looming image of Bottom with his ass's head, monstrous ears bedecked with a circlet of pastel posies! And as if that wasn't enough, next to him, coyly poised, stood another figure: Bambi, Walt Disney's winsome fawn, sporting a jaunty straw bonnet woven with buttercups and bindweed.

I gaped in stunned fascination, while the two companions gazed blandly back, framed in their tumbling foliage.

* See *Bone Idle*

95

Gladys swung round, and in strangulated tones gasped, 'What is the meaning of this, Canon? Who are these ridiculous creatures?'

'Bambi and Bottom,' I mumbled.

'*What?*'

'Er, um . . . literary characters,' I explained helplessly.

'Typical!' she snapped. 'Trust you to want to be different. I've always told the bishop there was an odd side to you, and here it is!' She glared at me and then again at the offending objects, and said icily, 'You *do* realize that this smacks of paganism – indeed many would see it as a form of desecration. My husband will be most distressed.'

Huh! I thought, not half as distressed as having his youthful gaffes exposed in the *News of the World*. Were that to happen, papier-mâché models of Bambi and Bottom embowered in the west porch would be the least of his worries!

'Oh come now, Mrs Clinker,' I protested mildly, 'that's putting it a bit strongly, isn't it? I suspect it's just a merry prank of the Brownies. They are very fond of our animal brethren, you know . . . in fact they have a most beguiling guinea pig called Giles. It's a wonder they didn't put him in there as well!' I started to giggle, imagining the manic Giles playing slaughter among the roses.

She stared at me frozen-faced. Then putting a mark in her notebook and shutting it firmly, observed: 'All I can say, Francis, is that Brownies or not, in total I am awarding your parish a single point for misplaced effort. As you are doubtless aware, the maximum number is twenty. And I can assure you that St Botolph's will not be hearing further from the selection committee.' (It always strikes me as ironic that whenever Clinker is in a mellow mood or particularly needs my help he uses my first name. Not so Gladys, who brandishes the informal address as the ultimate slight.)

Yes, the Bottom affair had been a dispiriting business and I reflected ruefully that had Daphne Porringer been in place, we might have had quite a jolly time and a fair chance of success. As it was, with the good lady rolling the dice with His Highness in Monaco, we didn't stand an earthly . . .

However, there was a mild turn-up for the books that evening which made me feel considerably better. Theodore Pick from St Hilda's telephoned. Such approaches are invariably spiked with gloom and I did not relish an additional dampening.

'How did you get on?' he asked.

'Not all that well,' I replied guardedly. 'Don't think our display was quite what was required.'

There was a pause. And then he said, 'Hmm, neither was ours . . . not exactly.'

'Really?' I asked with interest. 'You seemed to reckon it was in the bag this time.'

'Ye-es, but that was before,' was the glum reply.

'Before what?'

'Before some joker left a cardboard cow under the lych-gate, with socking great udders *plus* its hind evacuations. She wouldn't award a single point!'

I smiled. Pick pipped at the post – wonderful. 'Ah,' I said with smug superiority, '*we* got one. For effort.'

18

The Vicar's Version

In spite of the strain he must have been under, Ingaza's commercial activities seemed unaffected and he had rung to say that he was visiting the Cranleigh Contact and would I be at home if he called in on the way back. As it happened, the meeting I was scheduled to attend that afternoon had been cancelled and I was at a loose end – or rather there was nothing pressing which could not be happily shelved.

He arrived just before five, and it being a little early for anything stronger, I produced some tea as a stop-gap. We had just got on to the subject of Lavinia and the dramatic change which had come upon her since returning from France, when our speculations were interrupted by the telephone. Leaving Nicholas with a fresh cup of tea I went into the hall and picked up the receiver.

It was Clinker's voice – but utterly incoherent. In fact to begin with, I couldn't understand a word: the volume and speed was just too much. Drink? It seemed unlikely. I concentrated harder and gradually random phrases emerged – 'frightful shock', 'too awful for words', 'thank God Gladys away', 'appalling'. But other than the fact that he was agitated, I could glean nothing.

For a brief moment the torrent subsided and I tried to elicit something useful. 'So sorry you are upset, sir. What exactly is the trouble? Perhaps you could give some details. What about your secretary – can't he help?'

'Certainly not!' came loud and clear. 'Anyway he's not here, nobody is. Just as well, far better without. You must get over here immediately, Francis! It's crucial. Don't waste a minute. Do you hear? Immediately!'

'Er, well, yes of course,' I said, more than startled. 'But, um, at the moment Ingaza is with me. Shall I bring—'

'Yes, yes, bring Ingaza – but nobody else, mind! And for God's sake not a word to anyone, do you understand?' I told him I did and would leave straight away. 'And when you arrive,' he added, 'make sure you come to the side door – the *side* door, and you can put your car round there as well.' With that injunction, he rang off.

I returned to the sitting room baffled and uneasy. 'Hor's in an awful stew,' I explained. 'I think there's something really wrong, but I couldn't make out what.'

'Heart attack?' asked Ingaza.

'No, no I don't think it's anything physical – voice certainly seemed strong enough. It's as if he's had an awful shock, and apparently there's no one else in the house. Gladys is away and the staff are off duty. Sounds pretty urgent.'

'Oh well,' he sighed, 'suppose we had better go and see what's bugging him, otherwise he might bust a gut. I'm low on petrol so it had better be your car – saves messing about.'

Bouncer was loitering in the garden, and the moment he saw us making for the Singer he shot ahead and scrabbled to get in. Since apparently time was of the essence it seemed simpler to take him with us than to inveigle him back to the house.

On the way I told Nicholas about the bishop's insistence we should use the side door.

'Typical of Hor,' he laughed, 'pompous even in dire straits. Personally, if I were a canon I should be pretty peeved to be so relegated!'

I laughed too and said that even Clinker wasn't as crass as that (though I wouldn't put it past Gladys), and presumably the main door must be temporarily out of order – jammed, or being painted or something.

As we sped along the Hog's Back I was reminded of the last time I had driven that way – at a snail's pace and lashed by early morning rain. That time too I had been en route for the Palace . . . blithely unaware of the news that Clinker had in store.

'I say,' I said, turning to Nicholas, 'do you think it's something to do with the blackmail? Perhaps he's had another threat or demand. He sounded fairly desperate.'

'Yes,' he replied, 'that's rather what I was thinking . . . My God, it's a bugger, isn't it? What I wouldn't give to get my hands on that bastard!'

'I know we agreed not to, but maybe it's time the police *were* approached. They're practised in handling these things discreetly and most of it could probably be kept under wraps – the actual nature of the thing, at least.'

'Don't bank on it,' he replied bitterly. 'Too risky. It's bad enough for me – no good for trade and I shall be a laughing stock if it gets out: Aunt Lil would split her bleeding sides. But it's even worse for Hor. I've told you before, the publicity would destroy him.'

'You're right,' I agreed glumly.

There was a pause, and then he said musingly, 'I wonder if the sod could be nobbled.'

'Nobbled?'

'Hmm. Put out of the way – quietly. I've got a pal who knows a chap who—'

'No, Nicholas!' I cried. 'Absolutely not – you must be mad!' And without thinking I revved us into third gear.

'All right, all right! Keep your hair on, old man, just thinking out loud.'

'Well don't,' I snapped, adjusting to fourth again. 'Out loud or otherwise.'

He gave one of those maddening giggles. 'Sorry, forgot. Touched a raw nerve there – here, have a cigarette.' He lit a couple of Sobranies. I took one, and puffing furiously pounded on towards the Palace.

*   *   *

100

Given the drama of the phone call, when we arrived I was vaguely surprised to see the bishop's residence looking complacently normal. Flanked by trees and well-tended lawns, it dozed peacefully in the early twilight, its stolid Victorian frontage exuding an air of unruffled ease. Like the incumbent, it seemed assured of its own probity.

I don't quite know what I had been expecting – chimneys ravaged by fire, windows smashed, a tree sprawled across the roof? All was calm, and there was certainly nothing out of the ordinary about the front entrance. However, following the bishop's instruction I dutifully ferried us around to the side of the house, and leaving Bouncer in the car, we presented ourselves at the kitchen door.

I yanked the bell-pull and almost immediately heard heavy footsteps.

Clinker opened the door cautiously, beckoned us in and drew the bolt across. Although clad formally, he looked creased and dishevelled and the usually florid cheeks were a sort of pasty grey. It crossed my mind that perhaps Nicholas had been right about the heart attack.

'Are you all right, sir?' I asked.

'Of course I am not, Oughterard,' was the testy answer, 'and neither would you be given the circumstances!' Despite the words, the irascible tone was reassuring and it looked as if imminent demise was unlikely.

'And what are the circumstances?' Nicholas enquired.

'I'll show you,' he said grimly, and led us through the dark kitchen, down a gloomy servants' passage and eventually into the front hall where he paused in the area of the porch – in darkness but with door slightly ajar. He hesitated, then flicking a light-switch and seizing the handle, he flung it wide.

'There!' he whispered dramatically.

There indeed ... Freddie Felter. On the floor, shot through the head. We gazed in paralysed fascination as the stark, garish light exposed every facet of the scene. He was slumped on his side, legs half drawn up and a bloody crater over his right ear where presumably a bullet had done its worst. He wore what looked like a Burberry rain-coat, and I noticed inconsequentially that his trilby had rolled into a corner. For some reason that hat riveted my attention and it was only afterwards that I knew why: Elizabeth too had worn a hat – a green one. But in her case it had remained firmly clamped to her head . . .

'Well this one's not going anywhere, that's for certain,' said Nicholas.

'But he *was*,' exclaimed Clinker. 'He had already reached the drive but I had to drag him back into the porch. I mean, I couldn't possibly have that spectacle lying on the gravel!'

The implications of his words struck home and we stared in disbelief. And then Nicholas said quietly, 'Look, Hor, why don't you tell us exactly what happened – for example, why was Felter here and how did he get shot? Just give us the plain facts. It will, um . . . well, it will sort of put us in the picture.'

'Yes, yes of course,' he replied, suddenly brisk and clear. 'You see, after meeting at Lavinia's party we had tele-phoned each other a couple of times to discuss *The Riddle of the Sands* – I was scheduled to give a paper at the Guildford Literary Society and was glad to get a few more angles on the thing. Anyway, he rang up one day and said that as he was likely to be passing and happened to have a rather rare first edition, could he drop in for a cup of tea and show it to me? Naturally I said I would be delighted and that since Gladys was away there would be plenty of time for a good jaw. However, I also knew I would be in London shortly and suggested that we meet there instead, but he seemed keen to come to the house so I left it like that. If only I hadn't this might never have happened! Still, easy to be wise after the event I suppose.' (You can say that again! I thought.)

'So as arranged he turned up, and to begin with he was extremely affable – charming, in fact. Then all of a sudden the smiles vanished and he showed his teeth! Said he had a transaction to complete and if I didn't cooperate I would suffer the consequences. Well naturally I had no idea what he was talking about and told him I wasn't aware of any

102

transaction. At which point he asked if I had enjoyed his letters, and when I asked what letters, he had the audacity to quack like a duck! At first I thought the man was mad, and then of course the penny dropped. Ghastly! He became no better than his letters – snide and brazen and too damn pleased with himself – beastly little braggart. I hated him!' He winced as if reliving the scene.

'What was he bragging about?'

'The number of people he had put through hell and the money he had earned as a result. Said he had a list as long as your arm and it was getting longer. Would you credit it?' Clinker gave a derisive snort. 'He then had the gall to put forward a proposition, saying it might "mitigate" my problem if I accepted. Disgraceful, simply disgraceful!'

'But whatever was it?' I urged.

'Had the nerve to say that although I was quite a fat catch, there were even fatter fish in the pool, and one in particular had caught his eye. However, the "dossier" was incomplete, and if I could supply the necessary details he would look favourably upon my own situation – and by implication yours, Nicholas.'

'But why did he think that you would be able to supply details?' Ingaza asked.

Clinker sighed. 'Because it happens to involve a rather eminent colleague of mine. He was wrongly accused of substantial embezzlement some years ago. There wasn't a shred of evidence, and I can assure you, absolutely no foundation. In fact the case never came to court. But Felter seemed convinced that there was mud to dredge up and that I knew certain undisclosed things which would help him to "piece it all together". In exchange for certain data he might be prepared to "waive" the present situation. I believe his proposal is what is known as a *trade-off*.' The bishop enunciated the term with distaste, and then clenching his fists, cried, 'I told him I had no intention of partici-pating in his sordid little scheme.'

'What did he say?'

'He said that I would if I knew what was good for me ... And that's when I knew I'd had enough. I didn't care

what might happen, I simply wasn't going to be brow-
beaten any longer by that insufferable creature! Somehow
the thing had to be dealt with there and then!'

'So how did you deal with it?' I gasped.

'Prayed.'

'*Prayed?*'

'Yes, Oughterard, P-R-A-Y-E-D. Doubtless you have
heard of the efficacy of prayer?'

'Yes, but—'

'*And* I was answered.'

'So what did the Almighty have to say?' murmured
Nicholas with interest.

'To clock him one.'

There was a silence as we digested this. Nicholas
coughed discreetly. 'Went a bit further than that, didn't it,
dear boy? Chap's covered in blood with a bullet in his ear.'

Clinker whirled round on him. 'It certainly did not go
further,' he rasped. 'Never even got that far, didn't lay
a finger on him . . . And kindly refrain from calling me
"dear boy"!'

'But sir,' I protested, 'he's been shot!'

'Very observant of you, Oughterard – but that had nothing to do with me. I would hardly have summoned you
both here if it did! Now pull yourself together, we have a
problem on our hands, it's nearly seven o'clock.'

I sat down on the porch bench, feeling rather weak and
not too keen on the adjective 'our'.

'What's seven o'clock got to do with things?' Nicholas
asked.

'*Because* that is when Ridley the Archbishop of York's
secretary is arriving with important documents regarding
my imminent appointment as His Grace's aide. It would
hardly look good if the man were required to step over a
corpse to gain access to my study. The final interview is
only a fortnight away, and I do not propose that this
wretched Felter should mess things up!'

We stared down at the mess at our feet, studying the
blood-encrusted tiles. 'So if you didn't clock him one as

directed,' said Nicholas, fumbling for a cigarette, 'what happened? I mean, what stopped you from having a go?'

'Wretched man roared with laughter. Said we were both too old for that sort of horseplay, and proof or no proof he could make it very nasty for me. Said he was already composing a juicy article to send to the newspapers. That made me even angrier, and I thought I would try biffing him one anyway, but he sidestepped and, still cackling, shot out of the study into the hall. I heard the front door slam, and, and . . .' Clinker suddenly lapsed into silence, staring ahead vacantly.

'So then what?' I asked gently.

'Well nothing, really,' he replied flatly, 'I sort of lost my legs, couldn't seem to make them work. Then by the time things were back to normal and I went to take a look, he had gone. Except of course he hadn't . . . He was still there, spread all over the gravel, just the other side of the porch door! Couldn't understand it, didn't know what to do! But I couldn't leave him there, could I? I mean, it's not the sort of thing you want right outside your front door. So as you can see, I brought him in here.' He gestured towards the shape on the floor, then with a groan slumped down next to me on the bench, his face in his hands.

'One thing's certain,' said Nicholas, 'there's no gun around so it couldn't have been suicide. Didn't you hear a shot?' Clinker shook his head bleakly.

'Perhaps a silencer,' I suggested tentatively, and asked whether he had heard anything at all – feet on the gravel, a car engine . . .

He looked up and shook his head dumbly; but then with a sudden frown, said, 'As a matter of fact, now you mention it I think there may have been the sound of a car – but I really can't be sure . . . it's all so confused!' He gave a despairing sigh, white-faced and woebegone.

And then I made a tactical error: I asked him if he owned a firearm. Big mistake.

The leaked stuffing came flooding back: 'Are you *still* insinuating, Oughterard, that I was responsible for this? The only weapon in the house is Gladys's air-gun for the rooks

– and that's having its stock adjusted at the gunsmith's. So kindly don't try going down that road! If you imagine that your bishop is given to picking off visitors to his palace like some Chicago mobster, you are out of your mind. Must be the quiet life you lead!' He glared angrily.

I suppose Nicholas was trying to be helpful when he said, 'But he wasn't any old visitor was he, Hor? I mean, a good defence counsel could probably drum up a lot of sympathy for dispatching a blackmailer, especially if it could be proved that—'

I thought for one moment Clinker would explode. 'There will be no need for a defence counsel,' he roared. 'Just because Felter is dead, it doesn't mean that I—'

And then he suddenly stopped. And fury was replaced by an expression of what can only be described as angelic bliss. He looked down at the corpse and then at Ingaza. 'The man is *dead*,' he repeated slowly and in awed tones. 'Do you realize what this means? We are off the hook, Nicholas, off the bally hook! We are *free*!' He stood up and began to pace around the hall, swinging his arms exultingly as if testing his wings in new-found air, and I rather wondered whether he might break into a triumphal dance – or go mad.

Actually he did something far more disturbing, for, suddenly, looking at his watch, he exclaimed, 'Good grief, he'll be here in half an hour. Quick, Oughterard, do something! And Nicholas, don't just stand there, good fellow, give him a hand!'

'Do? Do what?' I exclaimed. 'I mean we can't just—'

'Get him *off* the *premises* of course!'

'But where?' I asked helplessly.

'*I* don't know,' he cried, 'anywhere will do, just as long as he doesn't stay here! It's vital that Ridley doesn't notice anything – that man's got eyes and nose like a ferret . . . Now where on earth does Gladys keep the mops?' He thundered off into the nether regions while Nicholas and I were left alone, contemplating the visitor on the floor.

'Hor's got a point,' he said. 'If this Ridley chap is due any minute he won't take kindly to a stiff strewn in his pathway. It'll have to go somewhere else.' He must have seen my discomfort for he added, 'Look, if it's left here, not only Ridley but the whole world and his wife will know – police and press swarming everywhere, banner headlines and interminable questions leading to God knows what! Best thing is to remove the evidence and ask questions afterwards. After all, it's not the first time you've dealt with a dead body, so don't be so squeamish. Now come on and take his legs.'

Gingerly I did as I was bid, and with much grunting and straining we managed to heave our burden into the back seat of the Singer and thrust it into a sitting position. And leaving Clinker to wield the mop and welcome the Archbishop's secretary, we sped off into the night.

19

The Vicar's Version

The initial problem was the dog. To say he was startled at having a lolling effigy thrust upon him would be putting it mildly: Bouncer went unquietly berserk. And for the first five minutes it was like being transported in a mobile version of Dante's Inferno. After a while tumult subsided into mere tempest, then mercifully to indignant growls, and eventually into what I took to be shocked silence.

I glanced uneasily in the mirror and was relieved to see that Ingaza had had the good sense to push Felter's hat well down over his face, so one was spared too gory a sight. Nevertheless I shuddered to see the shapeless form propped mutely within two feet of my neck, and found myself pumping the pedal hard as if to flee its grisly presence.

'Could do with a cigarette, Nicholas, if you wouldn't mind,' I muttered. He lit one and passed it to me silently, and we drove on saying nothing.

As to where we were going I had no idea. In some ways it seemed easier not to think and to just keep driving: at least in motion one was spared the necessity of manhandling the cargo.

'Do you think Ridley has arrived yet?' I asked.

He peered at his watch. 'Twenty past seven. Probably just settling down to whiskies and sodas and Hor's offering him one of those putrid cigars.'

'All right for some,' I said, glancing again at the thing in the back.

Ingaza didn't answer at first, then he said musingly, 'You know, Francis, I must have been mad to have approached you in the Old Schooner that time – raving mad!* Just think, if I had kept my distance and remained on that bar stool, my life would be free of all this – blameless and trouble-free.'

'Huh! I like that,' I cried. 'That's rich coming from you. You've been on my coat-tails ever since we met. Just because I once asked you a simple favour, you've done nothing but harry me ever since. And as for being blameless, well that really is a hoot! *And*, I might point out, you're the one who is being blackmailed and got us into this fix!'

'Blackmailed? Don't know what you're talking about, dear boy. Who is blackmailing me?' he replied airily.

'What? Oh I see – very funny . . . No, actually Nicholas, it's not funny at all. It's ghastly! What on earth are we going to do with Felter? And what about Clinker – do you think he did it?'

'Question one, I haven't a clue; question two, shouldn't think so. He's not the brightest but surprisingly he's not a complete fool, and was also probably telling the truth when he said he hadn't got a gun. But that's hardly the point just now. The main thing is what to do with Chummy here. We can't go driving round in circles or we'll end up where we started – outside Hor's front door. He won't like that.' He tittered.

I put my mind to the niceties of disposal. 'Well if we're going to dump him perhaps it should be on hallowed ground. It seems better somehow.'

'Like in your graveyard, you mean?'

'Certainly not! It would create endless problems.'

'So what do you suggest?'

'Actually I was thinking of another parish – e.g. Theodore Pick's. St Hilda's has a very roomy porch and a

---

* See *A Load of Old Bones*

large settle. We could prop him up on that. There would be a hue and cry in the morning of course, when the cleaners found him, or the Reverend Pick before early service, but at least it would ensure the poor chap was given all due attention before the police took charge . . . Mind you,' I added, 'don't suppose old Theo would like it much, grumbles enough as it is.'

'Very thoughtful of you, Francis,' observed Nicholas, 'though I'm not sure about the "poor chap" part. Personally I think he was a creeping little shit. Still, you always were a bit soft – part of that witless charm.'

I sighed. 'Perhaps if I had been a little softer, Elizabeth Fotherington would still be plaguing her budgerigar . . .'

'Yes,' he remarked drily, 'life is full of cumulative complexities . . . And just think, you might have been married to her by now.'

'Never!' I yelped, almost driving into the ditch.

'Watch out, you idiot, you'll upset our passenger!' At that moment the other passenger decided to give tongue again, and once more the tiny space was rent with shrieks and unholy bellows.

'Can't stand much more of this,' said Nicholas. 'Better get to that church as soon as possible before my eardrums give out!' I pressed on grimly through the drizzling darkness.

As we reached the outskirts of Molehill before turning left for Pick's church, there was a blaze of lights ahead, and through the rain I could just discern what looked like a roadblock. I changed swiftly into second, and as we crawled nearer I could see uniformed figures with torches. Apart from a Ford Anglia some distance ahead, there had been no traffic on the road; but then to my horror I saw that the vehicle had been flagged down and seemed to be undergoing some sort of search or enquiry. Three constables were clustered around its boot and driver's window.

'Christ, that's torn it,' muttered Nicholas.

I braked, doused the lights and quelled the dog. 'Oh my God, you don't think they're looking for *us*, do you?' I whispered.

'Not unless Clinker's gone mad and dialled 999. Can you turn round?'

'No, there are ditches either side and I'm not risking it without lights. I'll try backing.' I engaged reverse and slowly trundled us backwards. This necessitated twisting round in my seat, and thus the manoeuvre was not helped by enforced intimacy with Felter's head. Mercifully the hat shielded me from the worst, but even so, fear and distaste were beginning to make me sweat and it felt like a terminal nightmare.

'Look, there's a recess there,' said Nicholas. 'Turn in and we'll shove him through the hedge.'

'But—'

'Just do it! Do you want the police thundering up to us? They may have heard the engine. We'll jettison Chummy and then drive on smoothly and say we've just come from the flicks in Guildford.'

'What about Bouncer? It's unlikely that we would have taken—'

'*All right* – so just say we've come from some bloody dog show! Now hurry up!'

We got out of the car, and flinching at every sound started to haul the now stiffening Felter out of the back seat. Finally, just as his feet were being dragged over the sill, I noticed Bouncer crane forward and give one of the ankles a surreptitious nip. The action was swift, silent and mildly vicious. Deed done, the dog retired to the far corner, and with a guttural snort curled up and went to sleep.

Panting heavily and with the cadaver at our feet, we took stock of our surroundings. Although it was dark, I realized that we were parked at the opening to a small path spanned by a wicket gate. Somehow the area seemed vaguely familiar, and peering at the gate I could make out a rectangular plaque. 'Cowslip Cottage', the lettering announced, 'No Hawkers. No Circulars'.

111

I froze. 'We can't leave it here,' I gasped. 'That's Mavis's garden over the hedge!'

'Who's Mavis?'

'Mavis Briggs – the one whose painting we lifted that time!'*

'Well in that case, she's lost a picture and gained a corpse. Lucky Mavis. Now *come on*, Francis – do you want the police on us?'

Once more we struggled with the burden, slipping and cursing on the wet grass, and finding a suitable dent in the hedge finally managed to bundle it through.

The weight may have been off our hands but the exertions had been gruelling, and I was left literally bowed and weak-kneed. Ingaza looked pretty ropey too, and we were just about to clamber back into the car when I heard him wheeze, 'Oh crumbs, there's its ruddy hat! May as well have it,' and holding the brim between finger and thumb tossed it over the hedge to join its owner. I remember thinking vaguely that Mavis wouldn't be too pleased if it landed on her winter pansies.

Looking back on things it seems remarkable that we were able to negotiate the police barrier as well as we did. Perhaps we had become anaesthetized by the journey's horror, blasé at the shedding of our load, punch-drunk from gothic pummelling. But whatever the reason, we sailed through the obstruction as cool as proverbial cucumbers.

Obeying the signal I slowed to a stop and, winding down the window, heard myself saying with beaming voice, 'Good evening, Officer, what can we do for . . . oh, it's Sergeant Withers, isn't it? Must be something serious if they've put *you* in charge. But very reassuring all the same! So how can we help?'

'Good evening, Canon,' he replied affably. 'No, nothing serious, it's just Mr Slowcome mounting another exercise.

* See *Bones in the Belfry*

He's been to one of those courses he's always going on – Roadblock Tactics this time. Judging by the sheaf of instructions we've been issued, you would think none of us had stopped a vehicle in our lives! Bit of a waste of time if you ask me. Still, as I am sure you would agree, when He on High speaks, you jump to it – sort of.'

'Indeed,' I replied jovially, 'I know just what you mean. But you disappoint me, Sergeant, I thought it must be at least an escaped convict. How dull! Anyway, I expect you want some details, do you?'

He nodded, notebook poised. 'Just the usual.'

I gave our names and professions – clergyman and distinguished art historian (sounded better than dodgy picture dealer), and explained that I had just fetched my friend from Brighton and we were returning to my vicarage; the journey's purpose had been for pleasure and we had not stopped anywhere en route.

He wrote it all down slowly, then looking into the back, said, 'Ah, I see you've got old Bouncer in there. Being good, is he? Looks a bit sleepy.'

I refrained from explaining that he was worn out with baying at corpses and biting their ankles, and instead lapsed into a graphic account of the dog's antics as he had besported himself along the Brighton promenade and chased rabbits on the Sussex Downs.

As we drove away, Nicholas sighed and said wearily, 'Look, I know you were a rising star in the Dramatics Society at St Bede's, but there's no need to overdo it: anyone would think you were auditioning for a part in *My Fair Lady*!'

'Huh! *Arsenic and Old Lace*, more like.'

20

The Dog's Diary

'As a matter of fact, Maurice, I don't feel too well,' I told the cat. 'I've had a very hairy time, *very* hairy. In fact, so hairy that you are lucky to see me still here!' The cat yawned and said he couldn't be too sure about that, and what was I on about anyway? So I told him to take a deep breath and pin back his ears. Being Maurice he said he had no intention of doing any such thing, but if I cared to explain he would guarantee not to walk away.

I thought that was a bit RUDE and normally I would have done something about it tootie-sweetie! But do you know what? I didn't feel up to it. After all, I've had a VERY NASTY SHOCK, which I'll tell you about.

It all started when I had just come back from knocking over Edith Hopgarden's dustbins with O'Shaughnessy. We had managed to scoff some nice tit-bits, then having a bit of time on our paws we went and shouted at Stem Ginger the cat down the road. (He quite likes that as he lives with a very boring family and enjoys a dust-up now and again.) But after that O'Shaughnessy said he had to get back to his mistress as otherwise she would be screaming blue murder and refuse to give him his evening nosh. 'Can't have that,' I said. 'No grub: awful nightmares!' So we said cheerio and I went home to the vicarage.

When I got there I saw that big black car parked in the drive, the one which belongs to the Type from Brighton

114

and which we went to France in. I was just putting my leg up on one of its wheels when the two of them – F.O. and the Type – came bounding out of the house and rushed towards the vicar's car. I could see they were in a hurry, so I thought, Ah ha! If Bouncer plays his biscuits right they will take him too!

So before they had a chance, I whizzed ahead, hurled myself against one of the doors and scrabbled like hell.

'Get off the paintwork, bloody dog!' bawled the vicar. Of course I took no notice, so he opened the door, saying, 'Oh all right then, if you must,' and shoved me in.

We set off smartish and soon got to that bit of road called the Hog's Back. (I keep looking out for hogs but never see any. But one day I will, and then there'll be a racket!!) Anyway, F.O. likes that stretch, and so do I because usually we go VERY FAST, and if he's in a good mood he'll sing his head off – hymns mostly, but other things too such as 'Run Rabbit Run'. Now that's *really* good – all about bastard bunnies, and guns and farmers and chasing the beggars! Still, there wasn't any singing that afternoon as the two of them were too busy nattering. Don't know what about (wasn't listening really, too busy watching for hogs) but something was on their minds. I can always tell, it's the old sixth sense.

After a while we drove down a long drive and came to a big house where they parked. I jumped out pronto for a sniff and a leak, but then F.O. put me back inside and told me to be a good boy. I don't mind being left on my own as it gives me a chance to mee-use – as Maurice would say – or to have a quiet kip. But after all that rushing about with O'Shaughnessy I didn't feel like doing much *mee-using* (takes it out of a chap), so I curled up and went to sleep – like a good boy.

When I woke up it was nearly dark. And I was just thinking it was time to be going home, and wondering what F.O. would give me for supper and if I could wheedle some extra rations, when the door was suddenly wrenched open and this GOD-AWFUL THING came in!

Whew! It was ten times worse than *anything* the cat brings home! Really made my hackles stand up, it did. Dead humans in daylight and in open spaces are one thing, but that doesn't mean you want to be crammed up against them in the pitch dark and with no cat to keep you company. Oh no! And that's what I told F.O. and Gaza in no uncertain terms. Gave it to 'em good and proper, I did. 'Shut up and be a good dog,' yelled the Brighton Type . . . Be a good dog, my arse! He should have tried sitting where I was – in the back on a stiff's lap!

Still, things looked up because when at last they started to drag the goon out of the car I managed to get in a really good bite on its ankle. Mind you, it was a bit of a let-down really. You see I'm what the Frogs call a bone *con-o-sewer*, and I can tell you that this bone was NOT in the top bracket! Left a very nasty taste in my mouth. (When I told Maurice about this he said that he was sorry about the poor quality of the ankle, but that there are times when we all have to suffer for our principles and I had done a noble thing . . . I don't know what 'principles' are, but I think the cat was saying I had done well. Howzat, then!)

So after giving it that bite I felt much better and went to sleep – chuffed that whatever else happened to the thing, Bouncer had jolly well got in first and LEFT HIS MARK. That was good . . . But what's not so good is that it will be quite a while before I try to jump into the vicar's car again. After all, you never know what might be there!

21

The Vicar's Version

We arrived at the vicarage in a state of mild catalepsy (including, I think, the dog, who leapt into its basket, and as if grasping at the comfortingly familiar, immediately shoved its head down to inspect its nether regions). Also in search of comfort, Nicholas and I repaired to the sitting room where we took solace in whisky. We sipped and cogitated.

'Well, at least that's Felter fixed,' he observed at last. 'So what's next on the merry agenda?'

I winced. 'Mavis Briggs.'

'Hmm, you can count me out of that one,' he said drily. 'I'm off first thing in the morning. There are some things that even the strong can't take.'

'So you're staying the night, then?' I asked.

'If the spare room is remotely habitable and its owner agreeable I think I just might. Nerves a trifle fragile. Besides, the petrol's down and most garages are shut – and I certainly don't want to risk another encounter with some hare-brained police cordon!'

I was glad of his decision for my mind was a whirligig of fears and questions and I needed company. The first question of course was who on earth had done it.

'You know,' I said uneasily, 'there's nothing really to suggest that it wasn't Clinker. I mean, I know he denied it and so on, and seemed as shocked as we were, but you can never tell with that sort of thing, and it's amazing how some people genuinely believe in their own stories. Dispatching someone is a pretty big psychological upheaval and—'

'Oh yes,' he agreed, 'and of course you would know about such matters.'

I ignored that and continued to ponder the question. 'As we know, there was an awful lot at stake, particularly for someone like Hor: status and reputation are crucial matters to him. And in any case it's not as if he has only himself to think about – there's always Gladys. ('Always,' was the grim response.) If Felter was taunting him in the way he said, it's quite possible he suddenly lost his nerve and out of blind panic shot him, then hid the gun intending to dispose of it later.'

'Like you did with those binoculars,' Nicholas helpfully reminded me.*

'Look, I should be grateful if you would stop bringing me into it all the time! It's discourteous and irrelevant!' I glowered at him and he had the grace to look mildly apologetic.

'I told you, nerves a bit fraught – leads to unthinking remarks. And you are quite right: Clinker is the first one the police will suspect. Only one on the premises, easy opportunity. Except that I don't actually think it happened like that. I'm pretty sure he's on the level . . . But even if he isn't, it's hardly anything to do with us. After all, it's not as if we would "bring it to the attention of the authorities", is it?'

I took another sip of whisky. 'No,' I said, 'no we wouldn't . . .'

'Good. Glad that's settled. Now, assuming I'm right and that he *is* telling the truth, let's consider possibilities.' There was a long silence during which Maurice wandered in, and ignoring me, turned his attention to the guest. Settling at Nicholas's feet, he toyed daintily with his shoelaces while

* See *A Load of Old Bones*

now and again giving a speculative tweak to his trouser turn-up. Nicholas shuffled his feet irritably.

'Don't do that,' I warned. 'He's pretending you are a fieldmouse and will pounce if he senses resistance.'

The fieldmouse rolled his eyes to the ceiling. 'Your creatures, Francis!'

'But,' I continued, 'if Clinker didn't do it, someone else did. Must have followed him to the Palace and lain in wait. But what puzzles me is how did Felter get there in the first place? Hor just said he had "presented himself". Presumably he didn't drive otherwise his car would have been there when we arrived. A taxi is possible I suppose, but in that case it would surely have waited while Felter was conducting his business.'

'Unless he paid it off, intending to stroll back to the railway station.'

'Stroll? It's nearly four miles!'

'Oh well, perhaps he was a keen cyclist.'

'Huh! He would have had to be fanatical to slog it all the way down from London. And even then he must have left the bicycle somewhere. And no point in hiding it if he was going to leap back into the saddle and pedal home again.'

'Of course, we don't actually know that he arrived from London,' said Nicholas more seriously. 'Could have been staying locally and just sauntered over.'

'What, like in a hotel or pub, you mean?'

'Possibly, but maybe at a private house close by.'

I sighed. 'Yes, I suppose the thing to do would be to check out all the likely places within a half-mile radius where he might have been . . .'

'Just a minute, Francis,' exclaimed Nicholas. 'Don't get carried away, dear boy! It hardly matters how the bloody man got there. The main point is that he is mercifully dead and that thanks to us nobody knows he was at Clinker's place anyway.'

'Except the murderer,' I murmured.

'Except the murderer. Which brings us back to the original question. Discounting Hor, who?'

'Gladys?' I suggested hopefully. 'Perhaps she never went away at all, but somehow learning of the rendezvous and knowing more than she let on to Clinker, hid in the bushes and just as the visitor was leaving plugged him at close range with the air-rifle.'

Nicholas grinned. 'Don't get your hopes up! Besides, according to Clinker the rifle was having its stock done – easily verifiable.'

'There's also the *why*,' I went on, discarding my reverie.

'Well that's obvious. According to Hor he had a long list of victims, he and I certainly weren't the only ones. Somebody had had enough and thought it time to exterminate the little toad.' He paused, and then chuckled. 'Anyway, it wasn't me, was it? I was with the Reverend Canon Oughterard – an impeccable alibi. And being with you, I also know for a fact that you haven't been up to your tricks again!'

'I do *not* get up to tricks!' I cried, scattering the cat and spilling my whisky.

'Keep your hair on, old cock, just testing.' He stood up, stretched and yawned and announced his departure for bed. 'I suggest you do the same. Busy day tomorrow – Mavis and all. You'll need a good night's sleep!'

I groaned and followed suit.

Of course I didn't sleep – or not until much later when I snatched a couple of hours before dawn. Instead I lay awake reliving the nightmare, thinking of Clinker (possibly similarly engaged), dreading the kerfuffle that was bound to erupt the next day and asking myself incessantly who had done it, and why on the bishop's premises . . . always assuming, of course, the resident to be innocent.

As I lay staring into the darkness, I heard the onrush of rain pelting the windows and toolshed roof. That's all we need, I thought: corpse waterlogged as well as bitten . . . I turned fretfully on my side and closed my eyes, trying to shut out the vision of the sodden body and willing a sleep that refused to come. Lids closed, mind wide open.

Our conjectures had been vague to say the least, and I was still puzzled by how Felter had arrived at the house. The Palace was relatively secluded and even if, as Ingaza had suggested, he had been staying locally, he would still have had to cover almost a mile along the main road and then a further distance down the long drive. Elderly, fastidious, and apart from the sailing, not notably the outdoor type, it seemed unlikely that he would have walked. So why no car? The answer was suddenly plain: because he had not been *followed* but *taken* there by someone else! Clinker seemed to think he may have caught the sound of an engine shortly after discovering the body. Well, sound or no, it did seem perfectly feasible that Felter had been dropped a little way from the house – perhaps among the trees in the drive – and with the business completed, intended returning to the vehicle to be whisked away. But clearly his driver had had alternative plans: to ambush him as he left the house. And with no one but Clinker at home to observe proceedings, had performed the task and slipped safely away. If this were indeed the case it would mean that Felter had known his assassin, who, given the nature of the visit, might presumably have been a confidant: a confidant turned turncoat.

Perhaps, perhaps. 'If ifs and ans were pots and pans . . .' My mother's voice echoed languidly down the years, as, befuddled by fruitless speculation, I at last slipped into a curiously dreamless sleep.

'Well, I'm off now,' announced a brisk voice from the doorway. 'Mustn't keep old Eric waiting. I used your telephone last night to tell him I wanted a slap-up breakfast the instant I arrived. He gets fractious if the porridge overcooks. Still, at this hour of the morning I should get a clear run.' Ingaza paused, and then added cheerfully, 'Better give yourself a good one too – you'll need it!'

He disappeared and I heard the front door slam. The dog barked and I slid beneath the bedclothes.

22

The Vicar's Version

It was Savage who received the first onslaught. He had gone over early to tune Mavis's piano, and had been met halfway up the path by an avalanche of frenzied screams. 'The police, the police,' the banshee voice had shrieked, 'they'll be here at any minute. I thought you were one of them. It's disgusting!'

He explained to me that being blind, he was particularly sensitive to sound and that the cacophony was like being blasted by loudhailers from hell. 'Gave me a nasty turn, it did,' he complained. 'I mean, a racket like that's not what you expect when you're minding your business en route to tuning a lady's piano.'

'No,' I sympathized, 'I am sure it isn't.'

Apparently Mavis had clutched his arm so violently that he had dropped his tuning fork. 'Fell into the long grass. I spent ages scrabbling about trying to find it. The ground was sodden and I got my trousers all wet. I can tell you, Mrs S. was none too pleased!'

Plying him with more of his wife's fairy cakes that he had kindly brought, I asked what happened next, and he told me that while he was still on all fours with Mavis caterwauling above, there was the sound of a police car roaring up the lane, its clanging bell adding to the rumpus. The next thing he heard was Sergeant Withers saying, 'What are you doing down there, Mr Savage?'

'What does it look like?' Savage had said. 'Searching for a body, that's what.' He paused in his account, smiling wryly. 'Given the circumstances, Rev, it wasn't the best of answers, but at that stage I didn't *know* the circumstances. If I had, I might have said something else. As it was, it set Mavis off again and Withers got all shirty and asked if I knew something that he didn't. Anyway, eventually they took themselves off to her back garden and found the thing.'

'And did you find your tuning fork?' I asked.

'Oh yes. Under the bloody tortoise.'

After he left I polished off another fairy cake and decided that the best place for respite from telephone and callers was the church. Apart from Savage, I was reluctant to discuss the matter with anyone; but I also knew that in a small place like Molehill, untoward events invariably embroil the vicar, and that it would not be long before I was inundated with excited news-bearers eager for a reaction. Still dazed by the whole nightmare, it was the last thing I was ready to face. But the balloon was poised for take-off, and well before lunchtime the parish would be agog with Mavis's discovery.

Thus, with Bouncer trotting docilely at my heels, I repaired to the sanctuary of St Botolph's. The dog's dutiful adherence was untypical and I put it down to the chastening effect of the night before. I felt pretty chastened myself, and it would be a relief to sit quietly in one of the side pews and get my bearings before being engulfed by the tidal rush of rumour and gleeful speculation.

We had just reached the lychgate, when round the corner strode Colonel Dawlish, preceded by a prancing Tojo. Seeing Bouncer, the West Highland emitted a piercing snarl of recognition, to which my companion responded with a throaty 'Gurtcha!' Greetings of a less acerbic nature were exchanged between their owners, and after a brief pause Dawlish asked if I had heard about the body in Mavis's back garden.

'Yes,' I admitted cautiously, 'all very unfortunate.'

'You can say that again!' he replied. 'You know what it means, don't you?'

'Er, well I suppose—'

'It *means* that we shall all be plagued by yet another volume of lamentable verse. Only this time it won't be about Mother Nature's benison, but the frailty of life's natal gift and how death is "but a whisper away". You'll see.'

'Alternatively,' I murmured, 'about the beatitude of the quaintly unexpected . . .'

'Exactly. Either way, after this she'll really have the bit between her teeth and there'll be no stopping her! Won't be long,' he added darkly.

'So, ah, what is she doing at the moment?' I asked casually.

'According to Edith Hopgarden, torn between taking to her bed with shock and milking it for all it's worth in every tea shop on the High Street. Still, you'll find out shortly when you visit her.'

'What?' I said, startled.

'When you visit her – you are going, aren't you?'

'Well, I hadn't really thought that far . . .' I began.

'Oh she'll be expecting you,' he said confidently. 'After all, that's what you chaps do – comfort the afflicted.'

'Yes, of course.' I hesitated. 'But Mavis isn't exactly afflicted, she just happened to find the—'

'Ah, but that's how *she* will see it, mark my words! Take my advice – get it over with, you'll feel much better.'

'Will I?'

At that point Tojo gave a brisk bark and an impatient tug on his lead. 'That's my cue,' said the Colonel, 'can't keep the little beggar waiting.' And giving me a solemn wink, he marched off. Left alone, Bouncer and I wandered into the church, sat down and cogitated, the dog seeming as preoccupied as myself.

I sat for some time mulling things over, calmed, if not comforted, by the silence and familiar smell of polished wood and the ingrained legacy of incense. The early sun warmed the muted colours of the stained glass, and the ancient altar and flagstones gave anchorage to a mind adrift on confusion and fears. Current fears were focused on the immediate business surrounding Felter's corpse and our part in its disposal. But, I reflected, there was more. Much, much more. Far too much to confront at that particular moment ... A time to keep silence, and a time to speak? One day.

But regarding the present time, one thing was certain: Dawlish was right, I should have to go and visit Mavis. I glanced at my watch. Yes, just time to fit it in before the midday Intercessions and the blessing of the Brownies. I stirred Bouncer and we set off with resolute tread.

When I reached the vicinity of Cowslip Cottage, rather as feared there was a substantial police presence. There was also a cordon across the lane, a couple of press photographers; and clustered in an adjacent field a bevy of small boys mysteriously not at school. One had shinned up a tree with a pair of binoculars. As I approached I heard him yell, 'Cor, here's the vicar. I bet he done it!'

'Nah,' was the reply, 'not 'im, it'll be that organist – 'e 'ates everybody!'

I glared at them but felt a smug superiority in being ranked less suspect than Tapsell.

Approaching the cordon, I asked if it would be possible to see Miss Briggs as I understood she had had a great shock and might be in need of some moral support.

'Shouldn't think so,' answered the WPC gloomily. 'Done nothing but babble ever since we got here. Non-stop. Don't know where she gets the energy! Still, if you think she wants supporting I suppose you'd better go in. D.C. Hopkins is with her, *trying* to get his report right. He's done it once but Sergeant Withers sent it back – said it was a load of rambling whatsit.' (Mavis's narrative style is not known for its clarity and one could see the constable's problem.)

I entered the cottage with an uneasy feeling of déjà vu. The last time I had been there was with Ingaza, intent on our mission re the Spendler painting.* Then, except for the ticking of the cuckoo clock in the hall, there had been an eerie silence. Now, however, the ticking was submerged under a welter of gabble from the sitting room, and any sudden effusion from the cuckoo was doomed to be upstaged.

Gingerly I slid into the room.

'Canon!' she cried immediately, leaping up and scattering Hopkins' notes. 'I knew you would come to aid a damsel in her distress! You were so wonderful over my stolen painting – but this is much, much worse. A dead body amid the polyanthus!'

'Wasn't it the pansies?' I said rather thoughtlessly.

'No, no. His *hat* was on the pansies but the rest of him on the polyanthus plants – and I had only just put them in! Dreadful, dreadful!' I glanced at Hopkins, on his knees gathering his notes. He stared back with glazed expression.

Well, I did my best – i.e. poured a bucketful of oil and said how brave she was and that the whole town was buzzing with her name. This seemed to do the trick and I was able to make my escape comparatively unscathed. It wouldn't last of course, but for the time being I was a free man.

However, just as Bouncer and I were sidling into the lane, a couple of cub reporters bounded up asking if I had any particular views on 'the tragedy'. 'None,' I answered curtly. 'These things happen.' I hurried on, knowing I was likely to be late for midday prayers. On reflection, I think I could have phrased my response a little more judiciously. A headline flashed before my eyes: 'Murdered man is "just one of those things", announces busy vicar.'

Later that afternoon, having finished my stint with the Brownies and blessed both them and Giles (a particularly bellicose guinea pig), I went into town to get a haircut. The local evening paper was already on sale (rushed out

* See *Bones in the Belfry*

126

an hour earlier than usual), the front page proclaiming: MURDERED CORPSE FOUND IN LOCAL FLOWER BED. Out of resigned curiosity I bought a copy and took it home to read at leisure.

A prominent Molehill figure was faced with the discovery of a man's dead body lying in one of her flower beds this morning. He is believed to have been shot through the head. Miss Mavis Briggs (inveterate amateur poet, church bell-ringer and staunch member of countless local societies) was faced with the grisly spectacle when she went out before breakfast to feed the squirrels. 'I was very surprised,' she told us graphically. 'I mean, it's not really what you expect to find at that hour of the morning, is it?'

According to police information little is known of the victim except that he is likely to have been in his late sixties, was well dressed and had deep teeth marks on one of his ankles. It is not yet confirmed whether these had been inflicted by human agency or animal. As always the police are pursuing their enquiries with the utmost zeal and diligence, and Superintendent Slowcome is confident that the mystery will be rapidly solved and an arrest made.

This is not the first time that Miss Briggs has been embroiled in disturbing events. Readers may remember that not so long ago she had the misfortune to have one of her pictures stolen. Neither it nor the thief was ever found. We trust that there is no connection between the two incidents.

I laid the paper aside. Typical: only Mavis would be daft enough to go and feed squirrels!

I sighed and turned to Bouncer. 'And trust you to plunge your teeth in where they're not wanted. If you're not careful they'll be taking fang-prints soon. Ruddy dog!' He stared back gormlessly. And then, very slowly, began to wag his tail.

23

The Vicar's Version

'DOG'S MAULING OF CORPSE'S ANKLE!' blazoned the *Clarion's* headline. 'It is now confirmed that teeth marks on the ankle of the unknown murder victim found in a Surrey garden were not inflicted by human agency but most probably by a dog of fearsome disposition. According to our sources the injury occurred shortly after death. The mystery deepens as to why or how . . .'

And thus cheated of the possibility of 'human agency', the newspaper substituted lurid speculation regarding the size and savagery of the canine assailant. Of the human attacker little was said, presumably for lack of evidence, and by the end of the article Bouncer had assumed the proportions and ferocity of a Baskerville.

I slung the paper aside, lit a cigarette and cogitated. My instinct was to take to my bed for a week – or a year – until the whole thing was over, but unfortunately current demands prohibited such luxury.

The first demand came from the bishop: *The Times* had also briefly reported the incident of Molehill's mysterious victim, and Clinker, with a mind like a razor, had put two and two together. 'I take it this was your doing,' he trumpeted down the telephone. 'What on earth possessed you and Ingaza to leave it in that woman's garden? Surely you could have thought of somewhere more discreet.

Now the whole area will be in a state of hue and cry. It's too bad!'

Considering the awfulness of our experience, I felt the reprimand less than gracious, and with uncharacteristic boldness observed that since it was his corpse and nothing to do with me, he couldn't be too picky as to where it was deposited.

This produced a thunderous silence followed by a spate of throat clearing, while I waited for the next volley. This in fact was less a volley than a grumbling protest to the effect that it certainly was not his corpse, and neither was it his fault if Felter happened to have been dispatched on Church premises. There being no useful response to this, I enquired how his session with the Archbishop's secretary had gone.

'Quite good,' was the reply. 'In fact, between you and me, Francis,' (note the cajoling first name) 'it's virtually in the bag. Which is why discretion is imperative . . . a tactical silence is required. The last thing I want is for Creep Percival to get wind of anything. You do grasp that, I trust?' he added anxiously. Oh yes, I grasped it all right!

The next demand was from Primrose. She too had seen the item in *The Times*, and agog to hear more about the corpse in my parishioner's flower bed thought she might stop off for a night en route to stay with friends in Harrow. 'Besides,' she said, 'I want to know if there have been any more developments regarding *you know what*!'

'What?'

'You know, the *blackmailer*! I've got one or two theories which—'

'Yes, well, um, that's been rather resolved . . .' I hesitated.

'Anyway,' she continued briskly, 'I'll be with you on Friday, six o'clock sharp. So make sure you've got something decent to eat.'

With that injunction she rang off, and I was left staring at the dozing dog with its 'fearsome disposition' and propensity for manic mauling. I shifted my ankle.

That afternoon came fresh disturbance: Mavis Briggs. She accosted me in the High Street, and seeing my car asked if she could have a lift. To give her her due, she does not normally do this, but gesturing plaintively to her shin she explained she had tripped over the milk bottles at the front door and bruised her leg. 'It's the new milkman,' she grumbled. 'He's so disorganized, never in the same place twice!'

Encumbered with library books and shopping bags, she clambered into the Singer's rear seat, presumably imagining that there might be more space there. Mavis does not talk, she bleats. And it was not unlike carrying an under-the-weather sheep in the back.

I drove off, paying scant attention to the passenger's ramblings, my mind largely occupied with Primrose's forthcoming visit. I had got as far as remembering to buy some dry sherry (beloved of Primrose but not to my taste) when there was an exclamation from Mavis: 'What a *large* handkerchief – and look, somebody's initials. Perhaps it belongs to one of your clergy friends?'

'Hmm,' I said abstractedly, circumventing a small child dangling its foot over the kerb.

'F.F.,' the voice bleated. 'Now I wonder who that can be? Certainly not Archdeacon Foggarty, I know for a fact *his* Christian names are Auberon Peregrine – rather a mouthful, I always think!' She gave an ovine titter.

I glanced in the mirror to see her peering at a pale blue pocket handkerchief presumably plucked from the floor. 'It's mine,' I said quickly, 'Francis Philip.'

'But Philip begins with a *P*,' she protested. 'It can't be—'

'Not in our family,' I said firmly. 'Always an F.'

'Really, Canon? How very unusual, I've never come across—'

'Where do you want to be dropped, Mavis?' I asked abruptly, cursing Felter for his posthumous carelessness. It must have been pulled from his pocket when we were dragging him out – or pushing him in.

'Edith's house. I've got something *very* important to tell her!'

Edith Hopgarden and Mavis conduct a running skirmish in gossip and one-upmanship, and their relations are not so much cordial as spirited. I suspected therefore that this was to be a visit of careful briefing rather than social courtesy. How right I was! In the next instant she said, 'You see, I doubt if she has heard the latest development about my dreadful body!'

'Your . . . ?'

'The body in my garden. Superintendent Slowcome has told me personally that the police are convinced it was transported there by car and probably left on my premises to avoid the nearby roadblock . . . You know, Canon, in many ways that is a *great* relief!'

'Why?' I asked faintly.

'Well, it means I was not specially singled out, and that pushing that poor man through my hedge was simply a *faute de mieux*, if you see what I mean.'

Some *faute de* bloody *mieux* all right! 'Oh well, they're always full of theories at this stage,' I replied vaguely. 'Don't suppose it's anything more than—'

'Oh it's definitely a *fact*, Canon,' she breathed down my neck. 'The Superintendent himself took me aside and said: "Be assured, Miss Briggs, that's what happened all right, your garden must have been a godsend to him – or more likely *them* – and we're working on that very thing. Once we've established the victim's identity, it won't take long to find the person or persons responsible." Well, I must say I find that very reassuring. Don't you, Canon? This Mr Slowcome, he's so much more professional than that Inspector March, much more up to date!'

'Is that so?' I said, stopping hastily at Edith's house and wistfully recalling March's bumbling bonhomie.

'Oh yes, *much*,' she gasped, clawing her way out of the back seat, 'and of course he also told me about those tyre marks . . .' And thanking me and squaring her shoulders in preparation for Edith, she turned towards the latter's gate.

Tyre marks? Oh my God! Retrieving Felter's handkerchief from where Mavis had mercifully left it, and stuffing it firmly into my own pocket, I drove off at breakneck speed.

'I need a whole set of tyres,' I yelled down the phone. 'Get Eric to find some!'

'Can't you buy them yourself?' asked Ingaza indifferently. 'A full set is pretty expensive – besides, what's wrong with your local garage?'

'Not new ones – *used* ones of course. They must be put on immediately!'

'Bit risky isn't it, old man? I mean, I know you are a parsimonious bastard, but even you need to draw the line somewhere.' He gave a wry chuckle. 'Thrift is all very well, but breaking your neck is—'

'Thrift be damned!' I snapped. 'The police have found tyre marks by Mavis's hedge and there's bound to be a full-scale door-to-door enquiry. I've got to do a swap – and pronto!'

'Hmm,' he said, 'I see what you mean. A complete new set could look a bit obvious; and I suppose if it got about locally that the vicar had just ordered some fresh ones, new or old, they might just mark your card.'

'And yours,' I said sharply.

He sighed. 'Okay, okay. I'll get Eric on to it and he can bring them up. Always been keen to meet you, he has.'

It was not a keenness that was reciprocated. Parleying with Eric on the telephone was one thing, but the thought of being faced with his bludgeoning good cheer in the flesh, particularly at this juncture, was more than frazzled nerves could stand.

'Er, actually, Nicholas, if you don't mind, could you possibly bring them yourself? I mean to say, Eric hasn't been here before and, um, well, he might lose the way . . .' I trailed off feebly.

There was a crack of laughter. 'What's the problem, old cock? Afraid he might fancy you?'

I felt myself blushing. 'No. No, of course not. It's just that . . . well, I'm feeling a little tired at the moment, and—'

'And you just need Uncle Nick's hand on your brow; a sort of soothing poultice, as one might say.'

'I do *not* need a blooming poultice, or your hand! Just bring the bloody tyres, will you?'

'Absolutely, dear boy. Have no fear, Nick is here!'

Ten minutes later, with a large whisky inside me, I took my seat at the piano and launched into a curious medley of my own devising, involving Scarlatti, Edmundo Ros and Ivor Novello. It was what you might call esoteric and I don't think the dog liked it particularly, but it kept me sane and my mind off things criminal and cadaverous.

24

The Vicar's Version

'What on earth are you doing?' demanded Primrose. She stood on the threshold of the garage, suitcase in hand and looking extremely put out. 'I've been hammering on your front door for ages and all I got were roars from the dog! And why is Nicholas here?'

'Nice to be welcomed,' murmured Ingaza, rising from his haunches and smoothing his hair with a grimy hand.

'Yes, well, you see we've been changing the tyres, Primrose,' I explained apologetically. 'It had to be done rather urgently.'

'What, all four?' she asked, gesturing towards the discarded pile.

I nodded. 'There's been a bit of a problem, and, er . . . Anyway, let's all go in and have a drink, shall we?' I grabbed her case and propelled her towards the house, leaving Ingaza to sling the spares in the boot of his Citroën.

When he rejoined us Primrose had powdered her nose and was absorbed in the sherry. 'Not quite as dry as mine,' she observed, 'but I've known worse.'

I acknowledged the compliment and poured a gin for my co-mechanic. Mechanic? The term is inadequate. Given the circumstances, Nicholas had been a saving grace and I was grateful for his help. However, I felt less warmly when, in answer to my sister's repeated query about the tyres, he observed casually, 'You had better tell her, she won't be put off.'

Primrose replaced her sherry glass on the table and fixed me with an astringent stare. 'Yes, Francis, I think you had better.'

And so I told her the whole story. It took some time and she kept unnervingly silent throughout. But when I had finally finished, she said, 'If you want my opinion it was definitely Clinker – I always have thought he was murky. Anyway, why on *earth* didn't you tell him to take care of his own damn corpse? I would have!'

Ingaza giggled. 'You're too harsh, Primrose. Poor old Hor may be odd but he's no murderer – and as for taking care of a corpse, he'd have only made a hash of it.'

'As you did,' she replied coldly. 'Thrusting it through that woman's hedge!'

There being no answer to that, we lit fresh cigarettes and contemplated the dog.

The main topic at supper was naturally 'the situation'. 'It stands to reason it's the bishop,' declared Primrose. 'He's hell-bent on securing that post – much kudos and little work; and in any case, even if they don't appoint him he couldn't endure anything getting out about his Oxford lapse. You'll see – he did it in a crisis of terror. Mark my words!'

Her words were duly marked and duly ignored.

'Honestly, Primrose, I just don't think it's in him,' I said.

'That means nothing. One could say that about *a lot* of people,' she replied darkly, giving me a pointed look.

'Speaking as part of the "Oxford lapse",' interrupted Ingaza smoothly, 'I'll lay you a treble fee for your Canadian sales that he didn't do it.'

'Done,' she said swiftly, refilling her glass; and after a pause added brightly, 'Well if it wasn't Horace, perhaps it was someone who bore him a grudge . . . you know, thought it amusing to do the job on the bishop's premises and then sit back and watch events.'

'Huh,' I said drily, 'so that backfired, didn't it? Thanks to our ministrations, no events to observe! Whoever did it must be utterly baffled.'

'You mean poisonous Gladys has been robbed of her fun?' laughed Nicholas. 'But you're right – somebody must be feeling pretty puzzled. After all, it's one thing to have killed a chap, but quite another to hear no response from the person outside whose door you left the remains! Normally all hell would have been let loose with police and press everywhere, and photographs of the bishop looking pale and pained. Instead an uncanny hush. Rather disquieting I should say. What do you think, dear boy? You're the expert.' He gave a broad wink, and I glared.

'That's enough, Nicholas,' said Primrose sharply, 'you are being most unfair!'

I have noticed with my sister that while she has no compunction about needling me herself, she is generally quick to defend me to others. It was like that when we were children, and so it remains. I am grateful.

A thought struck me. 'Of course, she won't know yet presumably – but I wonder how Lavinia will take the news once it eventually gets out. She seemed pretty friendly with Felter at that party in Kensington.'

'And at the Brighton binge,' added Primrose. 'They clung to each other like limpets nearly all evening.'

'The great thing is to avoid any contact with her until it's public knowledge,' warned Nicholas. 'And that goes for Hor too. I wouldn't put it past him to let something slip in a thoughtless moment – like paying his condolences on the death of her friend! I'd better warn him . . .'

At that moment the telephone rang in the hall, and I got up to answer it. And returned at some speed.

'It's Slowcome,' I gasped. 'Wants to come round with a couple of questions – if it's not too inconvenient!'

'Well of course it's inconvenient,' exclaimed Primrose. 'Did you tell him your sister was here and we had only just finished dinner?'

I ignored that and turned to Nicholas: 'For God's sake,

leave immediately and take those tyres with you! Get rid of them, destroy them, cut them into pieces!'

'All right, old man, keep your hair on,' Ingaza replied, but he rose quickly. 'I'll leave in a tick, but I just need to christen your gents.'

'Surely you can hold on or use a hedge,' I protested.

'Certainly not,' he replied indignantly.

After what seemed an age of messing about, Ingaza left. And with the thankful sound of the departing engine in my ears, I scurried around tidying the sitting room and trying to create an air of bland innocence. This included replacing my sports jacket with one of shadowy hue, putting on my dog collar and strewing copies of the *Church Times* in prominent places.

'What *are* you doing, Francis? You're like a flea in a fit!' exclaimed Primrose. 'What about offering me a glass of port?'

'No,' I snapped, 'you'll have to make do with coffee if you must. It wouldn't look good.'

'Oh, really!' She took out her compact and applied lipstick. 'This Slowcome, is he good-looking?'

'Awful,' I said, searching vainly for a picture of the Archbishop of Canterbury to hang on the wall.

'And is he likely to turn up on his own?'

'Bound to be a sidekick, there always is.' I thought gloomily of the dreaded Samson, who, with Inspector March, had plagued me for months over the Fotherington affair. At least I should be spared his foxy presence. Too shrewd for Molehill, Samson had transferred to Scotland Yard where his sullen and questing eye was presumably striking fear into villains far above my league. Occasionally life grants small mercies.

The doorbell rang and I went to answer it with sinking heart.

Yes, there were two of them: Slowcome, of course, and a round-faced youth in a navy mac, carrying a briefcase.

I ushered them in, and made introductions to Primrose. The latter immediately assumed her lady-of-the-manor mode. '*Do* let me make you some coffee, Superintendent, you must be chilled to the bone on a night like this!' (It was in fact unusually mild, but such details are of little account to Primrose.) She made great show of taking their coats and settling them in the warmest places by the fire; then before going for the coffee, said to Slowcome, 'My brother tells me you are a lay-reader at the cathedral and that Bishop Clinker says you are an absolute stalwart, in fact the only one with real voice!' She laughed gaily and disappeared to the kitchen.

Absurdly she had hit the mark. For flushing slightly, Slowcome said, 'Very complimentary of His Lordship. One does try to do one's best, you know. A *steady* tone is what's needed – at least that's what I always think, and in my modest way it's what I feel I achieve . . .' (Modest way, my foot! Bumptious ass.)

'Ah,' I said earnestly, 'but of course it's not just a matter of tone and resonance, it's also interpretation, *intelligent* interpretation – that's what Clinker looks for in his readers. Not easily come by, I fear, which is why he's so thankful to have a veteran like yourself among the cohorts!' I chuckled conspiratorially.

When Primrose returned with the coffee it was to find us absorbed in the niceties and snares of public gospel reading. I say 'us', but in fact it was principally Slowcome pronouncing and airing his views, with me supplying an obsequious obligato. (Anything, anything to delay the 'couple of questions'!)

Primrose dispensed the coffee, and turning to the round-faced youth enquired whether he shared his superior's interest in public reading. The young man shook his head; but before he had a chance to reply, Slowcome said jovially, 'Thomas doesn't read, he *sings*. In the church choir, he is.' (Yes, I thought I had seen him before: Thomas Winjohn – one of the tenors, and always half a beat behind everyone else.)

'Really? How splendid!' gushed Primrose. She was clearly ready to initiate further diversionary discussion, but the boy got in first.

'Yes,' he said eagerly, 'and do you know, it was when I was on my way back from choir practice that I think I may have passed the car!'

I had taken a small sip of coffee, but it suddenly went down with a whoosh, burning my throat. 'Car?' I asked mildly. 'What car?'

'The one parked by Miss Briggs's hedge. The one we are trying to trace the tyre marks of.' He tapped his notebook importantly.

'Yes,' said Slowcome sharply, all thoughts of lay-reading vanished, 'and if your bike had had its lights functioning properly like a constable's ought, you might have seen something useful. As it is, you can't recall a thing!'

'Well, except that it may have been some sort of sports car . . . But like I said, sir, it was pitch dark and my dynamo had failed, and I'd got my head down against the rain. Wasn't seeing anything very clearly except the pot holes . . .' He trailed off, crestfallen.

'Maddening, isn't it, to have been so close?' said Primrose sympathetically. 'But I know how contrary those dynamos can be – always giving up just when you need them most! Besides, it's not as if you were even searching for a car. So easy to be wise after the event. Don't you think so, Superintendent?' She gave the latter a worldly smile.

Slowcome nodded briefly, and turning to me said, 'Now this is where you might be able to help us, Canon. I gather that on that night you and a friend were returning from Brighton and got flagged down at our roadblock. They tell me there was a Ford Anglia ahead of you. But can you recall seeing any other vehicle either in front or behind, say within a couple of miles of Molehill?'

Which would be best? To say I had seen nothing, or dozens? Helplessly I glanced at the dog for inspiration. Bouncer stared back and gave a single wag of his tail.

'The roads were very empty – but I think there may have been one,' I ventured.

139

'Can you remember its make, sir?' asked Thomas Winjohn briskly, clearly wanting to reinstate himself with Slowcome.

'A Humber . . . yes, a Humber Snipe. Or come to think of it, it may have been an MG.' I frowned.

Slowcome cleared his throat. 'Bit of a difference, I should have thought, between a Snipe and an MG.'

'Oh, Francis is hopeless on cars!' broke in Primrose. 'I remember when we were children – he couldn't even distinguish the Dinky ones!' She emitted a gale of laughter, while I was torn between being grateful for her intervention and feeling piqued at having my reputation with Dinky cars so traduced. They had in fact been my favourite toy and I had taken particular pride in my expertise.

'Still,' continued Slowcome, 'given that DC Winjohn thinks that the one parked by the lady's hedge *may* have been a sports model, and that those tyre marks show a fairly narrow width – who knows, what you saw just may have been the one. A long shot, but worth pursuing anyway.' He turned to his companion: 'That'll be your job first thing tomorrow – make a list of all MGs registered in the Surrey area and then you and DS Withers can have a go at them.' I closed my eyes, thinking of all the innocent MG owners about to be so plagued.

However, my sympathy was short-lived, for at the next moment Slowcome said, 'And now if you don't mind, Canon, perhaps we could take a quick shufti at the tyres on your vehicle – or rather DC Winjohn will. He likes doing tyres, it's his speciality – never happier than when he's on his knees measuring treads and such. Just give him the garage key, it won't take long. He's got all the necessary in that smart new briefcase of his – torch, camera, measuring stick, reference manual. He's got the whole works in there – haven't you, Thomas?' The latter nodded, though I was not sure whether with pain or pleasure.

'Goodness,' cried Primrose, 'is my brother on the suspect list? That'll be a novelty for him!' (No need to over-ice the cake, Primrose, I thought irritably.)

Slowcome gave an indulgent smile. 'All car owners are suspects at this stage, Miss Oughterard – even vicars. Bishops too I daresay!' He laughed complacently at his own joke, and I started to wonder how I might scupper his chances on Clinker's lay-reading rota.

With Winjohn doing his bit in the garage, we turned to other matters, i.e. Bouncer. 'Cheerful old boy, that one,' observed our guest. 'Looks nice and docile too. I like an obedient dog. In fact now that I'm out of London and settled in the country, I quite fancy getting something like that myself.' He gave Bouncer a friendly pat. The latter cocked his head on one side, presumably trying to appear cutely docile, but in fact looking mildly insane. 'Yes, nice little chap,' observed Slowcome, 'not like that savage cur that bit our victim . . . According to the pathologist it happened post-mortem, you know – all very peculiar, not quite savoury!'

'Yes,' I agreed quietly, 'very odd.'

I did not like the turn the conversation was taking and was thankful when the constable returned. However, though confident that the original tyres were well away, I still felt a pang of fear. Despite the failure of the wretched dynamo, supposing there was something familiar about the Singer that had jogged Winjohn's memory? I glanced nervously at Primrose who stared ahead, a fixed smile on her face.

The young man wore a solemn expression. And with briefcase grasped firmly in hand, went over to his superior and muttered something in his ear. They both turned to look at me.

'Are you aware, Canon,' said Slowcome accusingly, 'that you have got *two* punctures fore and aft and that the tread on the offside front is *well* below the permitted limit?'

'Good gracious,' I exclaimed, 'how dreadful!'

I think both of us slept well that night, and the following morning we reviewed matters over a large breakfast, prior to Primrose departing for Harrow.

'It's all very well your saying we should cut our connection with Lavinia and Turnbull,' she said, 'but we can't.'

'Why not?'

'Because Millie Merton wants me to exhibit in her Brighton gallery.'

'Who? Oh, *her*. Why? And what's that to do with the price of coal?'

'It has nothing to do with the price of coal but much to do with my bank account,' replied Primrose icily. 'And as to why, I should have thought that was obvious – I am a local artist of increasing national renown. She's lucky to get me.'

'Hmm. From what you told me about those peculiar abstracts, I shouldn't think your sheep and church pictures would fit in there, far too traditional.'

She gave an imperious shrug. 'Quality will always out, you know. Something that Millie Merton will doubtless learn.'

'But where do Lavinia and Turnbull come in?' I protested.

'They *come in* by being her friends and by Lavinia having specially recommended my work to the gallery. Actually, I think I was far too charming to her when she stayed overnight for its opening. She now seems to look upon me as a valued chum . . . Anyway, the point is that it rather commits me, wouldn't you say?'

Grudgingly I agreed that it probably did, but that I personally intended keeping my distance.

'If you can,' she retorted. 'Once it becomes known that that body is Felter's, they are bound to want to chew the cud. I mean to say, their friend suddenly turns up assassinated and, of all places, discarded in your parish . . . Well naturally they will want to hear what you think about it all. It's not as if you are merely a passing acquaintance. We *stayed* at Lavinia's house in France, supported her over her husband's death, we've taken tea with them both in London, and you and Ingaza were recently guzzling their champagne at her housewarming. You can't just cut them – even if Turnbull did murder Boris. It'll look so odd.'

'Oh really,' I exploded, 'it's too bad!'

She sniffed. 'More fool you for getting involved in the first place. If you and Ingaza had had your wits about you you'd have left well alone, or at least dumped the body somewhere else. Wigan, for example.'

'*Wigan*? Why there?'

She shrugged again. 'Well any place would have done, except Molehill of course.'

I began to feel the onset of an enormous headache, and thought wistfully of my bed and several aspirin. If she left for Harrow within the next twenty minutes, it meant I could get in a good two hours' snooze before sallying forth to confront Colonel Dawlish and the church wardens.

'Primrose,' I said winningly, 'would you like me to help you down with your suitcase?'

25

The Cat's Memoir

Needless to say, once he had recovered from the initial shock, the dog was in his element and swaggered around the garden gabbling incessantly about the 'the stiff that I savaged'. The dimensions of the ankle into which he plunged his teeth increased substantially with each telling; as did the rankness of the 'muttony' smell, which even now he swears pervaded the car for the entire journey. I very much doubted this last detail, but in his current heated state it was pointless to argue. Besides, I have to admit to a sneaking respect for the dog's tenacity in the face of distasteful circumstance. It is amazing what these humans think they can impose on the rest of us (not that F.O. ever thinks very much), and I consider that thrusting a corpse upon a sleeping dog is the height of ill manners. Naturally I did not say this to Bouncer, who needs no encouragement in the role of injured innocent. There was enough gilding of the Bonio as it was.

But naturally the gruesome drama went well beyond the dog and its fangs. There was, for example, another martyr claiming centre stage: Mavis Briggs. To decant the thing into that person's domain was an act of unmitigated folly! But with the vicar and the questionable Brighton Type at the root of things, what else could you expect? Increasingly I felt myself immured in a bedlam of bone-headed buffoons. But that, alas, is the fate of most cats . . . other than

144

tabbies. (With that breed foolishness goes with the genes, and the concept of lunacy naturally passes them by.)

As an example of such bedlam, the events of that past week had been a testing challenge to an animal of my sensibilities. However, a prolonged sojourn in the grave-yard sun did much to restore my natural bonhomie (so much so, that I found myself addressing an affable miaow to the Persian jezebel three doors down, who seemed surprised and scuttled in the direction of her voluminous mistress).

But still, despite renewal of spirits, I did not relish seeing a repeat of the rubber tyre episode! That performance might have been risible had it not been so disruptive of my peace and comfort. As it was, I was disturbed not once but *twice* by the vicar's mismanagement of the affair. The first occurrence was a Sunday afternoon – when he is normally out for the count on the sitting-room sofa and thus safely immobilized. Not so this time.

I had just finished a particularly choice lunch of cream and hake-cakes, and feeling well sated (and with Bouncer absorbed in his usual spider-hunt in the crypt) had repaired to the garage for a snooze upon the bonnet of the car. For a time this went very nicely, and I was slipping in and out of consciousness, musing about the days of boyhood under the tutelage of my redoubtable grandfather (he of the upstanding fur) and his brother the wily Marmaduke. What a heroic pair! And how patient with the callow kitten I then was! Ah well, another story perhaps, another time . . .

Anyway, there I was quietly absorbed in my reverie, when all of a sudden came a stupendous crash, and shattering the idyll a voice cried, 'Watch out you idiot, that was my blithering foot!'

'Bugger your foot,' was the nasal reply, 'what about my trousers? What the hell's that can of oil doing in the way?'

Instantly those dulcet days vanished and were replaced by the unsavoury sight of F.O. and the Brighton Type lumbering around heaving a pile of motor tyres!

I emitted a startled screech, followed by a series of piercing hisses. But to my chagrin no one took the least bit of notice – far too busy scrabbling around in the dust, levering away at the wheels of the car. It was too bad! And after a few seconds' rapid thought I leapt to the sanctuary of the shelf under the skylight. From here I monitored the scene in all its grisly absurdity.

Amid curses and swirls of fag smoke, the two of them crawled around the vehicle wrenching at hub caps, manipulating something the Type referred to as the 'bleeding jack', and with a metal rod yanking off one set of tyres and replacing them with another. It seemed a pointless, not to say noisy, pursuit, and I was puzzled. However, eventually the task seemed finished and they sat back on their heels, panting. Despite his exertions, F.O. looked relieved and I heard him say, 'Well at least that's done. One less thing to worry about!'

'Hold on,' said the Brighton Type, 'better dirty up the rims otherwise they might smell a rat. Trust some smart arse to notice recent activity!' And he started to smear the hub caps and tyre crevices with dust and mud from the garage floor. I regarded this with some curiosity . . . And then of course everything suddenly fell into place and my agile brain saw the light! It was something to do with tell-tale tread marks at the scene of the corpse's disposal! Bouncer had told me that it had been raining when they had stopped at the Mavis woman's hedge, and that F.O. had had to shunt the vehicle to and fro to get off the slippery grass. So perhaps that was what they were up to: foiling the police by eradicating clues. Having witnessed similar antics from F.O. in the past, I concluded this to be the case.

However, all I can say is that while explanation may satisfy curiosity, it hardly compensates for ruined peace. And I was just about to embark on a sulk when I heard a third voice at the garage entrance: the vicar's sister demanding to know what they were doing. Enough was more than enough and I made a hurried exit through the open skylight.

* * *

146

Such had been my haste to find a more suitable snoozing place that I left behind my Special Eye. This glass orb is an exquisite plaything, and if it were not to be trampled under some galumphing foot, rescue was imperative. Thus, when the vicar was occupied with his visitors later that evening, I slipped back into the garage via the still-open skylight and started to scour the floor.

Crouched by one of the back wheels I glimpsed the thing lurking under the chassis, and with a miaow of pleasure darted to retrieve it. Then just as I had it under my paw, there was a thud on the door and the rattling of a key in the lock. Surely F.O. wasn't planning a joy ride at this time of night!

No, not the vicar. It was, as Bouncer would say, some other joker – to wit, the round-faced youth who had arrived with Slowcome. I remained deadly still as he started to scan the tyres with a flashlight, then got down on his knees to commence a minute inspection of each one. The process went on for some time with much puffing and muttering and fumbling with tape measure. This item rather fascinated me, and seeing it momentarily discarded on the floor I couldn't resist giving it the merest tweak. A foolish move, for the youth lowered his head to peer under the sill and then cried, 'Oh my Christ, a rat! Get out you little bugger!' And grasping an old broom-handle, he had the gall to thrust it under the car where it made contact with my hindquarter.

Well, you can imagine my fury. Bad enough being assaulted in that manner, but to be actually mistaken for a rat was insufferable! Really, sometimes I think the obtuseness of these humans knows no bounds. Indeed I later observed as much to Bouncer, who nodded sagely and said, 'You are quite right, Maurice. And what's more, they're stupid.'

Anyway, the upshot of such churlish conduct was that in my haste to escape I was forced to abandon the Eye yet again. But fortunately, despite discomforted stern, I returned the following day to collect it. So all was well … albeit as well as anything ever *can* be in the vicar's household!

I imparted all this to Florence the wolfhound who is one of those rare canine breeds to display good sense. She listened gravely to my tale (though judging from the drooping eyelids may have been a little sleepy – too much horseplay in the park, I daresay) and when I had finished, murmured that such things must be a great trial for a cat of my calibre and suggested I went lickety-split to the graveyard to recuperate.

'You are so right, Florence,' I exclaimed, 'and I will go immediately!' She wagged her tail vigorously. And then with a languid wave of massive paw turned and ambled back to the house . . . Matey though Bouncer is, it is always refreshing to talk to one of reciprocal intelligence and whose remarks soothe rather than grate.

26

The Dog's Diary

It's just as well that Florence is around otherwise I don't know what the cat would do! He was in a rare old bate the other evening. The two goons arrived to interview F.O. about the car tyres and one of them mistook Maurice for a rat. And oh my backside, did the balloon go up! Thought I'd never hear the end of it. Spitting and hissing half the night, he was. No wonder I've spent most of the day down in the crypt trying to get a bit of kip!

Anyway, he's better now, as he went off to complain to Florence and she put him right like she usually does. Wolfhounds can do that – they have a knack of calming ruffled fur. A bit like a donkey with a horse. Maurice is what you might call a bit special and needs careful treat-ment. It's his nerves. Of course, my nerves are sound as a cricket ball, bone-solid you might say . . . except of course when faced with a ruddy great human corpse shoved on top of me! Still, as mentioned, I got my own back there all right.

But as a matter of fact, biting the bastard is not the only thing I did. Oh no! I'm getting pretty canny with corpses, what with the body in the wood and then the Boris person in France. It's living with the vicar that does it. I mean, it was me who dealt with those deeds in old Fotherington's pocket *and* took the Special Eye from the stiff by the pool. And now I've done SOMETHING ELSE. But I'm not telling the cat as he'll only get bossy and then take all the jam. Of course I don't *know* that there will be any jam, but in this life you have to keep your wits about you and snaffle things when you get the chance JUST IN CASE! As I've said before, no fleas on Bouncer!

Mind you, anyone would think that the vicar was smothered in 'em. Oh yes, he's a very nice master and all that, but as my friend O'Shaughnessy would say, he's a couple of studs short of a full collar. Or as you and I might put it, doesn't always know his arse from his whatsit.

Take the other day for instance. There I was, lying quietly in the long grass by the rhubarb, when he suddenly leaps out from his study, yelling, 'Oh hell and *dies irae!*' Now, I'm not too good on words – as the cat often tells me – but you don't spend time in the crypt with all those ghosts and mouldering tombs around you without picking up a few handy terms. And *dies irae* is one of them. I'm getting pretty smart on the old Latino and I know that it means 'Watch out! God-awful day ahead!' So when F.O. shot on to the lawn and started ranting at the buddleia, I thought to myself, Ho ho, Bouncer, time for more marrow-bone . . . better prime the gut for the next palaver!

Well, after I had visited my secret hidey-hole and had a few good gnaws, I saw that the vicar had gone back inside, so I followed him in. And do you know what? As I bounded into the hall, I nearly bashed into something – GUNGA DIN!

Yes, old Gunga, all beams and blubber, and I could hear his mistress shouting the odds in the sitting room.

'Cor,' I said, 'fancy meeting you here! Thought you'd gone back to London.'

'Yes, nice, isn't it?' he answered, wagging that joke of a tail. 'Thought you'd be pleased.'

'We-ll,' I said, 'I'm *surprised*.'

So we had a few matey sniffs, and then I asked if he had seen Maurice. He told me that he had but didn't think the cat had seen *him* as it had walked by looking the other way. 'Thinking about mice I expect,' he wheezed. (More like thinking about how to sidestep jumbo bulldogs!)

So I asked him again why they weren't in London and he said that Mrs T.P. was in one of her nosy moods and seemed to want to pick the vicar's brains about 'urgent matters'.

'Huh!' I barked. 'With the size of our master's brain, that shouldn't take long!' *I* thought that was very funny but he just looked vacant and started to scratch . . . slowly, because of being fat.

Still, he must have been chewing over my words, because when he had finished scratching, he said, 'Ah but you see, Bouncer, it *is* taking long because there is another lady with them and that's why he had to rush into the garden. Probably thought it was getting a bit crowded.'

'What other lady?'

'She's got a high, squeaky voice but sometimes it fades away like a dying gas jet.'

'Ah,' I said, 'that'll be Mavis Briggs. She's very fond of bulldogs. You go back in and sit on her lap, she'll love that.'

He frowned. 'Do you think so, Bouncer? I thought she looked a bit worried.'

'That's her usual look,' I told him. 'Give her a big kiss and she'll be much better – you'll see.'

'All right,' he snuffled, 'I'll have a go.'

He turned round and plodded back into the sitting room. The door was half open and I could hear the rumbling sound of the Tubbly's voice, the squeaks of Mavis and the vicar's ummings and aahings. And then suddenly everything went dead quiet . . .

But not for long, because the next moment there was an almighty crash of tea cups hitting the floor, a bone-busting squawk (a bit like those ducks in France) and the Mavis person shrieked, 'Keep him away, Vicar! He's going to eat me! Keep him *away*!' There was another crash, a howl from Gunga, and then the noise of the Tubbly booming out, 'My poor little boy! Come to Mummy then! Come to Mummy!'

It sounded like good sport, and I was just edging up a bit to take a crafty peek, when Maurice strolled by. He stopped, shoved his paw in my ribs and said, 'You've been at it, haven't you, Bouncer? You've been at it!'

You can't always tell what sort of mood the cat's in. So at first I didn't say anything – just put my head and tail down and peered up from under my fringe. But then he gave me another prod, purred and said, 'Bravissimo, Bouncer! Larks in the afternoon. Whatever next!' I *think* that is cat-speak for THE DOG DONE WELL . . . Either that or he had been at Gunga's saucer of gin!

27

The Vicar's Version

It wouldn't have been so bad if they had arrived separately; but appearing as they did, within ten minutes of each other, was – to put it politely – challenging. Neither would it have been quite so dire had Maud not brought Gunga Din. Faced with mistress and dog on their own I can cope fairly well, but the addition of Mavis Briggs created a situation of fearsome consequence.

It was Wednesday afternoon, generally a fairly slack period, and other than the crossword before Evensong I had nothing especially to do. So when an unexpected telephone call from Mrs Tubbly Pole announced that lady's imminent arrival, though surprised I was not unduly perturbed . . . That is to say until she revealed the purpose of her visit: to 'ferret out, my dear, a little more of your murky mystery!'

So acute are my personal sensitivities to the 'Fotherington Case' that my immediate reaction was one of frenzied horror. Was she really bent on its resurrection? First time round had been bad enough*, but to have her sleuthing yet *again* into that awful business was more than flesh and blood could stand. What on earth could I do?

'Why?' I asked faintly. 'I thought you'd already written one novel based on it – surely you don't need another.'

---

* See *Bones in the Belfry*

'No, no,' she said impatiently, 'that was *Murder at the Moleheap* – jolly good too, it was. But there's no more mileage there. What I want to know about now is this *recent* business in that woman's garden – the anonymous body. It's been in the newspapers but no details yet, so I just thought that my old friend in Molehill might have an idea or two.'

'Well he hasn't,' I replied. 'Not a clue.'

'You are so modest, my dear,' she chortled. 'There's more in that head than one might think!' There being no answer to that, I cleared my throat. 'Now,' she continued avidly, 'have you spoken to the garden owner yet? What has she to say about it all? You know, I have a theory that it may have been a lover whom she had tired of – blew his head off and then left him out in the rain while she was thinking what to do. Have you considered that, Francis?'

I admitted that on the whole I had not, and that given the lady in question, it seemed highly unlikely.

'Ah,' she replied darkly, 'but if you knew human nature as I do, you would realize that the improbable is always possible. I haven't been a crime writer all these years without discovering that it is often the most innocent-seeming who are the most dastardly!'

'Is that so?' I remarked drily.

'Oh yes. Anyway, I'll tell you more when we arrive.'

'We?'

'Well I know you would like to see Gunga Din again, and as you know, he is *so* fond of you! Expect us in half an hour. Toodle-oo.'

I went into the kitchen, cheered by her claim that there was 'no more mileage' to the Fotherington affair, and abstractedly started to assemble tea things; then, remembering the bulldog's penchant for gin, checked the level in the bottle . . . low. Too bad. I had no intention of sacrificing my après-Evensong comforts to those of the dog. He would just have to go without. Unchristian? Undoubtedly.

She arrived, vivid and volatile, accompanied as promised by her rather less than animated companion. He greeted me solemnly and rolled a bulging eye. Hmm, I thought, if he thinks that's going to produce the tipple, he's in for a disappointment. To my relief, however, Maud declared that the 'little boy' was on the wagon but that a drop of Schweppes in a saucer would be most acceptable. It evidently was, for after a few ruminative laps he went and sat quietly by the French window, gazing intently at two butterflies crawling up the pane.

With dog thus occupied and mistress firmly settled on the sofa, we turned – or she did – to things criminal, namely the abandoned corpse. Despite reluctance to get drawn into her speculations, it would have looked strange had I kept silent, and so I did my best to appear suitably intrigued. She romped on merrily, then asked why I was sure that her original theory about it being a despised lover was so unlikely.

I closed my eyes in a spasm of pain, and then opening them, said quietly, 'I think you will see why at any moment.' She followed my gaze through the window, to the front gate and the figure of Mavis Briggs purposeful with asparagus.

I do not like asparagus and I could have done without Mavis, but clearly both were to be my lot that afternoon and I coped as best I could – which was not terribly well.

Each visitor recognized the other from Maud's recent literary talk when Mavis had had the temerity to quiz the novelist about the importance of the 'moral dimension'. According to Colonel Dawlish, the author's puzzled response that as far as she was aware there wasn't one, had not won favour with Mavis, who spent the rest of the session tut-tutting loudly. ('Frightful racket!' he had complained.)

Initially, therefore, a froideur of mutual suspicion hung in the air, but I rather clumsily broke the ice by telling Mavis how much my guest sympathized with her dreadful experience with the body. It was meant to kill two birds with one stone – to mollify Mavis while at the same time slaking Maud's rampant curiosity. In fact it produced such a barrage of excited dissonance as each strove to wield her oar, that I was reduced to escaping to the garden under the pretext of seeing off the pigeons.

When I returned, although things had calmed somewhat I did not get the impression that they were entirely 'at one'. Despite their shared interest in the topic (Mavis as drama queen and Mrs Tubbly Pole playing amateur detective), I sensed that neither was overly impressed with the other – Mavis still doubtful of Maud's literary propriety and the latter clearly bored with her fellow guest's vapid prattle.

I was just wondering how to get rid of Mavis, or at least turn the conversation, when, grabbing the tea pot, Mrs Tubbly Pole splashed a dark stream into the visitor's cup and pushed the plate of buns in her direction. It was, I think, an effort to keep her quiet, which for a time it did.

During the pause Mrs T.P. turned to me and, cutting across both our companion and the previous topic, said, 'Tell me, Francis, have you seen much of Freddie Felter recently? I've been giving him some thought and come to a conclusion about which I'll tell you *later*.' She nodded meaningfully in the direction of the munching Mavis.

'Er, no, not really,' I answered vaguely, 'except at Lavinia Birtle-Figgins' housewarming. Saw him there briefly.' I shot a fond glance in the direction of Gunga Din, hoping to divert her attention, but the dog seemed to have disappeared.

'Was Turnbull with him?' she asked.

'Well, not with him as *such*. But he was there with Lavinia – helped her to organize the thing. They are quite close.'

'Hmm,' she brooded. 'So what's F.F. like these days? Still as slimy?'

I was about to give a non-committal response, when there was a neighing laugh from Mavis. 'F.F.? Weren't those the initials on that handkerchief in your car, Canon – you know, the one you thought was yours?'

'Oh, I've got handkerchiefs all over the place,' I said lightly, cursing Mavis's elephantine memory. 'Always dropping them!'

She laughed. 'Yes, but do they all bear the initials F.F.?' And turning to Maud she exclaimed breathily, 'Did you know that in the Canon's family, the name Philip is spelt with an *F*? Isn't that quaint? I've never heard of such a thing before! Have you?'

'Of course,' answered Mrs T.P. woodenly. 'It's a medieval derivation.'

'Well I never! But tell me, how—'

She never completed her question. For at that moment the bulldog came lumbering back, advanced slowly towards her, and with a guttural grunt hauled itself on to her lap. Here he floundered while Mavis screamed and sent buns and crockery flying. Undeterred, the creature proceeded to smother her in lavish and snorting endearments while the object of his affections drummed her heels and tried vainly to beat him off.

'Absurd!' I heard Maud expostulate. 'Just keep still and give him a pat.'

That was the last thing Mavis was going to do, and I rose hastily to pull the dog away. Indeed, such was my haste that I knocked over a small table of books, scattering the volumes in all directions. Then just as I was reaching for the dog's collar, with a cascade of squawks Mavis heaved the friendly one to the floor where he emitted an anguished roar. This coincided with a similar eruption from the owner. 'Come to Mummy!' bellowed an enraged Mrs Tubbly Pole. 'Look what you've done to him!'

Mavis's departure was swift and unceremonial. Mrs Tubbly Pole's was slower and more thoughtful. After she had demanded that I yield my remaining gin to soothe the victim's injured psyche, she tried to quiz me re the hand-kerchief. 'What was that bit about spelling your second name with an F?' she asked suspiciously. 'I've never heard such nonsense! There's more to this than meets the eye. If I were a private dick in one of my novels I'd say you had been giving that toad Felter a lift!' She gave a caustic laugh.

'Rather a long story which I'll tell you sometime,' I parried. 'But if you don't mind, not just now, Maud, I'm a little fatigued.'

After she had gone I surveyed the fall-out from their visit: the debris of broken china, far-flung books and squashed buns. Chewing dolefully on one of these, I set about tidying things up. With or without the gin, that evening's choral service would be a balm and therapy of which I had much need . . .

28

The Vicar's Version

As it happens Evensong did do the trick, and despite the run-in with Maud and Mavis, the continuing embarrassment of the flower fiasco, and not least the visitation from Slowcome, I returned home moderately refreshed. Indeed, such was the refreshment that my spirits remained buoyant until a late breakfast the following day. At this point, however, tensions resumed and I started once more to contemplate the mystery surrounding Felter and our ill-judged disposal of his body.

I munched my toast despondently and wondered what on earth I should do if the tedious Slowcome succeeded in linking us with the corpse. It wouldn't just be Clinker who was suspected of murder – we should all be in the can! And meanwhile the killer was loose, presumably well away and smug at the possibility of there being a ready-made set of scapegoats – or fall-guys, as the Americans put it.

I gazed at the dog snoring blissfully by the boiler and wished I could share its ease . . . Still, I thought, no point in crossing premature bridges. Even when Felter was identified (which he surely would be), despite my anxiety, I reasoned that there was nothing to make the police suspect the wretched man had ever been near the bishop's Palace – let alone in the Reverend Oughterard's car. *Except*, I recalled with a pang, the initialled handkerchief and

Mavis's babbling tongue . . . Nasty. (And I wasn't too keen on Mrs T.P.'s crack about my giving him a lift, either!)

The handkerchief, of course, I had got rid of – but not Mavis's memory, and there was no knowing when, or with whom, she might mention the thing again. It was a worrying problem and for the moment there seemed no answer . . . I sighed and returned my gaze to the sleeping dog, and wondered not for the first time how on earth it could see anything through that impenetrable mop. Looking at Bouncer put me in mind of Gunga Din and his owner's latest whim – a richly embroidered dog-coat to clothe his portly flanks. Absurd!

And then, of course, I had my answer: *embroidery*. Yes, not only would I resolutely stick to my yarn about the initials (modifying it to invent a family soubriquet for Philip – Fillo, perhaps) but I would get Primrose to embellish a dozen handkerchiefs to that effect. Thus, flaunting the letters *F.F.* I could blow my nose with casual panache and bamboozle the lot of them – Maud included! Primrose naturally was bound to grumble, but with a little cajoling and promise of remuneration she would soon yield.

I grinned, congratulating myself on the neatness of the plan, and in lighter mood poured more coffee and smothered the toast in peanut butter. I was just poised to bite into this when the telephone rang. It shrilled insistently and Bouncer awoke with a bark. There was no choice but to answer.

Still smarting from Gladys's visit, I was far from pleased to hear her husband's voice. 'I am in a call box,' the bishop announced, 'and will be with you in ten minutes. Kindly do not leave the house.' He rang off and I was left staring at the receiver.

'Oh, what the hell now?' I protested to the cat. 'What the ruddy hell now?'

.

MY LORD BISHOP, it said, *I KNOW WHAT YOU HAVE DONE*. That was all. Short, crisp, unadorned, unsigned.

I stared down at the paper in my hand and then up at its recipient, the stark monosyllables dancing before my eyes.

'When did this come?' I whispered.

'The morning delivery,' he replied. 'Typed brown envelope, first class, smudged postmark.'

I gazed at the black capitalized message, trying to make it speak, to see something in it other than those nine faceless words.

'But how on earth . . .' I began.

'I do not *know*, Francis! Obviously someone else. And neither do I know what it *means*,' replied Clinker, cheeks grey and drawn. 'An allusion to the past? Or to the disposal of the body? Your guess is as good as mine . . .' He paused, and then added ruminatively, 'What an effing bastard.'

I could merely nod, having nothing more useful nor more apt to say.

'She'll divorce me, you know.'

'What?'

'Gladys, she won't stand for it. Couldn't bear the scandal. She'll go to her sister in Brussels.'

I refrained from offering my congratulations. And instead said stoutly, 'Nonsense, sir, it will never come to that – and in any case, I'm sure Mrs Clinker would look upon this as a challenge. I can't see her being defeated by some malicious little guttersnipe, whatever the circumstances!'

Actually, despite my aversion to the bishop's wife – and even more to her sister, the appalling Myrtle – I think my words held a ring of truth. Presumably Clinker agreed, for he suddenly stiffened, and with a gleam of mild battle in his eye said, 'You are right, Oughterard, she wouldn't. And neither shall I. Whoever it is shan't get away with it!' But even as he spoke I could see the spirit slumping and the old fears jostling back: 'But if it wasn't only Felter – who else? Do you suppose there's a whole *gang* of them out there?'

I was silent, grappling with similar thoughts . . . But I grasped at a straw: 'You know, it would have been perfectly possible for him to have written that note earlier on, before visiting you, and for it to have got delayed in the post. There have been a number of strikes lately, the unions playing up again. Or maybe he had wanted to fox you and post it away from London, and gave it to someone else to mail at a later date, and then decided to approach you in person anyway.'

'Could be,' he muttered. But he didn't sound very convinced. As neither was I.

I know what you have done . . . It was the wretched ambiguity that was so puzzling. Obviously, if it meant the shifting of the corpse, then someone else was responsible. But if it referred to the Oxford business, it might just conceivably have been penned by Felter at an earlier date – although it was not in the style of the three previous notes. Those had been much more expansive – bantering, cocky; whereas this, apart from the mannered 'My Lord Bishop', was tersely deadpan. Nor was there any allusion to money, as there had been in the last one. If Felter had composed a fourth message prior to his fatal visit to the Palace, would he not have pursued the money aspect and made the demand more explicit? And besides, what had happened to the quacking duck? Had Felter grown bored with his puerile nonsense?

No, the straw was too pale and too weak: clearly another person was on the bishop's trail. And despite the sparsity of the letter's content, I felt a chilling fear. They were out to get him, all right – and quite possibly Ingaza too. But *why*, for God's sake? Clinker was well heeled enough but he was no millionaire, and Nicholas's funds were decidedly up and down. The wretched Felter may have felt he would try his luck with them for a single limited payment, but surely the financial potential was not enough to excite the persistence of a second pursuer? And even if it were, why continue to be so oblique? Why not just demand the damn money and be done with it?

Perhaps, I thought with a surge of anger, it was indeed the Oxford folly and some sanctimonious pygmy was intent on stirring mischief less for monetary gain than the satisfaction of massaging the egos of the righteous. Clinker's gaffe may have been years ago, but the police still took a disproportionate interest in such 'deviant' behaviour and he was right to fear the threat of social disgrace – if not gaol itself. Yes, whether simple blackmail, malicious revenge for some past slight, or a perverted sense of moral justice – whatever the motive, the bishop's position was highly precarious . . . But then, of course, if it were the other blunder, disposal of the body, such a revelation could be equally dire – and substantially worse if they pinned a murder charge on him!

'Have you spoken to Nicholas?' I asked.

He shook his head. 'Telephoned as soon as I read it, but that strange Eric person told me he had gone to visit an "old auntie" and wouldn't be back till later . . . I didn't know Ingaza had an aunt – and in any case, why should he suddenly need to visit her, for Heaven's sake? I don't believe a word of it! The fellow asked if I wanted to leave a message or my name, and when I said that neither would be necessary, he had the nerve to say, "Right-o, Bish, I'll tell him when he's back." The effrontery!' Clinker glowered, the note momentarily eclipsed by the impudence of Ingaza's cheery house mate.

'Actually,' I murmured, 'it's true, he does have an aunt. Aunt Lil. Probably taking her to the Eastbourne bandstand. They go there sometimes and then stop off at Fullers for tea and ices, and walnut—'

'Oh, blow the aunt!' cried Clinker wildly. 'What about *me* and this damn letter? I tell you, I shall be ruined and Creep Percival will dance on my grave!' Not with that gouty leg, I thought.

Indeed, Creep Percival's inability to dance was the one certainty I had in the matter. However, I tried to calm the bishop as best I could, assuring him (with failing conviction) that things were bound to blow over and to think of Mother Julian.

'Why?' he asked.

'Er – well, you know, sir, "All things shall be well, and all manner of things shall be well . . ."'

He regarded me glassily, and then said: 'You may recall, Oughterard, that Mother Julian was not about to be accused of sodomy or of unlawfully concealing a corpse. Had that been the case, she may have been less sanguine ... Now if you don't mind, perhaps you could offer me something a little more sustaining.' He stared fixedly at the whisky decanter, and I hastened to find a glass.

As we sat sipping and brooding, there was the shrill of the telephone, and I got up wearily, assuming it might be Colonel Dawlish complaining about the deputy church warden. In fact it was my sister's voice, but without its usual briskness.

'Are you alone?' she breathed.

I told her that the bishop was with me.

'Where?'

'Not at my elbow, if that's what you mean. He's in the sitting room, guzzling my Scotch. I say, Primrose, have you got a sore throat? You sound a bit hoarse.'

'Hoarse?' she hissed. 'I am unsettled, Francis, unsettled!' Before I could ask why, she said, 'I have just received a very peculiar communication – most peculiar.'

'Oh yes? Turnbull proposed marriage, has he?'

'Don't be facetious,' she snapped, 'this is serious.'

I said that I was sure it was and that I was all ears.

'Well there's not much to hear, actually. It's a message of some brevity: "What price the Canada geese?"'

'No idea. What are you talking about?'

'Oh really, Francis!' she expostulated at full volume. 'Go back to Clinker and I'll phone you later when you are more *attuned*!'

'But Primrose—' I protested. The line went dead; and perplexed, I returned to my visitor.

He prosed, fulminated and finally left. And thankful but worried, I went into the kitchen and started to open a tin of meatballs.

I was just throwing these into a saucepan and heating

the stove, when light and alarm dawned: *Oh my God, she had had one too!*

Narrowly missing the sleeping cat, I sat down heavily at the table and pondered her words: 'What price the Canada geese?' My sister had only one connection with Canada: the paintings that she and Ingaza palmed off as original eighteenth-century pastorals and from which they made a 'pretty packet'. It was a project and collaboration that had always perturbed me, but little had I thought that the gravest danger would be from blackmail. But that was obviously what it was, and judging from the note's cryptic economy, it came from the same source as Clinker's.

Shelving the meatballs, I lit a cigarette and brooded. Perhaps there *was* an outside chance of its being a coincidence . . . No, not even an outside. The provenance had to be the same. The person pursuing Clinker had also set their sights on my sister – and presumably, because it was their joint venture, Ingaza too. I groaned. Back to square one with a vengeance!

But who could possibly suspect that Primrose's painting activities were anything other than above board? Courtauld shenanigans apart, until snared in Ingaza's silky web, Primrose had led a life of patent, if impatient, rectitude. There was nothing dubious either in her past or her persona to suggest artistic chicanery. It would seem, surely, that the writer of the note had discovered the deception entirely by accident. But how? A chance remark? Unlikely from Primrose and certainly not from Ingaza. A loose tongue among the latter's cronies? The Cranleigh Contact? Or . . . a picture of Eric, garrulous amidst beer and darts, sprung to mind, but I banished it instantly. No, at St Bede's Nicholas had been attended by satellites of a sly discretion, and it was unthinkable that his present chum, though lacking their social grace, would not share that essential quality. Raucous though he might be, Eric was no blabbermouth.

I sighed, went into the hall and dialled. 'Ah, Nicholas, glad to get you. Nice time with Aunt Lil?'

'Knackered,' was the terse reply.

'All in a good cause,' I answered vaguely. 'Um – afraid I've got some bad news.'

'You're coming to Brighton.'

'No, worse. Hor and Prim have both had blackmail letters – or at least I think that's their object.'

There was a silence. And then he said slowly, 'You mean since Felter?'

'Yes,' I said firmly, 'since Felter.'

The response was explosive and unprintable.

29

The Vicar's Version

I am not energetic, but given the circumstances I felt that an early evening stroll would help clear the mind and calm the spirit. This being the aim, I did not take Bouncer.

Others might have chosen Foxford Wood for a peaceful ramble – and from a distance it did look inviting. But for reasons earlier detailed,* for me it had become forbidden territory, so I settled for the local park, a pleasant enough spot beloved of dogs and small children. At this hour fortunately the latter were largely absent, being presumably occupied by supper or prep. Thus the place was virtually deserted and I wandered slowly, enjoying the solitude. Gradually, amidst begonias and scent of box the day's revelations receded somewhat . . . although I knew that the lull could only be temporary.

However, temporary or not, it was slightly marred by the sudden sight of Mavis and Edith Hopgarden lurking by the lily pond. Edith was busy laying down the law – her gestures unmistakable – and had not seen me. Mavis clearly had, and for one dire instant I thought she might come trailing over. But instead she tossed her head and looked away. Evidently I was in the doghouse over the Gunga Din debacle. Small mercies . . .

* See *A Load of Old Bones*

After pausing to feed the ducks, I made my way back to the vicarage via the churchyard and cobbled lane. A figure was moving briskly down it: Colonel Dawlish, stick and newspaper tucked firmly under one arm. He greeted me genially and asked if I had seen the latest news.

'What news?' I replied, wondering if the government had fallen or the Test been lost.

'That cove in Mavis's garden. He's been recognized.'

'Ah,' I said guardedly, 'is that so? And, er, who is he?'

'Name of Felter, lived in North Oxford apparently. A retired accountant they seem to think.'

It would have been nice to have been able to reply, 'How curious,' or something equally non-committal, and feigning all ignorance, walk on. As it was, I affected astonishment and exclaimed in my best thespian tone, 'How extraordinary – I met a man called Felter only recently at a soirée in London. But I don't suppose it could possibly be the same!'

'Unusual name,' Dawlish said, 'you never know, could well be the same chap. What height was yours?'

'Well, not very tall,' I replied hesitantly.

'There you are then. Just like the corpse! A little squit.' He drew himself up to his own six foot two, and added, 'Mark my words, old Slowcome will be on your tail before you can say knife!' He chuckled. '"Last observed, the victim was seen conversing with the Reverend Francis Oughterard at a *private* rendezvous in London."' And with a cheerful leer and thrusting the evening paper into my hand, he went on his way.

I pondered his words, wondering how long it would take before Felter's social calendar was checked and the interviews begun. They were probably at it then, methodically working their way down Lavinia's guest list . . . Oh well, time would tell. I entered the house and went into the kitchen where I was met with a scene that occurs regularly every six months or so: Bouncer's basket ritual.

This is an elaborate performance which involves the dog dragging the contents of its basket – rug and debris – on to the floor. Bits of bone, gnarled toys and generally one or two of my old socks lie strewn in haphazard array, while the dog sits on his haunches staring and sniffing at each. This can go on for a good half-hour, and any attempt to tidy things up is met with bared teeth and sepulchral growls. I have long since learnt that my role in this ritual is to show admiration and keep my distance. Whether the display is for my benefit or as a means of impressing the cat I can never be sure. Certainly Maurice participates – by crouching statue-like and fixing the wares with gimlet eye. At the end of the allotted period, i.e. when the stuff is retrieved and returned to the basket, the cat gives a long miaow and stalks away. It is a curious and unvarying business.

Thus, to pass the time and not wishing to incommode the dog, I lit a cigarette and started to scan the Colonel's paper for the Felter article. I found the item and was about to start reading, when for some reason I glanced again at the mess on the floor. In the midst of the usual rubbish lay a small, black, shiny notebook – one of those smart ones with a slim pencil slipped down the side. I was intrigued. What was the dog doing with something like that? It certainly wasn't mine, so where had he got it? Besides, what on earth did he want with it? Hardly typical of his usual stock! I resisted the urge to pick the thing up, knowing that the gesture would not be appreciated. Instead, curbing my curiosity for a safer time, I returned to the newspaper article.

The information was predictable, providing nothing more than the bare facts: Frederick John Felter, sixty-nine, divorced, retired accountant, house in north Oxford for the last fifteen years, keen traveller, member of the local chess club and experienced yachtsman. Neighbours were shocked, saying he was a very nice, respectable gentleman who kept himself to himself and not the sort you expected to get murdered. (Whatever that might mean!)

There was, however, one detail that startled me. Apparently there was evidence to suggest that his house had been broken into – with desk and safe showing signs of 'vigorous exploration', though money seemed not to be the object of the search. According to the reporter, the police were reluctant to confirm a connection between the two incidents, and local residents were being advised to keep a vigilant eye on their household security.

It could of course have been a total coincidence – an opportunist Joe Burglar trying his luck on an empty property. Though if that were the case, what about the money? Either there was none or it was not what the intruder was after ... Odd. My thoughts were interrupted by a noise from the cat and I realized that Bouncer's 'show' was over and we could all go home. I watched as the dog with much panting and badgering laboriously dragged the things back into the basket. Then with a dour look at me, as if to say, 'Don't you dare,' he pottered off.

Having missed lunch I felt hungry, and was about to re-heat the abandoned meatballs and see what else I could throw into the pan, when I remembered Primrose's threat to telephone once I was more 'attuned'. I wasn't sure if that condition had arrived, but noting that it was nearly half-past six realized she might call at any minute. Rather than risk interruption of supper I decided to get in first.

'I see what you meant about the geese,' I said. 'Has Nicholas contacted you?'

'Yes, we've got to work out how to put the lid on this Canadian operation. The horse may have bolted but we've got to do something! He's coming over tomorrow afternoon to discuss things.'

'Or you could go there.'

'What, and risk meeting Eric? No thank you! Besides, I want you here as well.'

'Well,' I said doubtfully, 'I am a bit pressed at the moment, it's getting rather a busy time – you know, weddings and so on ...'

'Ah, so you don't want to give your sister support in her hour of tribulation?'

'Well, it's not that, Prim, it's just that—'

'Oh very well then, I shall just have to cope on my own!' The martyred tone cut no ice for I did not doubt

170

Primrose's ability to 'cope'. However, I was flattered to think I was needed, and after a brief hesitation I capitulated.

'Good,' she said briskly, 'and you can stop off at that shop in Alfriston and bring some of that nice chocolate cake they do. Now don't forget!'

Supper over and my instructions for the following day duly accepted, I turned to Bouncer's basket. Its owner was otherwise engaged, so with a furtive glance at the cat, I flicked back the blanket and smartly appropriated the notebook.

30

The Cat's Memoir

'But didn't you mind him taking that thing?' I asked
Bouncer. 'I mean, usually you make an appalling hulla-
baloo if any of your toys are interfered with.'

'That's as maybe,' answered the dog. 'But this time I
think it could HELP!'

'Help? Help what?' I replied, adjusting my ears.

'Help the vicar of course, he's getting more and more
wound up. So I filched the thing from the stiff's pocket just
in case.'

'In case of what?'

'In case it could HELP F.O.!' he shouted. I cogitated
while he shoved his water-bowl around with his nose, the
usual sign of pique.

'I see,' I said quietly. 'So what made you think it might
be efficacious and why did you not inform me of your
remarkable sleight of jaw?'

The shoving accelerated, and retreating a few paces, I
prepared for flight.

'If you MEAN why did I do it and why didn't I tell
you: it was because my sixth sense said I should and
because I knew you would go on and on like what you
are doing NOW!' He made a lunge but I skipped sideways
... unfortunately colliding with our master's feet as he
entered the kitchen to remonstrate. He stumbled, dropped

his cigarette and cursed; then seizing us both by our scruffs pushed us out into the garden, ramming shut the pet-flap.

'Now look what you've done,' grumbled Bouncer. 'He'll forget all about us and we shall be here for hours and miss our feed!' He had a point.

'Not if I jump up on the study window sill and push my face against the pane while he's working. For some reason that always unsettles him.'

The dog snorted. 'I should think it would! I mean, it's not something you'd like to see too often, is it? A blooming cat's face all flat and furious, squashed against the glass glaring at you. No fear!' And he began to scuffle about in mock agitation.

I was too busy gathering myself for the jump to take much notice; but he suddenly added, 'Do you remember how you used to do that with the Fotherington bird when you belonged to her? Gave her the screaming abdabs, it did!'

I smiled and miaowed reflectively. 'Indeed,' I acknowledged, 'and sometimes I think that had I persisted and perfected my technique, F.O. would not have had to go through all that trouble in the wood.'

'You mean she would have taken one look at you and pegged out anyway – sort of murdered by the mog!' He gave a throaty chortle.

'Well,' I began, 'I wouldn't put it quite like that, but—'

'Mind you,' he continued, 'if that *had* happened it would have saved us a lot of messing about. We wouldn't have to keep protecting him and wondering what he was up to all the time.'

'Yes,' I agreed musingly, 'with my mistress dead but the vicar blameless, just think, we could have spent a life of consummate ease!' I hesitated, and for the dog's benefit revised my words: 'That is to say, Bouncer, we could have had a jammy number.' There was silence as we contemplated that vision.

Then, giving a thoughtful burp, he said, 'But you know what – except for my bones, your haddock, the church crypt and the Veaseys' fish pond, there wouldn't have been much to do, would there?'

'For those of us with resourceful minds,' I remarked pointedly, 'there is always something of—'

'Like bollocks,' said the dog.

'I *beg* your pardon! Kindly refrain—'

'Come off it, Maurice. You know I'm right. We'd have become bored and fat like Gunga Din . . . Now, chop chop! Up on to that ledge and start staring. I want my GRUB!'

Later that evening and having secured our food, we decided that the best policy was a low profile . . . that is to say, I instructed the dog to keep quiet and mind its manners. 'We shall know if this notebook thing is of any significance by the way the vicar reacts. A subtle vigilance is required,' I explained.

Bouncer nodded, settled in his basket, heaved his flanks and, shutting one eye, kept the other trained obsessively upon our master. At the same time I took up my position by the boiler, and silent as a garden gnome watched him lynx-eyed . . .

Nothing happened. He sat staring aimlessly into space, crunching peppermints and blowing smoke rings – simultaneously. Typical!

I became impatient and could already detect the sound of stertorous grunts from the dog's basket. It was time to expedite matters. The notebook still lay on the top of the draining-board where F.O. had carelessly flung it earlier. Quietly I edged over to the sink, and in one swift movement leapt on to the board and gave the book a brisk nudge with my paw. It fell to the ground – along with a clatter of accompanying crockery.

'Bloody cat,' was the explosive response. 'Now look what you've done!' He bent down, scooped up the debris and took the notebook back to the table and began turning the pages. The noise had woken the dog, who with a baleful bark scrambled out through the pet-flap.

For a while there was silence, and then an anguished exclamation. I watched as F.O. stared intently at one of the pages. 'Down in black and white,' he gurgled, bits of humbug spraying all over the table. 'Little so and so!' He had in fact gone quite white himself and I rather suspected that Bouncer's 'helpful' retrieval might prove less of a blessing than a blight. I sighed . . . clearly further crisis was looming.

31

The Vicar's Version

I was on the point of inspecting Bouncer's trophy, but suddenly remembered I had not yet written my monthly address for the parish newsletter. Its deadline was nine o'clock the following morning. Having been late in submitting the previous month's copy and not eager to risk another wigging from Colonel Dawlish, I hastened to the study and began making notes.

I had been at my desk barely five minutes when I was interrupted by a spate of disgruntled animal noises. I strode into the kitchen, sorted them out and thrust the disputants into the garden. 'Cool your paws there,' I muttered, and returned to the labours of the newsletter.

There was further interruption: Maurice glowering fiendishly and yowling for his fish at the window. But bit by bit, and to the chummy accompaniment of Wilfred Pickles and other radio stalwarts, I eventually got the thing done and thankfully returned to the kitchen to forage for humbugs and black coffee. I sat at the table, reflecting on the day's events, and was just lighting another cigarette when out of the corner of my eye I suddenly caught sight of the cat on the draining-board; the next moment the floor was strewn with cutlery and broken plates. With a screech the creature leapt to the sanctity of the boiler from where he watched and purred happily as I swept up the pieces.

Amidst the mess was also the notebook from Bouncer's basket, and with mild curiosity I started to scan its pages. This took a couple of seconds, for it was empty except for what looked like some sort of list on the first page. I examined it idly, then with more attention, and finally with alarm. It read as follows:

Dr Wentworth ? Likely
M.C.? (poss. adultery)
The Hon. Mrs Wyvoe – ditto (multiple)
R.? tba ✔
Prof. Goring – plagiarism
Hayward MP – fraud ✔
Sir L.L. – fraud & call girls
H.C. – buggery
Judge N. Yes – tba
P.O. fakery tba
Ing. – See C & O. NB jug. Useful
Angela Dillworthy – dope peddling

Despite the varied and in places cryptic references, it would seem these were all persons having one thing in common: impropriety. And two names struck me immediately, Hayward MP and Sir L.L. The first was presumably William Hayward, colourful Labour MP for a Yorkshire constituency and in the news recently for resigning his seat on grounds of ill health and 'family reasons'. The second could only be Sir Lionel Lucy, prominent West End backer and vaunted philanthropist. As to the others, well at first they meant nothing (though the Hon. Mrs Wyvoe with her multiple escapades sounded fun) ... And then suddenly three of them meant a great deal! My gaze riveted on the references H.C., P.O., Ing. Had the annotations been less explicit I might have persuaded myself of some coincidence. As it was, buggery, fakery and a prison sentence could surely mean only one thing: Horace, Primrose and Nicholas. Oh my God! Mechanically I unwrapped another humbug and lit a cigarette, grappling with the implications.

177

Obviously those listed were under surveillance. By whom – the Law? But were adultery and plagiarism crimes? Dishonourable conduct perhaps, but not generally police matters. No, this was nothing official . . . this was surely a blackmailer's agenda. One such as Freddie Felter might compile? Exactly! But in that case, how on earth did Bouncer . . . ? 'Oh my sainted aunt!' I groaned. 'The car, it was in the car!' If the chap's handkerchief could work its way from his pocket, so probably could a small notebook. What with the dog's back-seat antics and us having to heave the freight in and out of the cramped space, there had been quite a mêlée. It must have fallen in the manoeuvres and for some reason the dog had picked it up – thought it was a trophy perhaps for biting its ankle. I inspected the rest of the notebook: the pages may have been blank, but they certainly had the mark of chew upon them. Possibly the dog itself had pulled it from Felter's pocket. After all, judging from the amount of snuffling and growling going on, anything could have been happening!

As I reflected upon the curiosity of the matter the sheer luck of the thing suddenly struck me. With a shiver I thought of what might have happened had the notebook remained in Felter's coat pocket. It would have been found by the police, subjected to the closest scrutiny, the list of names examined, conclusions drawn, those featured identified, followed up and questioned . . . Well, Bouncer's agency or not, at least he had brought the thing to my notice and thus removed it from harm's way. I grinned, wondering what Sir Lionel Lucy et al would think if they knew that the Reverend Canon of Molehill held certain embarrassing data in his possession. Fed up, I imagine.

And then I thought of the dog again, and went to the French window to call him for bed. 'Bouncer,' I yelled, 'good dog, come on. Come on in now!' He didn't, of course.

Despite relief at having secured Felter's list, I wondered if any more such details might come to light from the police investigation. They would certainly be scouring his house for personal data, and thus there was surely a chance that other incriminating tit-bits might be found. Besides, what about the *recent* communications? Not surprisingly I slept badly, the night beset with dreams and fears and long intervals spent staring at the darkness.

The next day I arose tired and dispirited and was glad that it was my morning for inspecting the hymn lists in the church and checking the proceeds of the charity boxes. Enforced repose amidst the shadows of St Botolph's wouldn't go amiss – indeed was more than welcome.

At that hour the place held a seductive serenity, and before commencing my domestic duties I paused to sit in one of the pews and contemplate . . . Contemplate what? This and that and this and . . . And then inevitably, and as so often, Elizabeth's face swam into mind, and not for the first time I wondered what the hell I was doing and whether I would ever do anything different . . .

'Canon,' the voice cried, 'I was going to telephone but here you are!' Wearily I looked up to be confronted by Mavis sporting a straw hat and paisley pinafore. Evidently it was her turn for the vestry cleaning. I smiled briefly, rather surprised that she had not scurried past, still smarting from the bulldog incident. No, it takes more than that to deter Mavis. She hovered determinedly and I realized that something of moment was in the air.

'Canon,' she fluttered again, 'I have a little problem and would welcome your advice. It's, ah, a trifle delicate really. *Embarrassing*, in fact.'

'Well,' I replied with sinking heart, 'I'm sure it can't be that bad. What have you been up to – raiding the collection box?'

'Of course not!' she tittered. 'But it's something I've got to *report*.'

'To me?'

'No. To Superintendent Slowcome. It's about that dreadful night before I discovered the body.'

My attention flared and I asked her cautiously what it was.

'Well,' she replied, flushing slightly, 'I don't think it's the sort of thing one can discuss here – at least not in so many *words*.' And she gestured vaguely in the direction of the altar and the pulpit. 'Perhaps we should go outside – away from these hallowed precincts.'

Somewhat startled, I nodded obligingly. 'Er, yes, of course Mavis, if that's what you feel.' And taking her firmly by the elbow I propelled her out into the sunshine.

She trotted down the path, then presumably deeming we were at a respectable distance from the church porch, turned and said, 'You see, I've been so distracted by this whole matter, quite apart from having to order new border plants – all flattened of course – that I quite forgot to mention something which the superintendent might find useful . . . I mean in pursuing *clues*.' She gazed at me, intent and wide-eyed.

'So why don't you tell him?' I asked woodenly, fearing it might be the handkerchief.

'Well that's just it. I don't quite know how to! And I wondered if you might suggest . . . After all, it's not the sort of thing that I am used to—'

'What are you talking about, Mavis?' I muttered impatiently. 'What exactly do you have to tell him?' I felt worried and wished to God she would get to the point.

'As you know, my cottage overlooks the lane. It was quite a damp night but rather warm, and I had my bedroom windows wide open. Morpheus was upon me and—'

'*What?*'

'I was fast asleep – in the land of dreams. But for some reason I suddenly woke from my slumbers and overheard something on the other side of the hedge – something of possible *significance*! But then I nodded off again and it quite went out of my head until today . . . It's funny the way that can happen. Do you ever do that, Canon? It's so strange because sometimes—'

'What was it you heard, Mavis?' I enquired through gritted teeth.

'A man's voice.'

'Oh yes, and what did it say?'

She lowered her head and started to whisper. I lowered mine but couldn't hear a word.

'Sorry, Mavis, you'll have to speak up.'

She cleared her throat and hesitated. And then seeming to brace herself, and staring me boldly in the eye, enunciated crisply, '"Hold the fucker's legs, can't you? Do you want me to get back to Brighton with a bleeding hernia?"' She closed her eyes, shuddered, and then added, 'Although now I come to think of it, he may have said Worthing, or Bognor possibly. One of those south coast towns . . . Yes, Bognor perhaps.'

My first instinct was to roar with laughter, but that was swiftly replaced by numbed horror as the implications hit me . . . Brighton. That was exactly what we had told Sergeant Withers at the roadblock! Indeed, so keen had I been to supply authentic detail of our business that I had given him a vivid account of Bouncer's liking for the Brighton sea-front. If Mavis told her tale to the police, surely the Brighton reference might ring bells. Too clever by half, Francis!

Perhaps, I thought wildly, I could offer to go to Slowcome on her behalf and then conveniently forget. But knowing Mavis she would hardly let slip the excitement of another interview, and in any case was bound to bring it up again at some point. I clutched at a straw: her erratic memory. If she could forget something as crucial as Ingaza swearing about the corpse and be vague about the mentioned town, with steady repetition Brighton might be overlaid by Bognor. After all, they both began with the same letter. It was some distance along the coast to the west of Brighton and with Worthing in between. With a bit of luck, and assuming Mavis kept its name in her head, no significance would attach to Ingaza's Brighton domicile as recorded at the roadblock.

'Bognor! Well I never,' I exclaimed. 'And I thought it was so respectable! Why, I remember during the war how dull the troops found it. Nobody ever wanted to go on leave there. "Bally Bognor" we used to call it. Hastings was so much better. Well, fancy those thugs coming all the way from *Bognor* to dispose of the body!'

'Yes,' agreed Mavis excitedly, 'and Bognor is where the deed may have actually been committed. Good gracious, I must tell Mr Slowcome straight away what I heard. It could make all the difference!' (Couldn't it just.) She stopped, and then stammered, 'But I'm not sure that I could possibly repeat the exact—'

'Don't worry, Mavis,' I said gallantly, 'you won't have to. I'll come with you if you like, and I'm sure together we can produce a suitable substitute!' I beamed encouragingly.

'Oh what a relief, Canon,' she squeaked, blushing again. 'That would be such a support!'

And that is what we did: beetled off to the police station and in euphemistic terms told the desk sergeant all about the awful man who was so eager to get back to Bognor without incurring a hernia.

'So you think it was a Sussex resort, Miss Briggs?' asked Slowcome slowly.

'Oh *yes*,' exclaimed Mavis, 'Bognor to be precise. I wouldn't make a mistake like that!'

Later, taking me aside, he asked if the witness was reliable. 'Absolutely,' I replied gravely. 'Miss Briggs may appear a little airy-fairy, but she has a memory like an elephant.' He nodded, and seeming satisfied wrote something briskly on his desk pad.

Also later, after the witness had garrulously departed, he made sly enquiries of me regarding the cathedral's new gospel-reading rota, clearly intent on getting himself picked to play a major role in the forthcoming centenary celebrations.

'I daresay the good bishop has me marked down for something or other,' he remarked casually. 'And of course as one of the *old hands* at the podium, I should be more than happy to offer my services. These occasions are always a bit fraught and the public can't abide mumblers! They appreciate an experienced reader.'

You mean one who likes the sound of his own voice, I thought sourly; but with an ingratiating smile I assured him that I would certainly relay his kind offer to Bishop Clinker. He seemed satisfied and I hurriedly took myself off home to down a much-needed Scotch.

32

The Vicar's Version

The following morning was more congested than usual, the proposed visit to Primrose necessarily entailing a compressed schedule. One of the compressions was a now painfully early meeting with Colonel Dawlish to discuss the new sidesman – a sallow gentleman hastily recruited to fill a gap.

'He'll have to go,' fumed Dawlish as we stood in the church porch. 'Does nothing but pick his nose and drop the plate – half-crowns rolling all over the shop! Besides, Edith Hopgarden has taken against him and you know what that means!' I did, but was curious to know what form this particular gripe took.

'Says he lurks in the aisle and leers at her and she can't concentrate.'

'Concentrate on what? The psalms?'

'Giving the glad-eye to Tapsell in the organ loft.'

'Oh well, he'll have to go then,' I agreed mildly.

'Done!' said Dawlish with satisfaction.

I had hoped that might conclude matters and that I could slope off back to the vicarage for a belated coffee, but he clearly had more on the agenda.

Tapping me smartly on the shoulder, he said, 'You know you said we needed some new fund-raising proposals?'

I nodded.

'Well, I've got one: a dogs' talent contest. We could have them all parading in your garden, put 'em through their paces and charge owners five bob a head. Couldn't be simpler! What do you think?'

I had a momentary vision of Maurice confronted by hordes of roaring canines, and also of the baby next door ... That'll give them both something to yowl about, I thought grimly.

'Um, well,' I began, 'I'm not sure whether—'

'It'll be just the thing,' he urged eagerly. 'And you'll see, my Tojo's bound to scoop a prize. Cocky little devil, best prancer in the neighbourhood!' (And biter, I mentally added.)

'Yes, it's a thought,' I acknowledged vaguely.

'Good, good! I'll have notices drawn up and set the whole thing rolling. Just leave it to me.' He took off to the lychgate, untethered the waspish Tojo, and together they belted out of sight.

'Oh Lor . . .' I sighed.

Tasks completed, I bundled Bouncer into the Singer and hared down to Sussex – remembering just in time to make a detour via Alfriston to pick up the chocolate cake.

When I arrived Ingaza was already there, and I rather gathered that to soften the 'Canadian geese' threat he and Primrose had already worked out some kind of exit strategy from their project.

Turning to me he said, 'I've explained to my Canadian contact there's a revival of interest in that type of thing among British collectors, and that such pictures have become as rare as hens' teeth, making supplies impossible ... Means the loss of a few fat cheques of course, but in the circumstances better to be—'

'Safe?' I asked with some asperity. 'Don't bank on it! I doubt if our friend will suspend activities just because you've ceased trading. I always thought this commercial racket was highly dangerous and now look what it has led to!'

'Stop being so pompous, Francis,' cried Primrose. 'Besides, it most certainly was not a commercial racket, as you so delicately put it. It was an artistic enterprise of wit and imagination and a valuable chance for the Canadians to own artefacts remarkable in their resemblance to the rustic originals. Personally I think one was doing them a thoughtful service . . . And by the way, did you remember to bring the cake?'

I assured her that I had remembered, adding that I just hoped the blackmailer was the only one fly enough to have detected her hand in the paintings, otherwise all denials would be useless.

'Possibly,' cut in Nicholas smoothly, 'but you do have your *own* problems, don't you, dear boy? And if this chap has nosed out the Canadian thing, who knows, you could be the next on the list along with the rest of us. So let's work out who the bastard is.'

'Exactly,' declared Primrose, 'and then we can take him out.'

'*Primrose!*' I cried.

'Only joking . . . at least I think I am.' She stood up, and taking the cake from me went off to make tea.

While she was gone I let the dog into the garden, then produced Felter's notebook for Nicholas and explained how I had found it.

'Clever little bugger, your dog! Sharper than its owner.'

I ignored that and gazed out at the lawn, watching Bouncer as he rambled and sniffed among the rhododendrons, guessing that it wouldn't be long before he trotted off to view the rabbits. I just hoped the chinchillas were safely caged and not hopping about.

Turning back, I saw Nicholas studying the list, apparently with some amusement.

'What are you grinning at?'

He pointed to one of the entries. 'Angela Dillworthy – I knew her years ago. Bought some pictures from me. Doped up to the eyeballs even then . . . and now she's pushing the stuff. Well, what do you know! Hubby won't like that, nor the sponging brother – unless they're in on it too of course.'

'The Dillworthys?' asked Primrose, returning with the cake and tea things. 'A *very* suspect family in my opinion, not quite on the level. Why are you talking about them?'

I explained that one of their members had been marked down for blackmail by Freddie Felter, and described again how I had found the notebook in Bouncer's basket.

'There you are then,' she said triumphantly. 'I bet they all got together and there was a collective bumping-off.'

'That's as maybe,' drawled Nicholas, reaching for a large slice of the chocolate confection, 'but even allowing for your poetic imagination, Primrose, that doesn't tell us who the devil is on our trail *now!*'

There was silence as we sipped, munched and cogitated. And then I said musingly, 'Oh, I can tell you who it is.'

Nicholas raised a quizzical eyebrow, while my sister also looked sceptical. 'Who?' she challenged.

'Turnbull . . . And I bet you he also killed Felter.'

At that moment Bouncer bounded in, covered in mud and bits from the compost heap. He tried to scramble up on to the sofa, but was met with such an eruption from its owner that he slunk away to the rug. But even there he was not safe. 'Francis,' Primrose expostulated, 'you *must* put him in the kitchen! I've just had that thing cleaned and I'm really not prepared to have dirty marks everywhere!'

Dutifully I hustled him into the kitchen, gave him a wink and returned to the drawing room.

'Now, what were you saying?' she continued.

'Turnbull. I think he's behind this – the notes and the killing. We know he has blackmailed before and more than probably murdered. Nothing else fits.'

'But why should he kill Felter? They were on good terms – at least that's what Lavinia seemed to imply.'

'Yes they were. But suppose Freddie had found out or knew about the dispatching of Birtle-Figgins. After all, he was also an old family friend of Lavinia's. The two of them were quite matey. Remember how you described them at the Brighton gallery launch – stuck to her like a leech, you said. She could easily have let drop something about what happened in France, or even perhaps told him directly – she's not exactly reliable! From what we've learnt of Freddie, both through Mrs Tubbly Pole's account and Clinker's recent experience, he was pretty insouciant in his pursuit of victims. I bet you he had started to put the thumbscrews on Turnbull as well, and Turnbull wasn't having it.' I paused, drained my tea cup and carefully detached the icing from my cake, reserving it for the final splurge.

'Hmm, all sounds a bit speculative . . .' said Primrose. 'But of course speculation doesn't necessarily make it wrong. We know that Boris Birtle-Figgins was threatening to expose Turnbull's shady business dealings in France and thus ruin his career, *and* we have seen the evidence linking him with at least one, and probably both, of those two deaths. If he could kill twice to preserve his reputation in France it's equally likely that if threatened again, and just when his professional plans are going so well, he would do it again.'

'Could be,' mused Nicholas. 'After all, what's another killing? Might as well be hanged for three as for one. I expect those are your views, aren't they, Francis, dear boy?' He grinned.

'Shut *up*,' I muttered.

'Francis doesn't have any views!' said Primrose indignantly.

'Oh he does sometimes,' Nicholas replied, still grinning, 'and in this case he could be near the target. The only thing is there's no mention of our man on Freddie's list. Horace, Primrose and myself feature only too clearly, but not Turnbull. Not that that means much, I suppose. After all, one doesn't have to feature on a list to achieve distinction.'

I took the notebook from him and pointed to the letter *R* with its *tba* addition and the tick. 'Could be Rupert – Rupert to be arranged,' I suggested.

'Huh,' observed Primrose, 'should have made the arrangements more watertight!'

'You see,' I went on, 'that tick might suggest that he had already set things in motion, made his approach – i.e. the "arrangements" had been put into practice. And Rupert took umbrage – as he had in France with Lavinia's hubby. It was probably he who drove Freddie to Clinker's place and then attacked him as he left. In fact I wouldn't mind betting it was he who broke into Felter's house afterwards, searching for any stuff about himself. '

'So that all hinges on the letter *R*, does it?' enquired Ingaza.

'No,' I replied testily, 'that initial is merely an additional possibility in a picture of cumulative detail.'

I rather liked that last phrase and was annoyed when my sister gave a stifled laugh.

'What's so funny?' I asked coldly.

'Well, I daresay we shall be able to test out that theory before too long, or at least have another look at it. Remember we've been invited to the inaugural reception for the opening of Rupert's Oxford language school.'

'Not me!' I said quickly. 'I know nothing about it and have no intention of risking further association. I told you ages ago that getting re-involved with Turnbull would be dangerous; and after what Maud Tubbly Pole told me about how he beat up that boy in India, let alone what we take to be his recent record in France, I am convinced of it. So kindly count me out!'

'Too late,' she replied. 'I've accepted and so has your bishop. Seemed rather eager. *I* think he's taken a shine to Lavinia.'

'Hmm,' murmured Ingaza. 'Should that be the case and Turnbull is indeed the one, old Hor had better watch it otherwise another note might come winging his way! I doubt if Gladys would appreciate learning she had *two* rivals.' He smirked.

'I am still not going,' I said. 'I shall plead illness.'

'In which case I shall telephone Mavis Briggs and urge her to bring you some gruel,' responded Primrose sweetly.

I scowled and turned to Ingaza. 'Have you been invited, Nicholas?'

'No, but I might go all the same.'

'What for? I should have thought it was in your interests to keep as low a profile as possible. In fact, if I were in your shoes I would take Aunt Lil on a long cruise lasting several months!'

'Not Aunt Lil, you wouldn't.'

'But why on earth do you want to go?'

'Could be a chance to get the lie of the land, to see if there's anything in his manner to support your theory. And if there is . . . then, well, one might . . .' His voice trailed off and he lolled back on the sofa, twiddled his signet ring and smiled wistfully – a mannerism which at St Bede's had invariably signified impending trouble.

'Might what?' I asked suspiciously.

'Turn the tables. Give him a taste of his own medicine. After all, *we* know about the French business – or think we do . . . I take it you do still have that piece of evidence which you so cleverly unearthed?'*

'Yes,' I said uneasily, 'I have, but I really don't think—'

'Nicholas is right,' agreed Primrose. 'He might consider us easy pickings, but he's in a far worse position himself – as Freddie probably made clear!'

'And Freddie's bloody dead!' I reminded her.

Suddenly there was loud barking from the kitchen.

'Hold on,' Primrose said, 'I think that's the phone. Drat! It's probably the Smithers wanting me to make up a bridge four. Won't be a minute.' She left the room, while Nicholas and I smartly divided and consumed the remains of the cake. We were just about to return to the subject of Felter's notebook, when Primrose came back looking flustered.

'That was Millie Merton,' she announced. 'She's got Lavinia and Turnbull staying the weekend and wants to bring them over.'

'Rather you than me, can't abide that woman!' said Nicholas. 'When?'

'Now, actually.'

'What!' I yelped. 'I've told you, I do not want to meet either of them!'

'And I certainly don't want to see the Merton woman, she's already poached two of my clients,' Nicholas added.

* See *Bones in High Places*

'Too bad. They are on their way and they'll think it odd if you disappear, especially as I said my brother had so enjoyed Lavinia's housewarming and would be delighted to see them again. Besides, I want to keep in with Millie, there's a good chance of her exhibiting some of my paintings.'

'Oh really, Prim,' I protested, 'that's a bit much! Besides, I've got to get back to Molehill . . . Busy day tomorrow. Funerals.'

'Liar,' she said briskly. 'Now hurry up and help me get the place tidy, those cushions are in an awful mess.'

'I'm off,' announced Nicholas stiffly.

'No you are not,' she replied. 'After all, it was you who was saying you wanted to go to their Oxford thing to see the lie of the land. Well now's your chance. And if you don't cooperate I jolly well won't come to applaud your tango exhibition at the Old Schooner. The competition's being broadcast on the Light Programme and the contestants with the loudest claps get the prize *and* the lolly.'

He made a face and mooched into the garden.

I had to hand it to my sister. A bit like Ingaza himself, she knew the right wires to pull. 'Snake Hips Ingaza' was a soubriquet in which Nicholas took sly satisfaction; and his prowess on the Brighton dance floors and in certain arcane nightclubs was surpassed only by his talent to run an art dealership of maximum flair and minimum probity . . . Yes, winning the competition mattered, and Primrose knew it.

'*So* lovely to see you again, Primrose!' Millie Merton gushed. 'Oh – and Nicholas too. Long time no see!'

'Two weeks ago at Lavinia's flat,' was the dry response.

'Ah yes, one so easily forgets these things . . .' She drifted off to examine a bowl of lilies.

'Bitch!' he muttered under his breath.

Primrose whisked Millie into the hall to admire a new painting and Lavinia followed. The latter had brought Attlee, sporting a filigree harness. He looked morose, and

I watched with some sympathy as his little bandy legs spindled after his minder.

Left alone with Turnbull, Nicholas and I exchanged pleasantries, asking him about the new language school and his plans for its development. He spoke enthusiastically about the patronage from the Foreign Office and also his hopes to establish links with some graduate school in India. 'Jaipur, actually,' he volunteered, 'they seem very keen.'

'Oh yes,' said Nicholas blandly, 'you were at St Austin's, weren't you? Oddly enough, one of my customers was speaking very warmly of you only recently – name of Timms – said he remembers you well when you were in the sixth form and being tutored by your friend Freddie Felter. He was a housemaster then, wasn't he? Timms seems to recall you both returning to England at the same time . . . Must have been an awful shock for you and Lavinia, him turning up dead like that!'

For a moment Turnbull was silent, his face expressionless. And then he said quietly, 'Yes, it was. Awful. Poor old Freddie, an extraordinary business! We shall miss him.' Before he had a chance to say anything further, Millie Merton had zoomed up, and taking him by the arm, inveigled him on to the terrace to admire the line of the South Downs in the westering sun.

I glowered at Nicholas. 'For one who was reluctant to stay this afternoon, you've certainly made your mark,' I fumed. 'What on earth possessed you to mention Timms? You do realize that was the name of the boy Rupert and Freddie victimized! And I don't believe for one moment he's a customer of yours. Besides, how did you know the name?'

'From you. You mentioned it when you were telling the tale you heard from your novelist pal. I'm quite good on things like that – little trifles.'

'Well this is no little trifle,' I snapped. 'You've as good as told him you know about the Jaipur scandal, and he's bound to assume you've discussed it with me. I suppose next you'll tell him we suspect him of other things too!'

'Nothing so crude,' he replied smoothly. 'I just thought that a mild hint wouldn't go amiss. What you might call a little needler, dear boy, just to see the reaction – the only problem being that little Miss Fig Face had to come and put her galumphing oar in things, otherwise I could have pushed him further.'

'Do *not*,' I hissed, turning to fix a ravishing smile upon Lavinia.

She smiled back but said pensively, 'You know, Francis, I simply can't get over dear Freddie's death, and such an awful way to go, too! It really has rather unsettled me. He was so entertaining and with such a wonderful sense of humour!' I rather doubted whether Clinker would share those particular views, but in my best clergyman's voice – and possibly with a modicum of sincerity – I launched into the appropriate condolence.

However, this rather lost its momentum when she suddenly exclaimed, 'But the *amazing* thing is his being found in that woman's garden so near you. It does seem strange! After all, he spent most of his time in Oxford and London, so what was he doing in Surrey, I wonder?'

'Ah, but they say he was, er, *dispatched* elsewhere,' I said quickly.

'But that's what makes it all the more peculiar. Why kill him in one place and then take him to tiny Molehill? And *you* must have been pretty shocked too when you heard about it. I mean, you had only just recently met him at my party – and then his body is discovered so close by. Ghastly!'

I agreed that it was more than ghastly, and enquired if she would care for an early cocktail. My own need beginning to be acute, I was relieved when she said she would.

I went into the kitchen to see what I could find but Nicholas was ahead of me.

'Where does your sister keep her drink?' he asked.

I directed him to a cupboard. 'But at all costs avoid the sherry. It's lethal.'

'Better give it to Millie Merton, then.'

* * *

Cocktails sipped and the ritual perambulations of the garden complete (with gormless chinchillas duly admired) it seemed likely the guests would soon take off. Indeed Millie Merton was already making noises to that effect, announcing loudly – for Ingaza's benefit, I suspected – that they were dining with a *most* distinguished art critic that evening and they really shouldn't be late. ('Distinguished, my arse,' Nicholas had later opined. 'Can't tell a Tintoretto from a Margaret Tarrant!')

'We can't go yet,' exclaimed Lavinia, 'Attlee's disappeared. He's wandered off somewhere and I can't see him anywhere!' And marshalling Primrose and Nicholas she set off with them to scour the shrubbery.

Turnbull laughed and offered me a cigarette. 'That dog,' he protested, 'it rules the roost. Will of iron and silent as the grave. Not quite sure what Lavinia sees in him – though a change from Boris, I suppose . . . How's yours these days?' He gave Bouncer a friendly pat.

I was taken aback by this casual quip re the dead spouse, and to conceal my confusion hastily embarked on a catalogue of Bouncer's oddities. Turnbull seemed amused, stooped down to pat the dog again and began to talk wittily about the antics of his neighbour's cat. I was just getting drawn into the exploits of 'Tigger' when he broke off and, looking thoughtful, enquired if I knew when Bishop Clinker had last seen Freddie Felter.

Caught on the back foot I could only stammer that apart from Lavinia's party, I didn't think he had. 'Er, why?' I asked nervously.

'Well it's simply that Freddie had a spare first edition of that sailing novel the bishop seems so keen on – the one about riddles and sands – and he said something about wanting to give it to Clinker next time they met. I just wondered if he had managed to deliver it before the tragedy – seem to remember him saying he might drop it in if he was ever passing.' I was about to disclaim all knowledge, when he added lightly, 'Actually, that was something I forgot to mention to the Surrey police when they interviewed us – quite slipped my mind. Still, don't suppose it matters really, they're bound to have more pressing aspects to pursue . . . Have they been to you yet?'

'Been to me?'

'Yes, they seem to be doing a routine check of all those who may have spoken to him at Lavinia's party.'

'Oh, yes of course. Er, no, not yet, but I imagine it won't be long – the superintendent is pretty keen.' I smiled vaguely, wondering what I could say to get him off the subject, but wasn't quick enough.

'Must have been terribly distressing for the bishop to learn of Freddie's death like that – practically on his own doorstep, you might say. Awful shock!' His blue eyes regarded me earnestly.

'Yes,' I agreed, feeling mildly ill, 'most distressing.'

Mercifully, at that moment the search party returned with Lavinia clutching the errant Attlee.

'Where was he?' asked Turnbull.

She giggled. 'You will never guess – curled up with the chinchillas, fast asleep! Their cage door was on the latch and he must have hooked it open. He's such a sharp little thing!'

I glanced down at Bouncer and muttered, 'Missed a trick there, didn't you, old boy? Must be slipping.' He wagged his tail vigorously – though presumably less in agreement than to signal his desire to leave. It was a desire I shared and I was thankful when the visitors finally departed.

After they had gone Primrose said with satisfaction, 'That was rather productive, I consider!'

'Why?'

'I've got a contract out of the Merton Gallery.'

'Cultural suicide,' snorted Ingaza.

Despite my sister's scepticism over my run of funerals the following day, I had in fact been telling the truth and the first one was at an early hour. Thus, after her guests' departure, I declined Primrose's offer of supper and started my journey homeward.

A busy day ahead was not the only reason for my desire to get on the road. Given the circumstances, I had found the unexpected arrival of Turnbull and Lavinia a considerable strain, and their references to the Felter matter had been unsettling . . . so much so that I wanted time on my own to reflect before saying anything further to Primrose and Nicholas. Thus, shifting Bouncer from the front seat to the back with the enticement of an old bone from under the dashboard, I lit a cigarette and drove off pondering the significance, if any, of what had been said.

On the face of it their reactions had been entirely predictable: distress at the death of their friend, shock at its manner, puzzled surprise that his body should have been found in the vicinity of Molehill. Surely their words had been unremarkable . . . Or had they? Blandly innocuous or loaded with innuendo? Turnbull's allusion to Clinker's doorstep had more than rattled me, but was I being absurdly sensitive? It was after all a perfectly ordinary expression which anyone might use. Was there really any reason to see the coincidence as sinister? Other than nervous instinct, no. *But*, I nagged myself, what about his reference to Felter intending to deliver that novel to Clinker! Surely if the police learnt of that they would be round to the Palace like a shot . . . But they didn't know about it: Turnbull had omitted to tell them. It seemed a curious detail to have slipped his memory. The man wasn't a fool, he must have recognized it could provide a useful lead in establishing Felter's later movements. Yet he had dismissed it as being of little consequence. In which case why mention it at all – indeed, make such a point of asking me about it? *Because*, I concluded unhappily, the whole matter was a fabrication. Turnbull was just trying it on – throwing down a covert challenge, letting me know that he knew . . . Just as Ingaza had been doing to him over the Jaipur business. I groaned, stopped the car and let the dog out.

Propped up against a farm gate and watching Bouncer ambling blithely amid shafts of willowherb, I lit another cigarette and thought about Lavinia. Had she been part of the 'game'? Were her remarks also double-edged, designed to get me windy? If so, she had certainly succeeded. *But that's what makes it all the more peculiar. Why kill him in one place and then take him to tiny Molehill? And you must have been pretty shocked too when you heard about it. I mean, you had only just recently met him at my party – and then his body is discovered so close by!* Yes, she was quite right – it did look peculiar: Clinker and myself encountering Felter for the first time in London, only to have his corpse turn up jettisoned ten miles from the bishop's domain and in my obscure parish. Surely she had every reason to be intrigued. And yet, I fretted, had their separate concern over the locality of the find, their emphasis on the strangeness of its proximity to both me and Clinker been a trifle too harmonious – orchestrated, even? Both had been making exactly the same point, the one observation neatly reinforcing the other . . . Again my mind returned to Turnbull's metaphor of the bishop's doorstep; and again amid the perplexity I felt a sting of fear.

My cogitations were interrupted by the dog making clear its purpose of resuming the journey. And taking my cue I returned to the car, and once more we set off on the homeward path and the relief of bed.

33

The Dog's Diary

'It was a bit rum,' I told Maurice, 'and just as well you weren't with us, you would have gone all ratty.' The cat opened his mouth to make some sniffy answer but I got in first. 'You see,' I said quickly, 'it wasn't just the Prim and the Brighton Type who were there but the whole blooming lot – Turnip and the thin bird and a short one I didn't know (and didn't like much either), plus that little geezer Attlee. Far too many for you, Maurice, and all jabbering nineteen to the dozen. I mean, it was like what you say sometimes . . .' (I had to stop here, trying to remember exactly what it was he *did* say – it's not always easy) 'um, you know – when you wave your paws in the air and screech: "I can't tell you how awful it was: the noise, the *people*!"'

'And what about those purrnishus rabbits,' he asked, 'were they still there?'

I told him that they were, but that since I was on my BEST behaviour and hoping to get some special extras from the tea-table I thought I would give them a miss this time.

'In that case,' said the cat, all hoity-toity and pleased with itself, 'how do you know they were there? Your sixth sense, I suppose!'

I told him coldly that my sixth sense had better things to do than bother itself with bastard bunnies (or even

PURR-NISHUS ones), and I knew they were there because Attlee vanished and was found fast asleep between them.

'Peculiar,' said Maurice. 'I am surprised they didn't raise hell. After all, that's what they usually do if any of us go near.'

'Yes, you would have thought so,' I said, 'but old titchy legs seems to have a knack. He told me that he just went up to the hutch door, nosed it open, said nothing, pushed them apart with his elbows and lay down. They didn't do anything, too stunned I suppose. He said that one of them, Karloff probably, did begin to squeak, but thought better of it when he was fixed with a stern eye and told to pull himself together.'

For once the cat looked quite impressed. But we got on to other things such as Turnip and F.O. I said that this time my sixth sense was working overtime because I kept having the feeling that Turnip was somehow getting at the vicar and making him all hot and bothered – and that the thin lady hadn't been helping much either. It was like they were both watching F.O. to see what he would do – going so far and then holding back: 'Just like you, Maurice, when you play Tom Tiddler's Ground with the Veaseys' goldfish.' (That got him preening all right – fancies himself as a dab-handler of pond life.)

So when I had finished telling him about Turnip & Co. and that funny little Attlee fellow he asked what happened next, and I explained that by then F.O. was so windy, the next thing I knew I had been yanked into the car and we were off at a rate of knots . . . But I tell you, I soon put a stop to that! I mean to say, he hadn't even allowed time for me to put my leg up properly; just got it at half-cock when he hustled me into the car *and* shoved me in the back seat, if you please! And as I said to Maurice, Bouncer was buggered if he was going to stand for that, oh no! So after we had gone a few miles and our master was in the middle of mangling some hymn or other, I made it clear I wanted a run. So we stopped and got out, and I beetled around a bit while he leant against a five-barred gate smoking his head off and staring into the distance, twitching. He stood like that for ages and in the end it was my turn to push *him* into the car. Anyway, we arrived home at last and I was pretty glad to get into my basket for a good kip. After all that scent and such those ladies were wearing – it smelled really nice, all sort of old and hairy and earthy. Just the job!

34

The Cat's Memoir

Having accompanied the vicar on one of his Sussex jaunts, Bouncer had been in one of his superior moods, i.e. tiresomely cocky, and kept telling me how much he had enjoyed the sea air and 'those great rolling Downs'. Rolling Downs, my aunt's tail! What does he know about such things? The only time he ever meets a rolling down is when he and that maniac O'Shaughnessy roll the hedgehog down the hill! No, it's clearly a term he has picked up from the humans and has added to his repertoire of dubious mimicry. So there it sits, along with other choice borrowings such as 'Harrodsknightsbridge', 'How's your father?', 'Aiy don't maind if aiy do!', 'Poodle-faking ponce' and 'What a charming daughter you have, Mrs Ramsbottom!' He's only just learnt that last one, took him ages, and now he trots it out ad nauseam!

Anyway, as said, he had been taken to the sister's house in Lewes, and from what I could make out, despite all the rams' bottoms and rolling Downs, his visit there was not without interest. He told me there had been a whole crew of them gathered, all gabbling and slurping tea and gin, including Turnip and that female appendage he had with him in France. There was also some short job whom he hadn't seen before. He said that he didn't think the Appendage liked the Short Job much and kept shooting her poisonous looks – 'Like you do, Maurice, when you think the tabby might snaffle your haddock.' (Huh! If that creature so much as sniffs at my fish it'll get more than a poisonous look, I can tell you!)

I enquired if the Type from Brighton had been there. 'You bet,' he said. 'Oiling away as usual and fingering the chocolate cake. Never gave me any!'

'So is that all they did, drank and guzzled?'

'Oh no,' he said, 'other things too.'

I waited for him to continue but he bounded away in pursuit of butterflies and I had to call him back sharply. '*What* other things, Bouncer?'

'Oh, just things . . .' he replied vaguely.

He does it deliberately, you know – all part of the canine cussed nature. It used to madden me, but now I generally shrug and pretend to be occupied with something else. It usually works and the next moment he's agog with his news. However, that afternoon I was in no mood to play silly beggars, so I told him briskly that if he didn't hurry up and tell me I would pee on his marrow-bone. I have an aversion to bones so it is not something I undertake lightly, but occasionally needs must.

It did the trick and he launched into a long narrative involving the vicar and Turnip.

'You should have seen F.O. – getting in a right old sweat, he was! I mean, he tried to look calm and SOOSIANT but *I* knew he wasn't feeling at all well, not well at all. Kept rubbing his nose and twitching his little finger. Sure signs.'

'Really?' I said with some curiosity. 'Can't say I've ever noticed him do that.'

'P'raps not. But then you don't make a study of him. *I* do. It's what we dogs are taught as puppies. "Always watch the buggers, every inch of 'em, and you can't go far wrong!" Yes, that's what they told us. So you see, Maurice, I'm what you might call *trained* from birth.' He cocked his ears and looked smug.

I mewed impatiently. 'In that case, it is the only training you have ever had! A more unruly hound it would be hard to imagine – except for O'Shaughnessy of course. Now

202

hurry up and get on with the story!' And so he did, with all the customary embellishments and ribaldry.

But I have to admit that when he had finished I was worried. Quite clearly matters were tense with the vicar, and judging from Bouncer's description of the exchanges with Turnip and the Appendage, there seemed an aura of possible menace. And while I may not possess the dog's 'training' nor the much-vaunted sixth sense, it was quite apparent from F.O.'s demeanour the following day that something was afflicting that muddled mind. I just hoped for all our sakes that the muddle would unravel itself and we should be safe!

35

The Vicar's Version

Though mercifully overlaid by clerical duties, the fear engendered by my encounter with Rupert Turnbull hovered for most of the following day. It was not unlike a persistent headache – low-key, yet impossible to shift. Eventually, as a means of distraction, I decided to take the dog for a walk. Though it was earlier than his usual hour, Bouncer was raucously cooperative and we set off at a brisk gait.

We had just rounded the corner by Tapsell's house (me dragging the lead, fearful there might be a repeat of his previous performance) when I saw a slight figure carrying a large canvas bag, moving in our direction: Savage, on the homeward lap from his tuning rounds. As he drew near I hailed him and Bouncer gave a friendly woof; with a wave of the white cane he stopped and smiled broadly.

'Must be the vicar,' he said cheerily. 'Not seen you for some time, Rev! In fact I was just saying to Mrs S. only the other day that I thought your piano was well overdue – it's probably feeling a bit under the weather by now.'

I agreed that it most certainly was but that I been terribly busy.

'Ah yes, goes in phases, doesn't it? One moment slack, the next it's all coming at you every which way! Anyway, how are things? Winning, are you?'

'Not noticeably,' I replied. 'Treading water more like.'

'That's the ticket, ' he said cheerily. 'Just keep treading and *nil carborundum* – don't let the baskets, etc, etc.'

I told him that said baskets were currently proving rather recalcitrant.

He grinned. 'Don't worry, it'll pass, it always does. I've told you before – you should do as I do, get the old drums out and give 'em hell. A piano's *all right* in its place but nothing beats a pounding à la Krupa!'

I laughed. 'One day, Savage, I'll surprise you and come and ask for lessons, and do just that – and Mrs S. can teach me how to bake fairy cakes.'

'You're on!'

I felt a sudden pang of envious longing . . . Yes, to be amid the safe domesticity of the gentle Savages with all the time in the world and nothing more taxing to do than watch Mrs S. at her redoubtable baking and listen to him demonstrating the finer points and pleasures of jazz timpani. What could be nicer? Or more remote . . .

We fixed a date for the next tuning, and giving a tug to Bouncer's lead I was about to set off when he said, 'Mind you, you're not the only one who's busy, Rev. That Mr Slowcome, he's really at it, isn't he?'

'What do you mean?'

'It's Mavis's dead body. All over the place with it, he is – interviews, press briefings, mugshots in the *Clarion*, or so Mrs S. tells me. Even heard him on the wireless this morning talking about how a good copper is tireless in his pursuit of detail, however small or seemingly trivial, and that that was how he had made his mark as a tyro sergeant: "following minute leads that others had discounted". There was quite a lot of trumpet-blowing on that theme (trying to impress the Chief Constable, if you ask me). And then the interviewer wanted to know what lead, minute or otherwise, was being pursued regarding Molehill's murder victim, because from what he had heard the local police were getting nowhere fast.' Savage chuckled. 'He didn't like that, and said all cold and huffy that there was a great deal going on behind the scenes which naturally couldn't be revealed to the public. But what he *could* divulge was the matter of the dog.'

I started. 'The dog! What dog?'

'The barking dog from Bognor – at least that's where they thought it must have come from. He said that according to the witness – Mavis, I suppose – a voice had been heard outside her window talking about getting back to Bognor, but that she had also heard a dog bark. Slowcome being super-bright, assumes the dog was in the car during the unloading of the body and that it and its owners came from Bognor.' Savage scratched his head and added sceptically, 'Mind you, it all sounds a bit what you might call "recherché" to me. And besides, if I were the superintendent I wouldn't set too much store by Mavis's evidence . . . not what you would call exactly watertight, I shouldn't have thought! Still, I suppose he felt he had to say something positive. Any crumb would do!' He grinned again and, whistling tunelessly, went on his way.

I stared after him, cursing Bouncer and cursing Mavis even more. Not a word to me about having heard a dog! Presumably something must have jogged that addled memory and she had mentioned it to Slowcome after her recent interview. I cast my mind back to those grisly moments outside her cottage and our efforts heaving the corpse on to the grass. Certainly Bouncer had given the thing a crafty nip to the ankle but had he barked as well? Perhaps. After all, he had been roaring his head off for most of the journey.

As I was brooding thus, there was a light tap on my shoulder. 'Oh, Canon,' squeaked Mavis Briggs excitedly, 'I think I may have been able to assist the police even further with their enquiries – I told the superintendent that I was sure the miscreants had a dog with them and that it must have been the one that had inflicted those dreadful bite marks!'

'How do you know it wasn't a cat?' I said accusingly.

She looked startled and in a pained voice replied, 'Well, I think at my age, Canon, I can be relied upon to know the difference between a cat and a dog.' I apologized, explaining it had been a rather feeble joke.

This seemed to satisfy her and, mollified, she launched into a rambling account of how grateful Mr Slowcome had been for her information and how *so* much nicer he was than the previous Inspector March.* 'I mean,' she said, lowering her voice confidingly, 'he's what you might call a *gentleman*.'

'Is that so?' I murmured. 'Now tell me, Mavis, is there anything else you have been able to help him with?'

She frowned. 'Well not so far ... but you never know what other little *clues* may come to mind. I mean, when they first interviewed me I was so shocked that I could hardly think. But *now* – well, one's recollections could be invaluable!' Despite being encumbered by shopping bags and brolly, she contrived to clap her hands.

Dear God! I thought, and raising my hat said I had to hurry back to prepare for Evensong.

As I approached the vicarage (hastily reminding myself to ask Primrose about the handkerchiefs), I saw a black Wolseley drawing up at the kerb, and the next moment the passenger door was flung open and Superintendent Slowcome emerged. Reining in Bouncer, I composed my features into what I fondly imagined to be a sociable expression and enquired whether it was myself or the neighbours that he had come to see.

'You, actually, Canon,' he said. 'Sergeant Withers and I were just passing and thought we might drop in on the off-chance you were at home. Saves a telephone call in the morning. Have you got a few minutes to spare?'

I told him that I was a little pressed as Evensong was in an hour, but if it didn't take too long I would be only too happy to oblige. I ushered them into the study, tense at the prospect of questions re my encounter with Felter at

* Inspector March, with his assistant DS Samson, appears in the first three books.

Lavinia's party – for that was surely the purpose of their visit.

It proved to be the case. And as presumably with others on their list, Slowcome wanted to know how long I had known the dead man and was there anything in his demeanour which had struck me as unusual. I explained truthfully that since I had only ever met him at the party, I was not in a position to say whether he had been his usual self or not.

'So what was your impression of him, sir?' asked Withers.

I was undecided whether to tell them that he looked exactly like a man ravaged with fear and about to be shot to death at any moment, or to tell the truth and say I had found him entirely at ease and convivial. Prudently I opted for the latter.

'And did he mention what his immediate plans might be – whether he was going anywhere in the near future?'

There flashed through my mind Primrose's voice saying, 'I can't think why you didn't leave him somewhere else – Wigan, for example,' and I was tempted to recommend that they focus their enquiries on that particular part of the country and leave Guildford and its clergy in peace. Instead I said that I could not recall any mention of plans but that he seemed to be keen on sailing . . .

'You see, sir,' Withers interjected, 'one of his neighbours reports that the last time they had seen him he had been in good spirits and said he must hurry off to prepare for an episcopal progress. The neighbour didn't know what he meant by that – and neither do we, but apparently *he* seemed to find it very funny and even repeated the phrase. Seems an odd thing to have said. In fact, it is something we thought Bishop Clinker might be able to shed light on when we see him. He's on tomorrow's list and may have a suggestion.'

'Probably of no significance,' said Slowcome, 'but it must be followed up. Oh yes. As I always say, Canon, it is amazing how often the most trivial remark carries a weight of meaning. *Multum in parvo*, that's my motto – known for it, aren't I, Withers?' The sergeant nodded, looking suddenly bored.

I, however, was not. For having been initially shaken by Felter's remark and fearful of what the police might make of it (and suspecting that a question regarding the movements of bishops would send Clinker into a frenzy of panic), I realized that with luck I could pre-empt further probing. 'I doubt if the bishop can enlighten you,' I laughed, 'he doesn't know a thing about chess, never played it in his life!'

They looked at me blankly. 'Correct me if I'm wrong,' I continued, 'but I gather from one of the newspaper reports that Mr Felter was a keen chess player, leading light of his local chess society, apparently. I should think you will find that he was making a rather oblique reference to the bishop's move – you know, the one where the black bishop sweeps the board of the knight and other tiresome adversaries. It's a handy manoeuvre if you can work it, but it needs a bit of attention. Presumably that is what he was off to do – ponder his strategy.' I beamed helpfully while also praying that neither was au fait with the rules of chess. My own scant memory of it came from family squabbles in the drawing room after tea, when across the chequered board Primrose and Pa would lock themselves in mortal and voluble combat.

'Ah – yes,' said Slowcome, looking both puzzled and disappointed, 'yes, that would, er, fit, I suppose . . . Hmm. Sharp of you, Canon. We'll have you in the Force yet!' And with a few more words of wisdom and jocular patronage, he rallied the sergeant and took his leave.

I turned to the cat. 'Preparing an episcopal progress, my foot!' I exclaimed. 'Cocky little stinker deserved all he got!' For once Maurice seemed in agreement, for he emitted a piercing miaow which took me by surprise – though it may simply have been a demand for haddock.

After they had gone I began to think of Clinker. Did he know they were coming? Or were they giving him as little notice as they had intended for me, i.e. a telephone call in the morning? But even with prior notice, how well would he cope? With the memory of that appalling encounter looming over him, how equipped was he to parry their questions? Would his nerve snap? Would he stumble, make some thoughtless remark, something that would link him more closely with the dead man than he cared to admit? But perhaps I was worrying unnecessarily, judging him by my own incompetence. Yes, doubtless the bishop was fully prepared and had some smoothly honed narrative all lined up ready to fox and disarm . . .

Like hell! This was Horace Clinker, I reminded myself, not Nicholas Ingaza! I hurried to the hall and dialled the Palace number, eager to warn and if necessary advise.

'My husband is away,' announced Gladys. 'Surely you know that, don't you, Canon? In fact, I rather gathered he was expecting you to be there. Why aren't you?'

'Where?' I faltered.

'Crewe, of course . . . or possibly Carlisle. Well anyway, one of those northern towns. It's the annual Missionary Conference – this time something about the difficulty of their position in Mozambique. You always attend, you can't have forgotten!' Her voice had a ring of accusation.

I sighed. It was precisely because I always attended that somehow I had now conveniently forgotten. Custom can blunt the memory as well as sharpen. Besides, did I really need to know about the ins and outs of the 'missionary position' in Mozambique – or indeed anywhere? Whatever the locality, it was bound to be exhausting . . .

I started to invent vague excuses but she cut me short. 'Of course it's really none of my business how you organize your duties – and besides, I have other matters to consider: the police are coming here tomorrow. Practically first thing, so tiresome!'

'Ah yes, presumably about Mr Felter at Lavinia's party. Er – what are you likely to say?'

'Likely to *say*, Canon? I shall say exactly what I have been saying to the bishop: that I considered him a rather common little man and that it was a great shame that my husband and he were planning to meet again. Just because he jawed on about sailing in the Baltic and had read that wretched book Horace is so keen on, doesn't mean that one wished to become socially involved!'

'But they weren't, were they?' I said quickly. 'I mean, socially involved. They may have telephoned, but they didn't actually meet . . .'

'What? Well I don't know, really – quite possibly, I suppose. Horace sees all manner of people . . . But he certainly wasn't invited for lunch here!'

'Well,' I foolishly ventured, 'if you want my advice, I wouldn't—'

'I can't think why I should want your advice, Francis, but you are obviously keen to give it. What have you in mind?'

'It's, um, it's simply that given the circumstances – the appointment matter – it might be best not to mention anything at all about the bishop and the deceased having been in contact. I mean, you know how quick the police are to jump to conclusions – always getting the wrong end of the stick and spreading alarm and despondency. They, er – they do have a tendency to be rather *officious* . . .' I trailed off weakly.

There was a long pause while she presumably gave thought to Clinker's imminent elevation to the Archbishop's entourage. And then she said, 'If Superintendent Slowcome imagines he can be officious with me, he'll have to think again! I have heard all about police harassment and have no intention of inviting it. I shall spare them five minutes and no more. Silence is my policy and I suggest it be yours, Canon!' There was a loud snort and then the line went dead.

So that was a relief. With Gladys in granite-wall mood, Slowcome's chances of sniffing a lead were nil. I could rest easy for a little longer, and taking the opportunity went to the piano and embarked on a rousing keyboard version of *Tannhäuser*. The cat wailed pathetically, seized its woollen mouse and scuttled from the room.

36

The Vicar's Version

Lunch the following day was a somewhat onerous business. It took place in the parish hall and was one of those earnestly 'frugal' bread and cheese affairs put on periodically by the Vestry Circle to support the starving.

While applauding the intention I can never quite fathom the logic. The idea is that the world's poor will be the recipients of the saving made between such basic fare and the price of an average two- or three-courser. However, since seemingly fewer people are making luncheon their main meal (and with those at work often settling for no more than a sandwich) the gap between the two sets of prices is narrow. Indeed, partaking of the 'rustic' fare will sometimes involve an excess rather than reduction in out-lay – in which case a straight five-shilling donation might be both simpler and more lucrative. I have also observed that those still in the habit of consuming a full meal at lunchtime tend to stuff themselves so full of bread, cheese, beverages and assorted pickles that again the profit is negligible. I mentioned this once to a colleague who evi-dently missed the point, explaining that it was all about productive self-denial – 'practical penance' being the exact words, I think. Judging from the steady chomping of jaws, gales of hearty laughter and very moderate pro-ceeds, I see little that is either penitential or practical – and rather wonder what the starving poor might think. If I have the nerve (unlikely), one day I shall put a stop to the practice and urge instead greater generosity in the collection plate . . . *Do I digress? Then I digress* (as the noted Mr Eliot might have put it), and so back to the bun fight and its consequence:

There were two problems here – first the awfulness of the chosen cheese (not a mature Cheddar but some base imitation of pallid hue and matching taste); and second, a flanking attack by Miss Dalrymple and Colonel Dawlish regarding the latter's proposal that a dog show be held in my garden. For once both were in perfect unison and I was subjected to an enthusiastic briefing on its fund-raising value and the plans already in place for the categories and prizes. These seemed many and elaborate and I realized with dawning awe that the thing was a virtual fait accompli. However, adopting a brave face I enquired if there was anything in particular they would like me to do, and wasn't sure whether to be relieved or affronted when Miss Dalrymple said, 'Well actually, Canon, if you don't mind, you could go out for the day and take Bouncer and Maurice with you.'

The Colonel must have seen my look of surprise for he explained hastily, 'It's not that we don't want you, dear man, but I've lined up the stewards and judging panel, got the women organized with the tea and raffle, and so that only leaves the gate.' He paused, and with a sly grin added, 'Don't think that's quite your forte, is it, old chap? Bit of a problem at the Christmas party, wasn't there – sorting the door-payers from the ticket-holders? Queues halfway down the road!' He laughed loudly and I gave a polite smile.

'And of course,' chimed Miss Dalrymple, 'there *is* the difficulty of Maurice. I mean – how shall I put this? – he's not exactly the most sociable of cats, is he?' I nodded in grudging agreement, while she went on to point out that while Bouncer was 'absolutely charming', he might not take too kindly to having his home ground invaded and perhaps turn 'a little tricky'. She was right there – when he puts his mind to it Bouncer is a past master at trickiness, and I could indeed envisage ructions of a spectacular kind.

Thus I was just thanking my lucky stars that I was being offered a heaven-sent let-out, when she said magnanimously, 'But of course we *would* want you back by six o'clock to award the special prize at the end of it all.'

'And what will that be?' I asked.

'A year's supply of Sparkling Chews for the dog with the whitest fangs – and *you* may do the final inspection!' She beamed encouragingly and strode away to hack off more of the awful cheese.

Yes, it had been a gruelling period and I was grateful to escape to the haven of my armchair and absorb the silence. Idly I picked up a copy of the *Church Times*. It is not the most enlivening publication but at moments of boredom or abstraction I will occasionally peruse it. For once the headlines were startlingly fresh: 'MOZAMBIQUE MISSIONARIES CASTRATED IN CREWE.'

What? But prurient shock quickly turned to disappointment as I realized my mistake. Alas, the mind can play a sleight of eye, and the words 'slated' and 'castigated' had somehow fused themselves upon my muddled brain. The reality was that Bishop Horace Clinker, attending the Crewe conference, was reported as having slated clerical inertia in foreign parts and in particular castigated the Little Band of Hopeful Brethren for its failure to garner converts to the Anglican cause. (Hardly surprising, I thought: confronted with a name like that, any self-respecting heathen would run a mile!)

But more interestingly the article went on to say that while the good bishop had made his customary mark at the conference, delegates were sorry to see him looking so drawn and tired and trusted that the strain of duty would not affect his expected appointment as the Archbishop of York's new aide. There was a photograph of him looking uncharacteristically tense – the result, no doubt, of the blackmailer's latest handiwork. Clinker infuriates me, but

I was even more infuriated to think of his being the target of such perverse and callous attention. No, there was nothing else for it – he would just have to go to the police, painful though that might be . . .

But how *could* he? And yet again I quailed at the enormity of the cost: revelations about his previous illegal liaison with Ingaza, failure to report Felter's death on his own doorstep, his deliberate silence over the identity of the body, and worst of all the distinct possibility that he would be facing a charge of murder . . . Yes, bad for the bishop – and not too good for the enchanting Gladys either. And naturally it would hardly stop there. The blackmail probings could unearth other things: Primrose's picture heist with Ingaza, Ingaza's own part in the ridding of Felter's body, *my* part in its disposal, not to mention obstructing and lying to the police . . . And if it was established that I had been less than frank in this current enquiry, might they not start wondering about my responses in the earlier one – the 'Fotherington Case'? The more I considered the ramifications, the more I thought I might be carried off by a quiet seizure. Indeed, I was just beginning to think that might be no bad thing when I heard the flop of the afternoon post on the hall mat. Morosely I went to investigate. There were only two items – a bulky manila envelope bearing a Molehill postmark, and a much smaller one.

I opened the larger first. It contained a wad of closely and rather badly typed pages, plus a covering note:

Dear Canon,

 It was so kind of you to agree to pen an introduction to the third volume of my Little Gems of Uplift and I am sure with your esteemed endorsement it cannot help but be a success! One never quite knows where the Muse may take one and I find that these days it increasingly leads me down the path of philosophy – a route that I trust will not be too complex for Molehill's worthy readers! However, I am certain that you will appreciate the little aperçus and finer subtleties that the verses contain and will thus have no difficulty in composing a commentary of perhaps three or four

pages. I so look forward to your appraisal, which I know will
do justice to the text!
   Yours most sincerely,
   Mavis Briggs (Miss)

Three or four pages! Justice to the text! Was she utterly barking? (Absolutely.) I stared, horrified, at the words and the accompanying sheaf of papers. A few moments ago I had been contemplating having a quiet seizure; my instinct now was to endure the drama of the kitchen knife.

Clearly an early whisky was indicated and I hastened to the sideboard, poured a drink and scavenged for crisps. There weren't any so I settled for Huntley & Palmers' Breakfast Biscuits. These are impossible to eat silently and Bouncer adores them. I threw him a couple and the room crackled with our joint crunchings and munchings. The cat appeared, emitted a long miaow and disappeared rapidly. I often think that Maurice is not entirely attuned to this world . . .

After a further glass I felt sufficiently fortified to open the second envelope. Its size was so slight in comparison that I guessed it held no fears.

Francis, couldn't get you on the blower, hence the enclosed.
We've got to stop the bastard, make no mistake. Just
received this. What do you think? Aunt Lil on my tail so
may not be here, but ring Eric.   *N.I.*

A message was enclosed. It read as follows:

So, according to your local rag you've netted £2,000 for
some 'long-lost' Eric Gill. I bet the sum is authentic, but as
to said item – probably as bogus as hell. No matter. It's a
nice little bonus which I am sure you can afford to forfeit.
Put it my way and we'll forget about the removal of the
bishop's nasty surprise – let alone your charming friend-
ship. Both still at it, are you? Doubtful – but the news-
papers would like to think so.

Transaction details: by 3 Sept cash to A/C 956355206, Bank of Gottfried, Zurich.

I leapt to the telephone; but as feared heard not Ingaza's voice but Eric's raucous twang. 'Wotcha, Frankie,' he began. 'His Nibs said yer might ring and seeing as 'ow it was you I made a special point of staying in and scrapped the darts.'

'Oh dear,' I murmured apologetically, 'I'm so sorry, I hope it hasn't caused too much—'

'Don't worry, old son,' was the cheery response, 'the other team are the Rottingdean Rotters – not werf turning aht for!' There was a caustic guffaw and I hastily adjusted the receiver. 'Anyway,' he went on, 'Nick wants to see yer. He's orf to see that Cranleigh twister on Thursday and wants you to meet him at the posh pub in Chiddingfold. Says he'll find it soothing after Lil.'

'Yes, I rather gathered he might be engaged with her . . . everything all right, is it?'

'All right? With that old baggage? You must be joking!' There was another mirthful explosion.

I laughed politely and asked if it was the Eastbourne bandstand again.

'Nah, the dogs at Kemp Town. Complained she'd missed the last two meetings and said what was the point of having a bleeding nephew if he didn't escort her to social whatsits? Mind you, it's not the *escorting* that he minds but having to lay out dosh for her drink and losses. And then of course there are the argie-bargies she has wiv the bookies . . . Gawd, he comes back like a poleaxed rabbit!'

I have to admit that the picture of Ingaza so discomfited was not uncongenial, and I made a mental note to keep the image in mind when next he made one of his outlandish demands. Clearly there was something to be said for Aunt Lil.

Thursday morning proved a little tricky. I was halfway down the High Street in search of slab toffee before embarking for Chiddingfold, when I was waylaid by Edith Hopgarden.

'Ah,' she said, 'all ready, are we?'

'Ready for what?' I enquired warily.

'To do Mavis's introduction, of course – the third volume of those remarkable gems of wisdom. I gather you are about to produce a glowing endorsement – or should I say a scintillating exegesis?' She barred my path with a stance of unsmiling challenge.

Edith's disdain for her 'friend' is trumped only by her dislike of me. I have few weapons in my armoury other than the knowledge of her rather tiresome liaison with Tapsell. Ever since I once encountered them in compromising circumstances she has taken against me; and as for myself, I have only to see a bicycle clip to be reminded uncomfortably of that abortive evening . . . However, this was not the time to dwell on such things, and if evasive action were needed I could always enquire after the health of Mr Hopgarden. It usually works.

'Yes, Mavis's literary energy is prodigious, isn't it?' I laughed. 'But I am sure the new outpouring will speak for itself and needs only a short paragraph from me.'

'Oh, she's expecting more than a short paragraph,' was the sadistic reply. 'Half a book of praise and perceptive analysis, I gather.'

'Don't think I can quite run to that,' I said jovially. 'Just a few choice words might fit the bill. And besides, Edith, since you think so highly of her talent, why don't *you* compose something for the next edition of the parish newsletter? A really full-blown encomium. You have such style and wit and she would be delighted! I'll put you down for it straight away.' I raised my hat, fixed her with a dazzling smile and rushed onwards to the toffee shop.

Driving over to Chiddingfold was a relief and a fear. Cocooned in the Singer I was safe from marauding parishioners, but the prospect of the luncheon topic was not a happy one and my mind was once more beset with anxious gloom. Chiddingfold is an attractive place, and as I drew up beside its small village green edged with trees and cottages, I thought wistfully of how nice it would be if the only agenda for our meal were the latest cricket scores or some government scandal. As it was . . .

I got out, sniffed the fresh air, and then seeing Ingaza's elderly Citroën sprawled at the side of the inn, steeled myself for trouble.

He sat in a corner gazing abstractedly at the menu, his lean fingers caressing a Bloody Mary, smoke curling up from a discarded Sobranie in the ashtray. For one who was supposed to have been poleaxed by his aunt he didn't look too bad, but I couldn't help noticing the prominence of his cheekbones and the signs of strain around the mouth. Yes, Clinker wasn't the only one being put through it. We were all on a knife-edge, and it would only take an accident or wrong decision and we could fall spectacularly. There flashed in my memory the image of a recent acquaintance plunging into a mountain ravine, vanishing God knows where . . . I shut my eyes.

'You look a wreck,' drawled the nasal voice. 'Better have one of these – perk you up and blow your head off!' He gestured to the Bloody Mary and offered me a cigarette. I took his advice, fetched the drink from the bar, took a sip and nearly exploded. 'Well that's brought colour to the boy's cheeks,' he observed. 'Now, have you heard from Primrose?'

'About a week ago I suppose. Why? Should I have?'

'I meant more recently than that. She called me yesterday – had another letter.'

'Oh my God, her as well! What on earth does it say?'

'Very little apparently. No preliminaries or anything, simply the payment details, i.e. the sum of £1,000 to be paid into a numbered Swiss bank account by the third of September. Smaller sum than mine and a different bank, but that was the instruction. Nothing else said.'

I took a thoughtlessly large sip of my drink, scalded my throat and gazed unseeingly at the menu. 'This is becoming appalling,' I muttered. 'What the hell can we do?'

'Play the sod at his own game,' he snapped. 'As I said before, we're possibly in a stronger position than he is – or at least no worse.'

'So you really do think it's Turnbull?'

'Don't you? You seemed pretty convinced earlier on.'

I nodded, and started to tell him about our conversation down in Lewes: 'Perhaps I was being oversensitive but I just had the impression that everything he said about Hor and Felter's death was somehow loaded, as if he was taunting me – guessing that we were the most likely ones to have taken the body.' I paused, then added, 'Mind you, things weren't exactly helped by you stirring things up over the Timms affair. He must have known what you were getting at. It was as if you were throwing down a glove, and now he's bloody well taken it up!'

He shrugged. 'Don't twitch. We'll have some lunch and then hatch plans.'

'Plans?' I exclaimed. 'How can we make plans? The whole thing is a frightful mess, the police are out of the question and we know from what happened in France that Turnbull is as cool as hell!'

'Getting our theology a trifle muddled, aren't we, old boy? In my time it was the burning fiery furnace, but of course the Church changes its views so often these days that one loses track ... Anyway, I can thoroughly recommend the Chicken à la King – the sauce is good and the creamed potato all nice and crispy. I also suggest we have a bottle of Montrachet.'

'You can't afford it,' I said acidly, 'you've got that £2,000 to pay.' He ignored me and waved imperiously to the waiter.

The wine was delivered and we set about our meal, and for a brief spell immersed ourselves exclusively in drink and chicken, carefully avoiding anything touching on blackmail. It didn't last of course, and by the time we had reached the apple tart we were back on the subject.

'So, if we are fully decided that it's really Turnbull, what do you propose?' I asked him.

'Confrontation. I think that the best thing would—'

'You mean beard him in his den?' I asked.

'*Beard* him in his *den*! My, what a quaint, old-fashioned term! Where on earth do you get them from?'

'It's what we learnt at prep school,' I said defensively. 'Lists of "handy" idioms.'

'Ah well, being but a grammar school product I was denied such lists. Doubtless there is a gaping lacuna in my—'

'But you read Classics at Merton, didn't you? Got a First. And then what, Nicholas, then what?'

He looked surprised at my question, or perhaps at the tone of insistence which possibly the Montrachet had given it.

'And then what? Well, the theology thing at St Bede's – you know that. You were there, if you recall. And since there was such a hoo-ha when they chucked me out I imagine you remember only too well!'

'Oh I'm not talking about St Bede's,' I said impatiently. 'Before – during the war. What were you *doing*? You've never said . . . I mean, you weren't in it, were you?' Yes, it must have been the drink talking; I had consumed nearly half a bottle, not to mention the lethal Bloody Mary, and it had clearly made me bold. Ingaza's reticence about the war years had always slightly puzzled me but I had been too diffident to ask. And now for some reason, suddenly at this quiet table in a country inn, I was pinning him down for an answer.

He raised a quizzical eyebrow and regarded me coolly; and leaning back in his chair, said, 'Well old cock, I wasn't a conchie if that's what you're thinking.'

'No, I didn't think you were – not entirely your style, I shouldn't have thought.'

He must have noticed the hint of sarcasm but shrugged good-humouredly and said, 'Wasn't batting for the other side, either – at least, not *that* other side.' He winked.

221

I cleared my throat and poured him the dregs of the wine, feeling rather a fool. Was I being unduly inquisitive? I wondered. Perhaps he had been a Bevin Boy and felt cheated of not being in the thick of things. Some did, I gathered. A clerk in the Home Office debarred service on account of flat feet? (But his feet weren't flat!) Or perhaps, I reflected, a tuberculosis case huddled in blankets on a sanatorium veranda, listening to the Allied planes droning overhead . . . After all, he had always been pale.

'Don't look so worried, Francis,' the voice mocked. 'Spoils the classical features! I'll tell you sometime . . . Perhaps. But meanwhile let's get that bastard nailed.' He ordered coffee and a couple of brandies, and puffing my humble Craven 'A's – the Sobranies having vanished in smoke – we discussed tactics.

No, that is not quite correct . . . I was given my instructions.

37

The Vicar's Version

Ingaza's plan and my instructions were simple and to the point: I was to attend the inaugural reception in Oxford and make all the expected noises, i.e. compliment Turnbull fulsomely on his acumen and enterprise, mingle with the other guests, express astonishment at the splendid facilities of the place and be generally impressed by the whole set-up. And then just when Turnbull was at his most flattered and disarmed, put the boot in by slipping him a copy of the two-line note I had appropriated in France. No words would be needed, the note itself would do the trick.

'You mean the trick of making him back off?' I had asked.

'Oh yes,' Ingaza had said confidently. 'With that staring him in the face there'll be nothing else he can do, especially if you murmur the magic name of little Inspector Dumont* in his ear!'

'There *is* something else he could do,' I had objected. 'What he did to Boris – bash my brains out!'

'Well hardly there in the midst of everything, dear boy – people might notice. And besides, he would know that the evidence was only a copy and that the original must be held elsewhere. Snuffing you out wouldn't achieve anything.'

* Dumont appears in *Bones in High Places*

'No it wouldn't,' I had replied impatiently, 'and neither will your damn fool idea. Really, Nicholas, you've been living with Eric too long. It's crude, rash and theatrical and I want no part of it!'

He had looked put out and retorted acidly that doubtless with my fertile mind I could devise something better. 'But you had better be *quick*, Francis – he's not bluffing, you know. He has the power to blow everything sky high, including your sister's reputation and very likely yours. The press will be only too delighted to learn that she has a vicar for a brother and they'll milk it for all it's worth. The name Oughterard will hold a stigma for life. And of course, if you want your bishop to be branded a nancy boy, let alone a possible murderer, then just allow things to take their course. And you can bet they will! Turnbull needs the money, and if he doesn't get it you don't imagine he's going to sit back without exacting some sort of payment, do you? Think about it.'

I had thought about it, and did think about it all the way home in the car. And although I recognized only too well the likely consequences of doing nothing, Ingaza's proposal struck me as wildly precarious. Shock tactics of the kind he envisaged might work in Jacobean melodrama, but hardly in real life or with one as cool as Turnbull. Besides, despite the weight of circumstantial evidence, and indeed my own instinct, there was still no absolute *certainty* that he was the one. Probable, yes, but definite? Hardly. No, the whole suggestion was a preposterous gamble and there had to be a better way.

Of course, underneath the rationalizing lurked something else: my own failure of nerve. Some people are suited to precipitating events and relish the risk. I am not one of those. And the one time in my life when I did turn protagonist had been a moment of horrific and gross disaster whose effects are remorseless . . . Thus I was loath to take centre stage in such a bald and uncertain initiative.

* * *

224

Back at the vicarage I fed the animals and started to tidy my study. The latter does not happen very often but I suppose it was a vain attempt to distract the mind and engage in something safely prosaic. However, despite my efforts at sifting papers and redistributing the general rubble, my thoughts were still riveted on how to deal with matters. I was annoyed, but not surprised, that Ingaza had put the immediate onus on me. After all, I thought ruefully, it was *he* who had been Clinker's inamorato, however briefly; and he who had persuaded Primrose to collaborate with him over the fake paintings to Canada. He was also considerably more seasoned at games of chance and daring than I . . . But then that had always been his strength (skill, rather): using others to procure his own ends. Memories of St Bede's came flooding over me and I remembered how suavely he had called the shots while poised mockingly in the shadows.

So absorbed was I in old memories and tidying old books that I didn't hear the telephone at first, and it was only when the cat started a peevish mewing that it caught my attention. Thinking it might be Primrose wanting to let off steam about her recent 'invoice', I hurried to lift the receiver.

'Is that Francis Oughterard?' asked a man's voice.

'Yes, speaking.'

'Ah, Francis,' said Rupert Turnbull, 'glad to catch you in. I have a little problem which I rather hope you might be able to help me with.'

Before I could muster thought or words, he had moved on: 'This is in strict confidence, you understand, but frankly I am rather worried about Lavinia. And as she's my cousin as well as being such a good friend I really feel I need to confide in someone.'

'Confide what?' I asked guardedly, wondering what on earth he was getting at.

He hesitated, and then said quietly, 'Well it's a little delicate, Francis, but actually I don't think she is terribly well . . . I mean, not well in the *head*.'

225

'Oh dear!' I exclaimed reassuringly. 'Er, in what way in the head?'

'From what I can make out, it's not so much mental as spiritual, as if she is undergoing some sort of' – here he paused, seeming to search for a term – 'well, what one might call a crisis of the soul.'

Crisis of the soul? Why should he want to telephone me about it! I fumbled nervously for a cigarette and nearly dropped the receiver. 'Anyway,' he continued, 'I know it's a bit of a cheek but I was wondering if you might possibly help her to sort matters out, help her to get things in perspective. You see, apart from Bishop Clinker, I don't really know any other clergymen, so it's a bit tricky. But that's what I think she needs – at this stage, at any rate – guidance from the Church, not Harley Street.'

I had a momentary memory of Lavinia in France, drearily garbed and gabbling incessantly about the hermit's bones with cranky Boris. Was it possible that despite the startling transformation, she was now having a relapse and reverting to the nut cutlets and earnest mysticism of six months previously? It seemed unlikely. But even if it was the case, it was hardly something I wanted to become involved with!

I scanned the hall, struggling to formulate some tactful excuse, and my gaze fell on my father, sepia and stern in an ancient school photograph. Ranks of blazered boys stared out anonymously, but I could always spot him – back row, third from the right: C. K. Oughterard, House Prefect; beetle-browed and ramrod-stiff. And I remembered his later words addressed to a less than ramrod son: 'Always respond to the call of duty, my boy, it's the least any of us can do. Fail in that and it'll haunt you for life.' He had been right, of course (though how did he know?). I sighed . . . Yes, forgetting to feed those hamsters and carelessly letting them escape on to the busy road had dogged me for years.

And thus with Pa and hamsters firmly in mind, I heard myself saying, 'Well if you really think I could be useful, then naturally I'll see what I can do. But perhaps you could give me a little more information . . .'

There was an audible sigh of relief at the other end and he gave fulsome thanks. 'That's such a weight off my mind! She likes you, you know, and I'm sure she will respond well to any counsel you care to give. It's all a question of nipping things in the bud, wouldn't you say?'

I was mildly flattered but still unclear. 'Yes, I should think so – but what things exactly? I would really need to know a little more about her difficulties before I could—'

'Oh, of course! You need to be put in the full picture – the only problem is *when*. It's not the sort of thing one can really explain over the telephone, but my problem is I'm stuck here in London, bogged down in the Kensington project – builders, staff interviews, equipment deliveries, etc. And it's all got to be sorted out before the Oxford opening in ten days' time. I don't suppose you could possibly . . . No, I'm sure you're far too busy.'

'Busy for what?'

'To come up to London, have lunch at my flat. We can chew it over and down a bottle of Fleurie. Seem to remember you rather enjoying that in France!' He laughed.

He was right, but a bottle of Fleurie was hardly enticement to go to Turnbull's flat!

'Ah, well,' I stammered, mind racing, 'not sure if I can . . .'

'I mean, I rather wondered if you had any appointments which you could combine with lunching here. I can tell you, Francis, I really want to get Lavinia sorted out. Poor girl, I think she's going through it.'

I was flustered but intrigued. Was she really ill? In which case, as Pa had directed, there was not much choice . . . On the other hand, how far (if at all) could I trust Turnbull? What was he playing at? *Was* he playing? There was only one way to find out, and the next moment I had said mechanically, 'I do have to go to Whipple's on Thursday to collect some shirts and be measured for a new cassock. I could pop in for a quick lunch if you wanted, but it would have to be—'

'Splendid!' he exclaimed. 'I'll be here, one thirty on the dot. I really appreciate this, Francis, you've no idea.' He gave me an address off Wimpole Street and after a few niceties our conversation ended.

I returned to the sitting room, stared at the cat and cursed myself for being so weak. It passed through my mind to seize the telephone again and tell him I had been horribly confused about dates and couldn't possibly get to London for at least two months. The problem was I didn't have his number, and it would mean going through all the palaver of Directory Enquiries. Besides, to suddenly cancel now would look so obvious and churlish . . . I stood studying the dog, chewing a peppermint and weighing things up. Resolution: I would ring Primrose.

'Sounds a bit fishy,' my sister said, 'though can't say I'm surprised about Lavinia going bonkers. Always thought she was fey. She was on cloud nine at her party and seemed in good spirits when they all came over to Lewes, but who knows, perhaps the gruesome fate of hubby has triggered buried insanities – even if she did engineer it!'

'We don't know that she engineered it,' I reminded her severely, 'and in any case, Turnbull suggested the trouble was some sort of spiritual malaise, not madness as such.'

'Well I think *you* would be mad to go to Turnbull's flat without some sort of reinforcement.'

'Such as?'

'Me. It's high time I paid another visit to Marshall & Snelgrove. I need a new corset, and they've got some very pretty patterned ones there and just the right size. Might as well go up on Thursday as any other day. You have lunch with Turnbull as planned and I'll meet you afterwards in that Greek coffee shop round the corner. If you don't appear by two forty-five I shall come up and see what's what!'

'In the corset?'

* * *

228

So that was the arrangement. And I didn't know whether to be pleased that I was doing something positive to confront whatever was going on, gratified that I might be of conceivable help to Lavinia, or scared witless in case I ended up as mincemeat. On the whole I thought the last unlikely, and yet for some ridiculous reason I decided to take Bouncer with me. He would be a companionable ally, and never having been to London before would perhaps enjoy the novelty of the city's lamp posts . . .

38

The Vicar's Version

I rang the doorbell and waited. Silence. I rang again, the dog fidgeted and there was still no response. I scanned the corridor, put my ear to the door and tried once more. Nothing.

It was a bit much, I thought. Turnbull issues an urgent summons, I break my neck to arrive on time and then he doesn't appear. Wretched man, had he gone out? But why? He *knew* I was coming! I stared at Bouncer. 'Some people,' I grumbled, 'are so ill-mannered!' The dog looked blank and burped. Baulked of the promised Fleurie, I began to tire of the whole thing; but before turning away gave a desultory rap with my knuckles. The door must have been on the latch for it yielded slightly. I gave a tentative push and the next instant it had swung open and we were inside.

'Are you there, Turnbull?' I called. 'It's Francis – Francis Oughterard.' Silence. Hesitantly I started to move forward but was restrained by a whine from Bouncer and a sharp tug at the lead. 'Oh do come on,' I muttered, 'and stop playing silly beggars, we've come to see the nice man.' Unimpressed, he sat down mulishly and refused to budge.

I let go of the lead and rather irritably called again to Turnbull, taking a few more steps into the room ... And there I found him: back towards me, slumped across a writing desk by the window, his right hand clutching a toppled wine glass whose dark contents had soaked lavishly into the blotting pad.

Apart from shock, my initial reaction was one of annoyance. He had specifically asked me to come, and despite inconvenience (not to say reluctance) I had agreed. And yet here he was, out for the count in a drunken stupor! It was the last thing I had expected, and I was just wondering whether I should seek the kitchen to get a glass of water either to administer or throw, when I heard a low growl from Bouncer. I glanced round and saw the object of his vexation: Attlee.

Indifferent to the other dog, the little creature stood poised in a doorway, staring severely at the crumpled figure draped over the desk. But in the next instant he had turned tail, and with a tart bark disappeared from the room. I gazed after him, perplexed. If Attlee was here, what about his owner? Turnbull had intimated he wanted a private talk and, given the topic, it had hardly occurred to me that Lavinia herself might be present . . . But was she? There seemed to be no sign or sound. Unless of course she was having a quick 'crisis of the soul' in the bathroom – or, like Turnbull, was also laid out in a pre-prandial torpor!

I was pondering this possibility when I heard a light footfall, and in place of Attlee stood his owner, suited, behatted and carrying a shiny handbag and smart travelling case. The air became redolent with Je Reviens.

'Ah, Francis,' she exclaimed, 'I hoped I might catch you before I left. I had been meaning to write but there has been so much to do what with one thing and another, and there simply hasn't been time! I hope you don't mind.' She flashed me a dazzling smile.

I had no idea what she was talking about. Where was she going and why should she want to write to me? My puzzlement must have been plain, for she said teasingly, 'Oh dear, you haven't a clue, have you?'

I replied rather coldly that I did not have a clue and wouldn't it be a good idea if before her departure we attended to her comatose companion? I gestured towards Turnbull's slumped figure.

'Oh, Rupert's not comatose,' she said, 'he's dead – or at least he jolly well ought to be by now, I gave him enough stuff!'

For a few seconds my mind was a static blank and I registered nothing except the ticking of the clock and Lavinia's smiling eyes. And then the blankness gave way to a kaleidoscope of gruesome images: Boris bludgeoned on the flagstones, Violet Pond's stark white legs upended in the potting shed, Climp sprawled in blood on the high plateau, Felter's frozen features inches from my neck in the Singer . . . and in precise and graphic detail, Mrs Fotherington throttled and mottled in Foxford Wood. The scenes shifted dizzyingly before my eyes, forms and colours blending and dissolving in protean nightmare. Strange the way the proximity of death stirs our subconscious.

'You look tired,' her voice said. 'Sit down and I'll get you a drink.'

I glanced at the fallen wine glass. 'No,' I replied quickly, 'it's quite all right. Please don't bother.' Gingerly I perched on the arm of the sofa and groped abstractedly for Bouncer's shaggy head.

She scrutinized her watch. 'I shall have to be going pretty soon. My seat's booked on the Golden Arrow and I couldn't bear some last-minute hitch. Travelling always makes me rather jumpy, doesn't it you?'

'Oh *yes*,' I agreed, 'always.' Then clearing my throat, I added, 'But before you go, might you have time to—'

'Explain? Of course. But I can't be too long – I'm not risking having my plans upset all over again!'

'What plans?' I asked dazedly.

'My plans to go to South America. Much safer there than here after all this kerfuffle!' Her eyes swept the room, resting momentarily on the figure by the window.

I looked in the same direction at what I now knew to be the very dead Turnbull. 'Why did you do it, Lavinia?' I ventured. 'I thought you were fond of him.'

'I *was*,' she sighed, 'but he turned into such a rat. And after everything I had been through with Boris and the

232

French tarts I simply wasn't having it! I had sunk a lot of money into those wretched language schools and the toad repaid me by having a walk-out with Millie Merton of all people! Well, I can tell you, I wasn't going to be made a fool of by that squat little thing. She's as rich as Croesus – obviously her only quality and presumably the attraction – so I was none too pleased when I found out about it. And added to that, he actually had the nerve to imply that I was under an obligation to him for ridding me of Boris . . . In a way, of course, that was true, but it's not something one cares to have pointed out.' She frowned. 'And then when blackmailing Freddie got wind of things and had to be silenced, I began to grasp the full extent of Rupert's ruthlessness and the danger of my own position. After all, I knew all the details of the French business. So in case he decided to dispense with me as well, I thought I would get in first. I think it's known as being ahead of the game. Isn't that the expression, Francis?'

Terrified, I assured her that it was. She nodded amicably, lit a cigarette and offered me one, but I was too unsettled to accept and instead gave a weak smile. 'Er, Freddie's blackmailing activities,' I murmured, 'didn't Rupert do a bit of that as well? I mean—'

'Oh yes. If you are referring to that last letter to your boring bishop, that was Rupert all right. He thought he might cash in on what Freddie had started. Had him down for £10,000, I think. One of the many. He discovered all the details when he broke into Freddie's house to rescue his own dossier. You know, it's amazing just how comprehensive and meticulous Freddie's notes were. Even had the dirt on your sister. My goodness, that was a turn-up for the books!' She laughed merrily. I did not.

'So Rupert wrote to her as well? As well as to Ingaza and Clinker.'

'Oh no! Not worth it. That was *me*. "What price the Canada geese?",' she trilled.

I stared aghast. 'You mean to say it was you who sent Primrose that nonsensical note and its follow-up?'

'We-ll, not all that nonsensical. After all, it rather hit a nail, didn't it?' She shot me a knowing look which I carefully ignored.

'I have no idea what you are talking about,' I said as icily as I was able, 'Primrose has no connection with Canada and the whole thing was exceedingly puzzling.'

'If you say so,' she replied sweetly. 'But Freddie used to go to Canada a lot and had a shrewd eye for pictures. He could spot a pastiche a mile off and seemed to have some knowledge of your sister's style – but we won't go into that now, life's too short.' And she shot another look at our dead companion.

Stunned though I was, I was also extremely angry. 'That's a bit much, isn't it, Lavinia?' I exclaimed. 'You may recall that you were a guest in my sister's house. She put you up during that gallery launch and you say you had the brass neck to send her that ridiculous missive. Frankly I think that's a bit rotten.'

She had the grace to look mildly abashed. 'Yes, that was rather naughty. But you see, helping Rupert over the Boris business gave me a taste for adventure, and – well, I suppose, power.'

'Power?'

'Sort of. You've no idea what a frumpish and tedious life I was leading in France with Boris and his mystical vagaries (not to mention those sordid liaisons). I felt so stultified and *mere*! So after his little accident, it was as if I was reborn and ready for anything!'

'Including blackmail for fun?'

'Well, yes. Freddie and Rupert seemed to find it amusing and didn't do badly out of it either, so I thought I'd try my hand too. But then Rupert became so difficult and bossy and it rather took the edge off things. And when he started seeing Millie, that was the last straw. Boris was bad enough, but Rupert was repressive *and* dangerous. Anyway, I am free of them both now and I'm off to Rio. A girl can have a good time there, and I mean to have it!'

I stared open-mouthed, trying to gather wits and a suitable response. But before I had a chance to do either, she added coyly, 'As a matter of fact, I shan't be entirely alone. There's rather a rich gentleman waiting for me. Very agreeable and . . . er, rather *old*. Convenient, really.' She gave a gay laugh and a broad wink.

I glanced again at the desk, and in as detached a voice as I could manage, said, 'I am not quite clear – Rupert invited me here for lunch, had some business to discuss, I gather. Did you know?'

'Yes, he mentioned it last night. It annoyed me at first as I had everything worked out exactly and was running to a tight schedule. But then I thought, oh what the hell, I'll just have to go ahead anyway! Which as you can see is what I did.' She smiled and flicked a piece of fluff from her jacket. And then leaning forward, said confidingly, 'You see, I rather think he was trying to get me certified – or simply have it rumoured that I was in the grip of some appalling depression. I overheard him telling a colleague that he was "fearfully distressed about poor Lavinia's mental state", and that he felt so helpless. Actually, I bet that's why he brought you up here: to have someone to discuss it with and to spread the word. A sort of corroborating device.'

'But why?' I gasped.

'As insurance, in case I started to cut up rough about that Merton cow and took it into my head to let drop a few hints about the French business. Then if that happened he could always say I was losing my marbles. But the point is, that might not have been enough for him. He could so easily have gone further, i.e. snuff me out and fake my suicide – suicide while the balance of the mind was disturbed, as they say. After all, he had done it before – and frankly, Francis, it was a risk I wasn't prepared to take. As I said, one does have to be ahead of the game!'

'I see,' I murmured. 'But even if you had started to accuse Rupert about what happened in France, in that case surely he could have retaliated with tales of your own involvement. I mean, he did rather hold a few cards of his own, didn't he?'

'*Exactly*,' she exclaimed. 'So whichever way you look at it, he simply had to go!' And opening her handbag, she withdrew lipstick and rouge and started to apply them liberally.

As I watched the subtleties of the ritual, for some reason the crazed white features of Victor Crumpelmeyer* came into mind. Lavinia's face was prettier and her speech more lively, but I couldn't help pondering why it was my lot in life to be thrust among the dotty and insane. Perhaps they were my nemesis for the Foxford Wood incident. But that had been a mistake, surely . . . Hadn't it? No, I brooded, on the whole probably not. Not really . . .

'My dear, I simply must fly,' broke in Lavinia's voice, 'I have no intention of boarding the Golden Arrow in a gasping heap. As it is, I shall have to walk to a taxi rank – I couldn't possibly have a cab pick me up *here*. Wouldn't be prudent! And I suggest you also slip out as quietly as you can. Look both ways!' She started to gather her things.

'Er, one minute, Lavinia,' I said quietly. 'Talking of prudence, was it wise to take me into your confidence in this way? I mean, how do you know that I won't – well, sort of blow the gaff on things? After all, in the circumstances . . .' I gestured vaguely in the direction of Turnbull.

She paused, adjusted her hat in the mirror and then said genially, 'Oh, I'll take a chance on that. You see, I think you did in Mrs Fotherington . . .'

The words tore at my stomach and I found it physically impossible to speak. Taking advantage of my silence, she continued, 'As it happens, Mummy was a bosom pal of Elizabeth's – they had been at school together – and she had all manner of theories about the murder. Simply wouldn't let it rest. So boring! Anyway, one of her pet sayings was, "Believe me, my dears, it was that parson person she was so silly about. There's much more there than meets the eye!" Naturally no one took a blind bit of notice of her – we never did. Besides, I was far too busy with dreary Boris in France to bother about Ma and her cronies, dead or alive. But after her dire warnings it was such a coincidence bumping into you like that at Berceau-Lamont!

* See *Bone Idle*

236

And at the time I thought you were rather nice – still do, really – but I also remembered Mummy's words, *There's much more there than meets the eye*, and I began to think she could be right . . . Yes, I bet you probably did do it. I've no proof but I rather suspect it exists all the same, and one day someone will dig it up. Meanwhile I'll leave you to that quiet life you seem to want – unless of course you try to upset mine. You might find that troublesome – I had good mentors in Rupert and Freddie. It's amazing what can be achieved with a few hints here and there . . . Now I *really* must dash. Rio here I come!'

'You've forgotten something.'

'What?'

'Attlee.'

'Oh, have him. A keepsake!'

For a few moments I sat rooted where I was, caught in the waft of her lingering scent and listening to the faint clicking of receding heels on the landing. Then there was silence and it was as if she had not been there – no trace at all except for the huddled effigy at the desk.

Pulling myself together, I grabbed Bouncer's lead, dragged him away from sniffing the effigy's trouser-leg (planning another bite?), scooped up Attlee and, following Lavinia's injunction to look both ways, fled the building.

'But what on earth can I do with Attlee?' I said plaintively to Primrose in the car. 'There's no question of my keeping him, it's quite enough with Maurice and Bouncer without having that little tike tottering around. And if Maurice thought he were going to be a permanent fixture, goodness knows what might happen!' I lit a cigarette and glanced in the driving mirror at the minuscule passenger seated next to Bouncer. It gazed back unwaveringly, then with a mild grunt settled down to sleep.

'I don't suppose you want him, do you?'

'Certainly not,' replied my sister, 'I thought he treated the chinchillas most cavalierly. Karloff was particularly put out. No, I couldn't take the risk. Besides, to be frank, I find him rather unsettling: he has a funny look. And then there are those long silences – one is made to feel such a fool! Have you thought of Mavis Briggs?'

'I try not to. In any case, we were brought up to be kind to dumb animals. To offer Attlee to her would be a gross dereliction of duty.' (And I thought again of the hamsters.)

There was silence as we trundled slowly out of London in the evening traffic. And then she said brightly, 'Well one good thing, anyway, I bought the corset – two, actually. I think I shall need a new dress to go with them.'

'Look,' I said, 'corsets aside, do you think Ingaza might oblige?'

'Oblige? You don't mean take Attlee, do you? Huh, I shouldn't think so. Though I suppose he might if he thought he could get a good price for him!'

'Well it wasn't so much Nicholas that I was thinking of – rather his Aunt Lil. He tells me she kept a mastiff for years and has never got over its loss. Perhaps Attlee might make an interesting alternative – sort of divert her attention from the nephew.' I grinned. 'In fact, come to think of it, he might be jolly grateful.'

'Worth a try, I suppose, though knowing Nicholas he's sure to find something to bind about. Eric could be a better bet . . . Now look here, Francis, are you *sure* you left no trace in that flat?'

'Absolutely. There wasn't a single person about and I didn't touch a solitary thing.'

'Really? What about the door handle? They'll check it you know.'

I shook my head. 'Been through all that before.* Gave it a quick once-over with my handkerchief on the way out.'

'Well, if you're sure – then do you realize that thanks to dear crazy Lavinia we are all off the hook? Two dead and one absconded to the arms of an old man in Rio! I think I

* See *Bone Idle*

238

might sample a little of your malt when we get back, and then among other things we can drink to Clinker.'

'To Clinker? Whatever for?'

'Oh, didn't I tell you? I read it in the early edition of the *Evening Standard* when I was waiting for you in the Greek cafe. Apparently he has landed the job – that appointment as aide to the Archbishop of York. I gather it was his performance in Crewe that clinched it: what the press calls his "spirited" castigation of the failing missionaries.'

A picture of Gladys came to mind, also spirited and plaguing the angels in seventh heaven . . . Why, she might never deign to speak to yours lowly again! And with that pious hope I pumped the accelerator and spurred us on to Molehill and the libations.

'My dear,' Mrs Tubbly Pole trumpeted two days later, 'you'll never guess!'

'Guess what?'

'That toad Turnbull – he's been found dead in Wimpole Street! Poison in his drink. It's all over the *Daily Sketch*!'

'Well I never!' I said. A response which, although limp, was at least true.

39

Colonel Dawlish's Report

I discovered his diary, you know – *and* disposed of it. Dynamite! But since I'm ninety now and, according to my wife, in my dotage, there's no point in blowing the gaff to all and sundry. And even if I wanted to, nobody would believe me. 'Old chap has finally lost his marbles!' they would laugh. Well, marbles lost or not, I can still think about it and marvel at how he kept going for so long, or indeed how he managed to fool so many people . . . But then I suppose that's just it – he didn't *set out* to fool anyone, not in a malicious way at any rate. Simply wanted a bit of peace and quiet (a wish I increasingly share). And I suppose it was that very simplicity of purpose and lack of guile that forestalled detection and kept him afloat . . . until the Mavis Briggs débâcle, of course.

Had he been more 'professional', more efficient or savvy, he would probably have fallen at the first hurdle. As it is, despite the vicissitudes and blunders, he eventually found a little of that peace he had always wanted and became to all intents and purposes a reasonably competent pastor . . . competent in that he rarely upset anybody, could occasionally preach an intriguing sermon and was generally regarded as a useful chap to have around. Which, when you think of it, is as good a thing as most of us can achieve . . . Yes, I make no bones about it: murderer though he may have been, Oughterard always struck me as fundamentally a decent cove, and frankly and despite everything, I am sorry he is no longer with us.

'So where is he?' you might ask. To which I reply: 'Sleeping soundly in a shady plot at the far end of the churchyard', a situation entirely suited to his particular needs and proclivities.

'But how did he die?' you might also ask. Answer: cut off in his prime rescuing Mavis Briggs from plunging to her death over the side of the church tower – an event on which even now she still dines out. Indeed, not only does she dine out on it, but she has been one of the foremost sponsors of that gigantic commemorative plaque mounted in St Botolph's nave. Among other adjectives, the terms 'Bold and Resolute' feature in large gilt lettering. From my knowledge of the subject and having read his diary, these are not the words that I would personally have chosen for his epitaph. But who am I to cavil at the description of one who is fast becoming not only a local legend and hero, but a latter-day Saint Francis, attracting pilgrims from as far afield as Basingstoke and Surbiton? (And his empathy with domestic pets, specifically cats and dogs, has been the topic of many an article in diocesan magazines – although I have to say he was never noticeably enamoured of my own late lamented Tojo.) Yes, quite a mystic cult has grown up around our Francis, and even Edith Hopgarden gets in on the act by asserting piously that she had always known there was more to him than met the eye – an observation as fatuous as it is accurate!

The last entry in his journal was about two years before his actual death. I don't know why he had ceased to write . . . presumably because he had dispensed with the main subject, i.e. the Fotherington affair, and got it out of his system. The extraordinary details of the tale and its ramifications had been told and relived: the worst was over, the future moderately unthreatened. One imagines he had no further urge or reason to put pen to paper (other than for the necessity of parish paperwork, a chore which he heartily deplored). Why add to the burden by continuing a memoir increasingly concerned only with the humdrum? For someone as rootedly idle as Oughterard, it was doubtless quite enough to cope with that humdrum without having to narrate it as well!

So, as far as one can make out, the final span of the Canon's life was passed without drama or incident – unless you count occasional brushes with the bishop's secretary and Tapsell the organist. But I think by then he was sufficiently inured to both gentlemen to take them in his lolloping stride; and as long as he had the companionship of Maurice and Bouncer and access to his fags, gin and piano, he seemed entirely content to play a benign and moderately helpful part in Molehill's less than bustling society . . . Thus the speed and sheer staginess of his end came as a terrible shock, particularly to those of us who were witnesses – of whom there were many.

It took place on a Monday – the Cubs' annual outing, an occasion which happened to coincide with a rather 'fashionable' baptism in the church. Oughterard never liked baptisms – the infants put him off his stride – but to give him his due he was punctilious with the protocol; and unless he had over-doused or let slip the subject, parents went away generally well pleased.

As I said, it was a Monday: to be precise the fifteenth of September, one of those gloriously sunny and mellow afternoons when one was glad to be alive and when St Botolph's tower, all moss and ivy, rose into the blue as if in some bright and enamelled painting. Picturesque it certainly was. But it was also rather noisy, as somehow Mavis Briggs had pressurized the scoutmaster into bringing his young charges to visit the belfry and thence to inspect the tower's medieval battlements. Ostensibly this was to give the youngsters a treat and a sense of Molehill's ancient history; in reality merely an excuse for her to stand against the flagpole declaiming those frightful ditties from her *Little Gems of Uplift*. A tyro reporter from the local rag had been dragooned into attendance and was required to take photographs of the whole spectacle, i.e. Cubs, battlements, flagpole, Mavis. The vicar had been invited along to complete the composition, but had regretfully declined, pleading a pressing date with a child at the font. 'My God,' he had muttered to me, 'never thought I should be so glad to be taking a christening! Perhaps I can spin it out a bit . . .'

And so that was the set-up: Cubs and Mavis up on the roof parading around and spouting verse, Francis in full spiel and regalia sousing the baby below. Both groups commanded a fair audience. Normally I would be busy on a Monday but that day was an exception; and since Tojo seemed in particularly vocal mode I had thought I would quell him with a brisk walk round the churchyard.

When we arrived the whole thing was in full progress: a contingent of Cubs playing tag among the gravestones, Mavis and the rest looking like Lowry stick figures on top of the tower, and rousing singing from the christening party in the church. I remember saying to Tojo: 'Listen to that, old boy, they're airing their lungs all right. The vicar should be pleased.' Dog didn't answer of course, and sat down and had a damned good scratch . . . And then, by jove, all hell broke loose!

Manic screeches suddenly erupted from the battlements, and when I looked up there seemed to be a sort of commotion – people leaping about and arms flailing. The old peepers weren't too good even in those days, so I couldn't make out the finer details, but clearly something was going on and the shrieking got worse. I was just wondering what the hell it was all about when Vera Dalrymple shot out of the south door, and pounding over to me cried, 'Do something, Colonel! Young Billy Hopkins has just come down the staircase and told us that Mavis Briggs is hanging off one of the gargoyles!'

'What's she doing that for?' I said.

'Not for pleasure, you fool!' she snapped. I was a bit miffed at that but said nothing. Indeed, I wasn't given a chance, for the next instant she had grabbed me by the lapels and was yanking me into the church, crying: 'The Canon needs you – he's dropped the baby and is going up to help!'

243

As she dragged me over the threshold I just caught sight of a cassock whisking around the open door to the tower. The singing had stopped and was being replaced by wails from the jettisoned infant and furious imprecations from the godparents who evidently felt the celebrant had deserted his post when most required. It had the makings of an ugly scene. But I didn't stay to watch and, putting Tojo in the charge of young Hopkins, I scrambled up the stairs after Francis.

I eventually caught up with him on the top landing. Somehow he had contrived to shove a cigarette in his mouth and was muttering something to the effect of 'Bloody Mavis, she'll be the death of me!' And of course as things turned out, she was . . . However, he wasn't to know that, poor fellow.

Anyway, we both got on to the roof and rushed to the parapet, and along with everybody else gawped over the edge to view the dangling Mavis. Well, she wasn't dangling exactly, but rakishly astride a gargoyle – an air-borne Lester Piggot, silent as the grave and legs flapping feebly. Glancing down at the turf so far below, I felt a trifle sick – as obviously did the scoutmaster, who was busy fainting in a corner and being supported and sworn at by a couple of nine-year-olds. To this day I can hear their shrill voices: 'Cor, Mr Philpot,' one of them piped, 'this ain't no bleeding good. You said we was s'posed to be ever ready . . . Look at you, then – ready for bugger all, that's what!'

But Francis was ready. 'Just typical!' he sighed. And giving me his fag to hold, started to ease his long legs over the side of the parapet. We watched, mesmerized, as he crawled along the ledge, and then lying flat managed to stretch down and grasp Mavis by her belt and then one of her arms. He pulled and pulled . . . until eventually others were able to lean over, grab a hold and gradually haul her up, inch by agonizing inch. We were riveted by that burden, desperately urging it to safety. And at last they had her: winched, waxen and whimpering . . . but safe. A collective cry of relief went up.

But at the very point of triumph there was a faint scrabbling noise and a flutter of something to our left, and before we realized what had happened, we saw a billowing surplice . . . and Francis Oughterard, like a swooping albatross or huge Pentecostal dove, was swirling earthward. Down and down through the sunlit air he flew, until finally, far below in the toy-town churchyard, he lay spreadeagled on the green sward like an obeisant neophyte . . .

As you can imagine, it was a terrible time for all of us: and not least for the wretched Mavis, who, wanting to make a splash for the photographer, had apparently taken it into her head to perch roguishly on the stone balustrade. Too damn roguish! She fell backwards, arse over tip. What did she think she was *doing*, for pity's sake – being a cover girl? She should have kept to her verses and crochet.

Still, the funeral was a success – tremendous, in fact. I made sure of that. Got 'em all out. A full church parade, you might say. Splendid show! Full congregation, Scouts and Guides, choristers, the Townswomen's Guild, the Young Wives, Mothers' Union (brandishing their flag), lesser and major clergy – even the bishop, that Clinker fellow and his satellites. In fact it was he who gave the address – insisted on it, moreover. Wasn't bad as those things go, except that he kept talking about the Canon having a safe pair of hands – not *quite* the metaphor I would have chosen – and being the mainstay of the middle path which, he opined, was the best track to follow. (Obviously didn't know about that middle path through Foxford Wood!) But on the whole it all went like clockwork and I made it my duty to see there was no slacking in the ranks. (Give some of these clergy chaps an inch and they'll take a yard off the ritual, and I wasn't having that! Besides, Francis wouldn't have approved.)

The sister was there of course. Recognized her immediately – tall with the same thin legs and nose as her brother. She had brought Bouncer with her, for once looking quite kempt (obviously groomed for the occasion) . . . And wouldn't you know it, just at the moment of committal, as the coffin was being lowered into the ground, that damned cat appeared: darted out from the bushes and settled itself on the rim of the grave, staring in. That got the dog going, of course. Dragged itself away from Primrose and joined the cat, and together they gave tongue. And how! For one moment I thought the sextons were going to drop the thing down head first! But then the racket stopped as suddenly as it had begun and they seemed to lose interest. The cat took to sleeking its whiskers and the dog had a good pee against an adjacent gravestone, and the interment continued with all due solemnity.

Yes, altogether it was a pretty good show – though there were certain characters that I didn't recognize and who struck me as being a bit odd. Shady, actually. Three of them: sober-suited all right, in black from head to toe, but sporting huge diamond cufflinks and outlandish tie-pins. One was muffled in a jet astrakhan – not the type of coat normally seen in Molehill, least of all in summer. Two of them were stocky and the third – the one in the coat – as thin as a lath. Rather a raddled cove, I thought, and distinctly lachrymose. Kept sniffing loudly into a yellow handkerchief. His companions seemed quite solicitous and supported him to the graveside, where with flashing cuffs and glittering pin, he loitered bleakly. They also supported him back again to the bun fight afterwards, though by that time he had produced a hip-flask the contents of which were being downed with impressive celerity. Being rather taken up by other matters, I didn't have a chance to approach and enquire their connection with the deceased. However, I did note that tearful though he was, the thin one was scoffing Vera Dalrymple's flapjacks at the rate of knots, while the others were making a highly focused raid on the fish-paste sandwiches. The sherry too was clearly appreciated. It was only later when I saw them sloping off in the direction of a black vintage Citröen that the penny dropped ... Ingaza and his henchmen, Eric and the Cranleigh Contact. I should have known!

* * *

So, all in all a good send-off . . . though where exactly he was sent *to* I am not sure. But then, you might ask, where are any of us going? Not the sort of thing one likes to delve into much, easy to get bogged down! And who knows what goes through a chap's mind when he's hurtling hell for leather to his death – or before, for that matter? After all, diaries don't tell everything. I remember that bit in the poem he chose for her anthem, something about ever singing of Heaven and hoping to have it 'after all'.* Yes, reading between the lines, I think it did weigh upon him; but it was as if the matter was being continually shelved – endlessly overtaken by too many events! Perhaps if he had found rather more of that peace and quiet he was always after, he would have been able to deal with it. And maybe he did in those last months. Who can tell? So all I can really say about Francis Oughterard is to echo what little Mr Savage remarked at the funeral: 'You know, Colonel, the missus and me, we rather liked the Rev. As vicars go, he wasn't a bad sort, was he?'

'No,' I had answered, 'he wasn't a bad sort.'

But tell you what, though, apart from his premature demise, there *was* a sort of retribution. After that giant plaque was erected in the nave, the Mothers' Union felt it was time that they had a look-in, and some bright spark suggested that the annual Elizabeth Fotherington Memorial Award (which of course Francis had originally established) should somehow incorporate the memory of its founder. Thus, for many years now, the commemorative anthem composed specially for the ceremony has also borne the name of the Canon of Molehill – i.e. has become 'The Fotherington-Oughterard Anthem'. It is solemnly played amid popular acclaim every December, and the whole event rakes in whopping funds for maintenance of the church boiler and other worthy essentials. For one so anxious never to have his name linked with that of his victim, Francis may well feel that Fate has played him a pawky trick!

* See *A Load of Old Bones*

40

Maurice's Epilogue

Naturally, I knew it would not last – nothing involving F.O. possibly could. However, I was surprised by the manner of the resolution – as, presumably, was he. Our master had always been clumsy, and falling off that ledge was fairly typical. I had to explain to Bouncer that human beings do not possess the same agility as cats, and if they elect to go crawling about on hands and knees in high places then they must accept the consequences.

The dog cogitated, rattled his bowl, and then said soberly that he thought it was 'meant': that lying there on the narrow shelf, listening to the bleatings of Mavis Briggs being winched up from her perch, the vicar had suddenly got tired (as he often did) and decided to call it a day – shut his eyes and just let go. I was not entirely convinced by Bouncer's view (I rarely am) but he may have had something. However, in the rather delicate circumstances, I thought it best not to argue the point and so steered the conversation in another direction, i.e. *our* future.

(I must explain that we were being temporarily housed by the owners of Florence the wolfhound. The latter had been her gracious self – although absurdly concerned for Bouncer, who of course played up to her for all he was worth. She rashly let him share one of her bones, a kindness of which he took full advantage. Being the lady she is, Florence affected not to notice and gazed into the middle distance while he made nauseous gurgling sounds and stripped the whole thing bare! Sometimes I feel I have failed with that dog.)

'Anyway,' I continued to Bouncer, 'I rather think that in the near future we may be renewing our acquaintance with those obnoxious chinchillas.'

His hackles went up. 'You mean those idiot bastard bunnies in Sussex?'

'Exactly,' I murmured.

'Why?' he roared excitedly.

'Because, Bouncer, from what I have gathered by keeping my ears well primed, I believe we are destined to live with our master's sister, Primrose. She is coming for us shortly.'

'Hmm,' he said, pondering, 'that should be a bit of all right. She likes me, you know.'

I was about to reply that unfortunately not everyone's taste is impeccable, when he had the nerve to add that since I had always made her slightly uneasy – and given our present dependence – I had better mind my manners!

'*My* manners?' I hissed. He grinned inanely.

My sulk lasted for the rest of the day, but having been offered some cream and tolerable sardines from the wolf-hound people, I was disposed to be genial again. Bouncer too was in a good mood – evidently relishing the idea of the chinchillas and the attentions from Primrose. (It did not seem to enter the dog's head that were he to show too much interest in the rabbits, their owner would be less indulgent. A prospect I found mildly amusing.)

'I say, Maurice,' he exclaimed, 'if we are good perhaps P.O. will give us some more toys, like sort of welcome presents. I could do with a new rubber ball – the one F.O. gave me has lost all its bells.' (Yes, I had noted that and was thankful for the small mercy. But sadly, nothing lasts.) 'And *you* might get a new woolly mouse!'

'Quite possibly,' I acknowledged. 'That would be most welcome.' There was silence as we contemplated the gift-laden future.

And then furrowing his brows and drooping his head, the dog muttered, 'Maurice, do you think F.O. is going to be *all right*?'

'Oh yes,' I replied, 'no doubt about it.'

'I mean, where he's gone – will there be any bones for him?'

'Heaps! Strewn everywhere,' I assured him.

'And gin and fags?'

'Of course.'

'And good loud music?'

I winced. 'Bound to be . . . harps and trumpets blaring all over the place!'

'And peppermints and gobstoppers?'

'Thousands.'

'Ah well, he'll be all right then!'

'Yes, Bouncer, never fear, he will be *all right*. And so shall we.'